Hannah Rials

Reclamation is a work of fiction. Names, characters, places, and incidents either are the product of the author's imagination or are used fictitiously. Any resemblance to actual persons, living or dead, events or locales is entirely coincidental.

For information address:
Audrey Press/Aletha Press
P.O. Box 6113
Maryville, TN 37802

Printed in the United States of America 2020

Editor: Mallory Leonard
Book Design by Andy Meaden

ISBN: Print 978-1-936426-19-5
ISBN E-Book 978-1-936426-24-9
Library of Congress Catalog Number on file

www.audreypress.com/alethapress

A NOVEL

Hannah Rials

Aletha Press

Dedication

To all the people who are struggling to believe in themselves, who have dreams to write their book but haven't—believe in yourself, anything is possible.

Acknowledgements

To the whole team at Audrey Press, who believed in me six years ago, and took on a very rough book from an overexcited teenager. Thank you for believing in me and my writing. It helped me to believe in myself, which opened every door.

To my parents, who have supported me since day one and continue to support me in more ways than I could imagine. I'm the luckiest girl in the whole world.

To all the teachers/professors/tutors, who have fostered my love of reading and writing. You saved my imagination!

To all of my friends who have sat through stressed out writing rants, who have read scenes, who have come to every book launch and told all the people about my book. You all mean the world to me.

To the one who gives me all the support, all the hugs, reads all of my uncertain scenes—you're the best in the whole world.

To the people of Grand Isle, who welcomed me into their community during book research and cemented my idea that this was where Cheyenne's story was supposed to end.

To everyone who has read my stories, the immense, biggest thank you of all! I never thought you would exist.

Contents

Prologue x
One 1
Two 6
Three 18
Four 28
Five 38
Six 53
Seven 67
Eight 75
Nine 89
Ten 96
Eleven 105
Twelve 116
Thirteen 124
Fourteen 130
Fifteen 134
Sixteen 146
Seventeen 157
Eighteen 164
Nineteen 170
Twenty 177

Twenty One 189
Twenty Two 201
Twenty Three 209
Twenty Four 219
Twenty Five 236
Twenty Six 235
Twenty Seven 249
Twenty Eight 257
Twenty Nine 269

Prologue
1850

Something wicked was coming. That wasn't a phrase that Marie Laveau used lightly, or ever uttered aloud. But on this day, she felt it in the pit of her stomach where her reason rested.

Marie set to work making gris-gris for each of her seventeen children that morning after she woke up in a cold sweat with the wicked feeling. Whatever it was stirring the stagnant New Orleans air was not going to harm her babies.

"These gris-gris better still be in place when I get back, you hear me?" she said, placing one around each of their necks.

Marie saw herself in her children then, especially the oldest, as she raised her chin to the air. Marie had to squash the pride that rose in her chest—a good mother didn't praise insolence. "Put that chin down before your neck gets stuck like that." She yanked her daughter's head down and patted her cheek. "You take care of these children while I'm gone, you hear?"

"Where you going, Ma?" Little Joe asked, wrapping around her leg and looking up at his mother.

"I gotta go talk to an old friend, child. I'll be back

soon." Marie unhooked him from her leg and continued about her work.

Her oldest looked down her long, narrow nose. "You don't have friends. You have enemies."

Marie let out a heavy sigh, letting her chin fall to her chest as she sent a silent plea to her ancestors, her protecting spirits, to give her patience. Sometimes seventeen children were too many. "Get out my kitchen. Go play."

She shooed them away with a wave of her hand, but a chill struck her as they stumbled out of the kitchen, shoving one another and shouting. Marie waited until they were gone to finish packing her basket: a package of turtle soup, some fresh, dirty rice, steaming green beans dripping with butter, and several heaping spoonfuls of banana pudding—John Bayou's favorites. Marie knew her old teacher well, and she knew his spirit would be hungry.

She also had a bottle of his favorite rum, the spiced kind her first husband used to make and sell at market. She only made it now because she knew the powerful men who liked it and would give a pretty piece of information for a bottle. John Bayou was one of those men.

She'd already called on her man Édouard to pull the buggy around, and he was waiting for her out front, his eyes cast down as she approached with her basket. He knew food wasn't the only thing she was carrying.

"Where we going today, Madame?"

He opened the door for her, holding out a hand

of assistance. But she placed her basket in the seat, gathered her skirts, and pulled herself up into the buggy. "The bayou, Édouard. I need to pay an old friend a visit."

She saw his face fall. He knew they were going to the area of the bayou where people never showed their faces, even in the light of day. They were going in deep, over the water, to the little marshland that no one ever visited. No one except Marie Laveau. "Yes, Madame." And he closed the door behind her, climbing onto the driver's bench, and taking up the reigns in his callused hands. Even the horse seemed reluctant to take his first steps toward John Bayou's grave.

Marie felt it the moment they were out of the city. The air began to move, but only enough that someone who'd lived in New Orleans their whole life would be able to detect the difference. When she took a breath in, the air froze in her lungs. She felt the wicked surrounding her and rapped on the wall of the buggy to urge Édouard faster. She had to get to John before it was too late.

The horse's hooves kept getting stuck in the marshes, but they were finally at the swamp crossing to John's grave. Édouard came around to Marie's door and again offered his hand to her. Ignoring him, she leapt from her seat with unnatural grace, allowing her work boots to sink into the bayou. Édouard handed her John's basket and went to find the boat that they kept tied up there for her purposes.

As Édouard pushed off into the swampland, the

wind picked up again, but it wasn't the chilling wind from before. This was a familiar breeze, a spirit that recognized the scent of her infamous dirty rice. And Marie smiled for the first time that day.

She waited patiently as Édouard tied up the boat, and this time, she allowed him to help her onto dry land. She didn't know what kind of ancient creatures were lurking below those waters, and she didn't have time to find out. Life was too damn short to be eaten by a water dinosaur.

Édouard waited in the boat as Marie made her way into the marshy land, watching carefully where she stepped so she wouldn't go slipping into oblivion. It always took her precisely 124 steps to reach John Bayou's grave. The cypress trees were falling over his tomb, which she, and she alone, had kept up. She set to work unpacking the basket—the candles to pull his spirit forward, the meal that would make his mouth water. She had her own gris-gris around her neck because even though this was sacred ground—she'd blessed it herself at John's burial—she had a nasty feeling that whatever the wicked was that was on its way was stronger than she was.

John's spirit didn't even require a chant to call him forward. He was waiting for her. That couldn't be a good thing. The wind stirred; leaves danced together to create a rustling music; there he was. Even though she could see straight through him, his prominent, strong features shone through—cheekbones that whistled through the wind as he walked and eyes that knew everything. She needed those eyes today.

"Hello, Queen Lady!" John's deep monotonous voice was soundless. But that was the truth with all spirits she'd found. "I see you've brought me some treats." His white eyes scanned the meal in front of him greedily. It had been a while since she'd visited. Marie watched as her food sunk into the earth, and John smiled in satisfaction. "How fares my city?"

"That's what I've come to ask you, doctor."

His hollow eyes bore into her face as he floated in slow circles around her. "Then ask, Queenie. Stop wasting your own time."

"What's coming, John? I feel it—something wicked coming to my city."

John clucked his tongue at her. "You haven't been listenin' to the whispers of the ancestors, Marie?"

She sucked her cheeks between her teeth, looking at him from beneath thick eyelashes. "The people have been demanding of late. I've had to block out the dead to get some peace."

John stopped in front of her, rustling her headscarf. "I taught you never to ignore the ancestors, fool." And he spat nothing at her feet, white eyes blazing in the dull sunlight forcing its way through the thick cypress trees. "You've lost your chance to stop it."

"Stop what, John? Stop playing games with me!" Her voice shook the leaves as panic tickled her heart.

"The other queen—the one of immortality and blood. She has herself a plan, a plan for all the power she's ever hoped for. She will walk on earth with no restrictions, like the goddesses before her. You could've stopped it, Marie, but…" he stopped with a shake of his empty head.

"What's this plan?" She stamped her food as hard as she could into the soft earth, not making much of a sound at all. "Tell me this instant, John Bayou, or so help me—"

Again, he danced around her, white eyes watching. "A goddess she thinks herself, indeed, playing creator with a new people, made of all the bloods and magics that will give her back what she's missed the most from her long, long life in the dark."

"Magic? But how? Celine would never work with her." Marie always did her best to steer clear of the witches, but she couldn't believe them that foolish.

"Things have changed, I hear." John was egging Marie on, and she didn't care for it, not at a time like this.

"What does she want from all of it?" Marie's lips chapped the longer John's frosty form floated in front of her. She held herself still so she wouldn't tremble. She'd told herself long ago she'd never tremble in a man's presence again.

"Walkin' in the daylight-like she used to, like they all used to."

"No, what does she really want?" Marie might not know Lamia, queen of the vampires, but she knew that women like her, they always wanted something terribly, something they could never have and would do anything to get it. Lamia wasn't doing all this work—creating an entirely new race, dealing with the witches—just to walk in the sun again.

When he smiled, John's teeth nearly blinded her. "Now, that's the right question. Thing is, no one has the answer."

"No one at all? Nonsense."

"Would you like to volunteer yourself, little queen?"

Marie flinched at the word "little." He had no right to call her that. He was dead, and she was still living, the one serving the good people of New Orleans, protecting the innocents who were still ignorant of the supernatural world that paralleled their own. He was ten-feet-under and doing nothing to help anyone, even when called upon.

"I'll do whatever I have to do to protect my people. No thanks to you."

"I don't think so, missy." Again, he got up real close to Marie, his ghostly glow darkening around her. "You came here asking questions. I gave you the answers. Don't you be sullying my memory just cause you don't like what I tell you."

"What do the ancestors say?"

"That the world is going to end." And then he's smiling and cackling. Marie wondered if this was what death did to the mind, decomposing it until all that was left were the essential bits. She wondered if her mind would decompose too once her time came.

"What do the ancestors want me to do?" The thought of facing Lamia invoked fear that sent pinpricks into her toes and knives into her stomach. But she'd do it, for the sake of her city and her family.

"Nothing yet, little queen. Just wait. We'll call you when we're ready."

"I don't want to wait, John Bayou. I want to stop this before it starts."

He chuckled again, and she wanted to smack the living daylights out of him. But that would do her no good. "Get back to your little ones, Marie." And then he was gone, and Marie stood shivering in the bayou, in the middle of summer.

After a moment, she collected her candles and made her way back to Édouard and the boat. She didn't say anything as she climbed into the bow, holding herself together at her elbows. She didn't think anything as Édouard rowed them back to the buggy. She let herself thaw.

On the ride back to the city, her shoulders relaxed, and her toes no longer prickled with pain. John's words ran a circuit through her mind, sprouting into all the possibilities, all the desires, all the outcomes. Her vision grew blurry as she tried to pinpoint Lamia's true desire. But it wouldn't come. Her mind was a mess of blood and children and sunlight and so very many fangs.

Marie's head was throbbing by the time the buggy stopped in front of her home. Every sound made her wince, and she thanked the ancestors and the gods that the sun had set. She accepted Édouard's hand down from the buggy, swaying on her feet, and handed her basket off to him. She didn't trust herself to hold onto it. She walked to the door, clutching her gris-gris.

Then the air changed—a little rush, a slight chill.

Marie stopped in front of the door and turned one eye over her shoulder. And there she was, Lamia, queen of the vampires, creator of an army of blood-sucking monsters. She stood tall, just feet away from Marie. And she smiled brightly, linking her long, white fingers together in front of her.

"Hello, Madame Laveau." Lamia's red eyes flickered down to Marie's muddied work boots. "I see you've been out to the bayou. Visit with anyone I know?"

Marie's heart froze in her chest. Air wouldn't pump to her lungs. She remembered to look anywhere but at the creature's eyes, and she did, at the still air above her head. "You're not welcome here."

"Don't worry, Madame." Lamia took a step closer, just a breath away from the house's boundary. Her red eyes glinted as her smile grew. "I just wanted to meet the infamous Madame Laveau, the Voodoo Queen." The vampire looked Marie up and down, from head to toe, and gave a slight shake of her head.

"Ma?" Marie nearly cried out at the sound of her son's voice. She whipped around, risking losing sight of the vampire. But there was Little Joe, running out the front door to hide in her skirts.

"Go back inside, boy. Go." She pushed him away, but he froze when he spotted Lamia, right at the edge of the boundary now.

"Hello, little one." The vampire knelt down

so that she was on eye level with Joe. Marie covered his eyes, turning him toward her.

"You stay away from my children, cretin." Marie's dark eyes flashed, and she started muttering a curse, but Lamia cut her off.

"Don't waste your voodoo on me, Madame." Lamia stood to her full height, eyes blazing down at Marie. "We're on the same side now. The witches and I have a covenant."

"I'm not a witch. I have no contract with you." She spat the words and pushed Joe toward the door. "Go back inside and tell your brothers and sisters to stay." Joe did as she said, with only a small glance back at the beautiful lady with the garnet eyes.

"I was hoping you'd have a different answer, Marie." Lamia shook her head, and her face fell into a deep shadow. "It seems that we are enemies then." Her voice was smooth, syrupy, a contrast to Marie's own harsh creole. "Such a shame."

"I'll see to it you don't get what you want, leech." Marie's boldness grew, and she took several steps forward, standing directly in front of Lamia. She was significantly smaller than her and gritted her teeth at having to look up at her. "Stay out of my city and away from my family."

Lamia wore an amused smirk on her lips as she bent over, leveling her gaze with Marie's. "You threaten my future; I will take away yours."

Lamia's darkening eyes flickered to the open door, where several of Marie's children stood crowded together, watching the exchange. Marie's blood chilled, but there was nothing she could do. None of them were making like they were going to move.

When she turned back to Lamia, the vampire's hand struck out, breaking through Marie's boundary. Her chilled, pale fingers traveled down Marie's cheek, neck, stopping at her collarbone. She clutched the gris-gris, and with one hand, yanked it free of Marie's neck. "You're going to need to be a lot stronger to stop me, Madame." And Lamia smiled, wiggled her fingers at the children, then strode away down an alley. Something wicked certainly had come into Marie's life, and she knew it wouldn't be the last time she felt Lamia's cold chill in her heart.

One

I thought I'd seen the worst during my Ascension. I thought I'd seen the worst when I found Eli chained up in Anne's basement. I thought I'd seen the worst when I watched the life seep out of my cousin Drake. But I was wrong about all of that.

I stand paralyzed, Lamia's cold hand locked around mine, as the sun continues to rise and she continues not to burst into flames. Her chilling smile grows as warmth creeps into her hand, the sunlight highlighting her sharply beautiful features. Cheers rise around us from her army of vampires, who are still shielding themselves behind their umbrellas and hiding beneath the growing shadows of the trees. I can feel Lamia's pride swell as she closes her eyes to the sunlight. Her now warm hand squeezes around mine, and the strongest sense of nausea rolls through me, nearly knocking me to my knees, but her hand holds me up.

The screams break through my paralysis, and when I turn my attention from my nightmare, my friends and family are rushing at the vampires, huddled together away from the sun. Witches warp in and out of visibility, and I see vampires drop and burn, and soon the sunlight is mixing with firelight. Shrieks of terror echo in my ears, and I try to pull away because I don't know whose screams are whose. My eyes won't focus on any face; it's all a blur of flames and wind and water and screams. Then I spot Eli in the center, and I try to rush at him, wrenching my shoulder almost out of its socket in the attempt. I yell for him, but even I can't hear myself over the fight. Bodies keep dropping, but I can't tell what side they're on.

When I look back at Lamia, I wince away from the look of pure power on her face. She leads Jason to my side and places my hand in his calmly as if the war that's been brewing hasn't just started, as if her army isn't falling.

"Don't let her go, darling." Her long fingers brush across Jason's cheek, and then she sets off for the fight, not flitting as I would expect her to, but at a slow, deliberate walk.

"Fall back!" I cry, struggling in Jason's unnaturally strong arms. "Get out!" Just when I think my voice isn't strong enough, Regina's head flickers toward me and catches sight of Lamia. She repeats my calls, pulling back the witches, and grabbing my family members where she can. But then my mom races toward me instead of in the opposite direction. And instead of following his mom, following his High Priestess like he should, Eli's running toward me too. Then Anne's following him, and I could nearly cry, because they're not only running toward me—they're running toward Lamia. And she them. She stops halfway to the retreating rebels, and just barely looks over her shoulder, meeting my gaze from the corner of her eye. A scream rips out of my chest. I go limp in Jason's arms, waiting for the worst.

Eli and Anne and mom stop in their run mid-stride, a glaze covering their eyes. Around them, witches are warping Deuxsang away, but there are vampires guarding some of my family. But those three—they are still. I wiggle around so that I'm eye to eye with Jason. I lock into his gaze and try to push myself through the mental barriers he's put up. He focuses so hard on blocking my infliction that he leaves the compulsion part of his brain unguarded, just enough for me to slip in, and he's in my hold. "Let me go," I whisper. He's still fighting me, and a headache blooms behind my eyes as he tries to shove me out, but I already have a hold. Slowly, his arms loosen around me, and I break away. The only people that remain are Eli, Anne, and my mom. And they stand paralyzed. I can hear whispers of Lamia's voice, directed at them, and just as I reach her side, all three of them turn away, almost in slow motion, as if they're all fighting the compulsion. They walk through the crowd of remaining vampires, around the bodies littering the ground, and when I move to chase after them, Lamia grabs my shoulder, her long nails piercing into my clammy skin. I keep waiting for them to look back, to fight her hold, but I know they can't. I don't know what she said, but I know they're gone.

When my knees crumble this time, Lamia lets me fall. I crash into the cold grass, and then the church bells ring from across the river, announcing the arrival of Christmas morning. Tears rush out of my eyes in a turret, and I can't stop them. I can't stop the heaving in my chest or calling out to them, calling out to Eli as he grows smaller and smaller until they all disappear. And I'm left with Lamia and Jason and a disheveled army of vampires, blood dripping from their fangs, some with burns on their faces or dripping wet or scars running down their arms. A few of the vampires work together to bring all the bodies together, witch, vampire, and Deuxsang alike, piling them up one by one. I watch through blurred eyes as they pull out lighters, leaning down to set the pile on fire. For the moment, I'm glad I can't tell who's bodies they are.

Lamia kneels beside me, her heels sinking into the grass. I wince as her hand falls gently on my head, and then she's stroking my hair in slow movements. "All will be well now. We're all together. Don't fret."

Chills overtake my body, and Lamia pulls me closer. I feel like I have no choice but to let her and keep watching the bodies burn. The frozen grass crunches as Jason approaches behind us and stands on the other side of me.

"It's started, hasn't it?"

"Yes, my dear. We have a lot of work ahead of us."

My body is numb as they lift me to my feet, holding me between them. The flame from the pile of bodies adds some heat to the stiffly cold Christmas morning. I try to remain in control of myself, of the nausea ripping through my stomach, of the tears that won't stop. But I can't. All the food I ate before, and the blood I drank last night before enacting my terrible plan, races up my body. They hold me up as my body empties itself of everything. Lamia tucks my frosted hair behind my ears and dabs the cold sweat from my forehead. Jason hands her a handkerchief, and a flash of Eli appears behind my closed eyes as he wipes the vomit from the corners of my mouth.

"Let's get our girl home, shall we?"

Before I know what's happening, Jason scoops me into his arms, wincing away at the stench of my breath. I try to fight him, wriggling in his arms, but he locks me in tighter. When I meet his eyes, I try compulsion, try slipping through his defenses, but my mind is blurry. A headache springs up at my forehead and races to the back of my skull, nearly knocking me out.

As I'm carried away, I spot the small army of vampires following behind us, their chins held high, smirking at me as if they've already won. But they haven't, not yet. I have no idea what's going to happen next, where my family is, but right now, I'm on the inside. And for the moment, Lamia's plan isn't to kill me.

Two

After a while, the vampires trailing behind us disappear, flitting back to wherever it is we're going. But Lamia takes her time getting us back, reveling in the warmth of the sun. I'm stable enough to walk on my own, though Jason insists on keeping my hand tucked into his arm, walking through the city like a Victorian courting couple. The Christmas lights are still on, even though the sun is high in the sky now, but the city is quiet. A few stray bands play quiet Christmas tunes halfheartedly, and it sends a pang through me. Christmas was the one time of year where I didn't feel others in my family, where they put whatever it was they had against me aside, and we had Christmas, a real, family Christmas.

Grams always baked her special Christmas pie with too many fruits to even count inside it, but then there was always a drizzle of chocolate inside. There were presents, and a tree, and lovely smells and pure happiness. My family was never as happy together as they were on Christmas morning, and I could never explain why. But the dissonant, mournful sound of this Christmas music shakes me to my core.

"Where are we going?" I finally ask, tired of wandering through the French Quarter aimlessly.

No one answers me as we approach an abandoned Royal Street, littered with trash from Christmas Eve partying the night before, and again, an unsettling feeling settles over me. This Christmas is so completely wrong. But we keep walking, Lamia leading us, my numb hand tucked into Jason's overly warm elbow, but he never looks at me. He stares straight ahead at Lamia's back.

"Did you enjoy meeting your sister?" I ask, boring a hole into the side of his face. If he would just look at me… but he knows now that I can break down his defenses. He won't take the chance, chicken. "She misses you, you know? A lot doesn't shut up about you, really. It can get annoying, but I see why. Your absence has left her to be your parents only victim."

"Those people aren't my family," he finally says, barely above a whisper.

"Of course they are. Yes, they're crazy, especially your mom, but they're still yours. Sorry."

A muscle twinges in his jaw, rippling under his skin. He tightens his elbow around my hand, and my knuckles crack. I try not to wince, try not to show him any weakness. But he still smirks, knowing that he caused me just a small amount of pain. Payback. I fall into silence, avoiding the memories that are shoving their way into my head, the good memories of this street, Eli and Mason rocking jazz clubs, and the painful memories of this morning. Then suddenly, Lamia stops under an awning in front of a crisp white building. Christmas lights decorate the awning, and garland wraps up the pillars. Lamia waits for us to catch up, then glides through the doors that a doorman swings open for us, nodding his head as we pass.

The Hotel Monteleone. I've heard of this place. Supposedly one of the most haunted buildings in the city, even if it has been rebuilt. A fitting place for the vampires' hideout. Every employee that we pass nods their head to Lamia, blushing and not quite looking at her directly. She keeps her head and eyes forward, not acknowledging any of the adoring attention she's receiving. Do these people know? Or do they just think she's a filthy rich heiress?

When I look up at Jason, he's smiling with pride, and it's absolutely disgusting. He's proud to be hers, to be a part of her plan. How could he? His brain must just be absolute mush. I can't help my jaw nearly dropping as we pass through the lobby, filled with illuminated Christmas trees, strings of lights, and garland everywhere. A solo piano player in the farthest corner gently plays so as not to disturb the guests but greet them with Christmas cheer when they come down for breakfast.

I'm still staring as the elevator doors closed around us, and I turn to Lamia, my chin held high. "I see you're sparing no expense here."

"Why should we? My family deserves the best of the best. Hotel Monteleone is the absolute best. A good place for you to recover, dear."

"I don't need to recover. I just need to get away from you."

"It's in your best interest to stay with us," Jason mutters, staring at the gold-mirrored elevator doors, still holding on to me.

"No, it's in my best interest to be as far from you all as possible."

"You leave us, and you die along with the rest. It's as simple as that."

"Jason, dear. Please let me handle this." Lamia puts her hand gently on his other arm, smiling without showing her teeth. "No one is dying today, my dear. Today is about rest and recovering and awakening. Don't fret."

"You murdered my cousin. You killed friends who sacrificed themselves for me." I try to keep my voice in control, but as the doors ding open, my words roar down the hallway. And I'm struck at the sight of the oldest vampire kid.

"Ah, Arlo, there you are." I'm double-shocked by actually hearing the kid's name. "Please show Cheyenne to her room and get her settled." Without missing a beat, Jason hands me off to Arlo, even when I try to wrench away. I stomp on his foot, and he growls as he bends over, sucking in air from the pain. "Control yourself, Cheyenne. We're here for you."

"I'm not buying into your lies," I spit in her face, fighting Arlo's hold on me. I'm getting very, very tired of people holding me back.

But all she does is smile back at me. "Arlo, please," and nods down the hall, to my new prison. The vampire kid has my arms pinned to my side as he leads me down the gold gilded hallway and slides an old-fashioned key into the lock. The door opens to a bright room with the largest bed I've ever seen in my life. Drapes heavier than the carpet let in the bright Christmas daylight, but only slightly. The walls are soft on my eyes—pale, peaceful yellow in calming stripes. And in that moment, I don't care where I am; I just want to go to sleep.

"Why is there a Christmas tree in here?" I snap, moving away from Arlo when his hand drops from my arm.

"Because Lamia wants you to have a very merry Christmas, princess." He sneers at me, but hands over the key. "I don't suggest trying to escape. Even if you don't see anyone, they're still going to be there, and they'll know if you try to run. You also won't make the jump out the window." He follows my eyes to the wall-sized windows. "She and Jason will be up with you shortly for a Réveillon dinner. She asks that you please wash yourself because you smell like a sewer."

Arlo turns, and when I grab his shoulder to stop him, he flits to the door. "Don't touch me, half-breed," he hisses.

"Why are you working for her?" I ask quietly because despite the bloodstains on his teeth and the hint of savagery in his eyes, I can still see how young he is. He can't really be all that happy about fighting in a war when he can't be more than 15 years old.

"Everything I do, I do because she made me a vampire." But there's a hollowness in his words.

They're a script he's recited over and over again for who knows how long. Does he even want to fight for her? "Merry Christmas." And then he's gone, and the lock clicks behind him. But now I know that if I try to open that door, it'll open. And I could run. But how far would I get?

So instead, I do as asked—not because Lamia' requests' it, but because I've started to feel like a sewer. The smoke from the pyre is still in my lungs, blood on my face, frozen sweat in my hair. My insides are still twisting from the sight of all those bodies, from watching the life drain out of Drake's eyes. I peel off my dirty clothes as the bathtub fills up with steaming water then submerge myself in the steam, letting my tears mix with the bathwater. I open my mouth to scream and feel the bubbles vibrating around my ears. But when the water gets lukewarm, and my skin starts to wrinkle, I pull myself out of the water and douse myself in gardenia soap and gardenia shampoo, taking comfort in the smell that surrounded Kara's garden in the summer. For a fleeting moment, I'd allowed myself to imagine a future where I had a home of peace, and I'd fill that home with the smell of gardenias. But now, the smell made me sick — sickly sweet.

I pull myself out of the bathtub and pat myself dry. That's when I notice the clean clothes perfectly folded on the marble counter—a thick, red wool sweater with black jeans and socks. They've left me toiletries, everything I need to make myself presentable for them, for whatever this meal is. Since I can't force myself to put on my old clothes, to smell that smoke, I wear the new clothes, hating how warm and soft the sweater is. I throw my old clothes in the trash, hoping to block the smell as best I can.

As I'm finishing the braid in my hair, there's a knock on the door. Never would I have guessed that Lamia, queen of the Council, would knock on my door. I wait for a moment, to see if she'll just barge in the way I expect her to. But when one minute passes, and then two, she simply knocks again, a bit louder this time. I hate that I open the door. If this is the way she's going to play this, I could just never open the door to her, figure out a plan, and get myself out of here. But if I don't open the door to her, I'll never get any answers either.

So I do it, despite the pit in my stomach. She's already smiling and pecks my cheek as she walks into the room, followed by Jason. I start to close the door when a hotel cart comes barreling through carrying trays and trays of food.

"You look quite lovely in red, dear." Lamia says from the head of the small table.

"What is this?" I ask, ignoring her compliment.

"A Réveillon dinner. You've never had one before, of course. It's an old Catholic tradition that this lovely city has kept alive."

"Won't you burst into flames if you eat it then?" I spit, grinding my teeth together at both her and Jason.

All 26 pearly white teeth flash at me as she laughs. "That's only if I drink the holy water, my dear. I don't plan on doing that. But now you know how to kill me, if you can manage to get your hands on some, but make sure it's real stuff, from the nuns, not the souvenirs they sell in the shops around here." Her smile doesn't falter, and Jason laughs with her, but it's forced. I can tell he doesn't like the idea of losing his new mother. What kind of game is she playing?

We're silent, just staring at each other as a flurry of waiters set out trays and trays of food with smells that are slowly calming my roiling stomach. They set out three empty glasses in front of us, then disappear just as quickly as they came. And I'm left alone with Jason and Lamia.

Lamia pours us all blood—human—from a black bottle, then lifts her crystal glass in the air. "To... awakenings." And her eyes crinkle as she smiles, waiting for our glasses to meet hers. Jason swiftly moves to meet her, their crystal chinking together, and he echoes her toast. But I sit still, silent, my lips pursed into an invisible line. They wait a moment more for me, then give up with a calm sigh.

"Well, dig in, my dears. This feast is for you to build up your strength." She and Jason lift the silver lids off of all the different foods, and now I remember Eli telling me about the Réveillon feasts. But his family always eats theirs at midnight, as Christmas Eve passes into Christmas Day. We got a little distracted this year, I suppose.

There are some odd smells coming from some of the food. The soup smells fishy, but not in a way that fish usually smell.

"Here, Cheyenne, try some Turtle Soup. You'll love it." Jason dishes up a serving of the odd-smelling soup into my bowl, and then they're both serving me everything: turkey, shrimp, ham, red beans and rice, cornbread, and potatoes. Even though it all smells delicious, there's no way I can let myself eat this. That would be submitting to her. I can't do that. I just can't.

But they stuff themselves, though I'm not sure how Lamia is doing that. I always believed that vampires couldn't eat human food. But she's eating everything on the table, and Jason is shoveling food into his mouth and is already on his third glass of blood. Lamia smiles every time my stomach growls and rumbles.

"You're not doing yourself any favors by resisting this meal, Cheyenne. It's not poisoned, I swear on my life."

"Well, your life really isn't worth all that much to me, thanks." I mutter, turning away from the table.

"Really?" Jason snaps, dropping his golden spoon into his soup. "Centuries of a life isn't worth anything to you? Do you have any idea what she's done for you, for all of us?"

Lamia quietly places her hand on his arm, smiling appreciatively, a mother admiring her son. "Jason, dear, it's quite alright. Cheyenne doesn't understand. That's what this meal is all about—our family coming together, learning the truth of our predicament. All will come together, my dear." She squeezes his arm, then turns back to her meal, sipping blood out of her crystal, but keeping her eyes on me.

For a while, the room is silent except for the clinking of silverware against plates and Jason's loud chewing. I still can't bring myself to eat any of the food, even though my stomach is betraying me with its sounds of desperation. Waiters come in and out to clear trays and plates away, and finally, they bring in a tower of little pastries, encased in stringy sugar and stuffed with cranberries. My mouth starts to water.

"Please eat something, Cheyenne. You need to recuperate after such a big night."

"I won't be eating anything that you give me, thank you." I turn my nose away from the beautiful dessert, fighting the urge to shovel it all in my mouth. I hate that this is what I'm thinking about, and not the fact that I'm no longer with my family, or the fact that Lamia just let them go. Why did she let them go? She had Eli right in front of her. She could've killed him easily. But instead, she had them turn and walk away.

"Very well. It seems you're ready to talk, my dear." Lamia lounges back into her chair, crossing her legs and her hands together. "What is it you want to say to me, then?"

I can't help my jaw-dropping or my eyes doubling. Who does she think she is—belittling everything that she's done in the last 24 hours, the last two centuries? Her words make me sick to my stomach, and now I really couldn't eat anything.

"You murdered my cousin. You made me a freak.

You took me away from my family. You're planning on murdering an entire population of living creatures just so that you can walk in the sun and rule the world. Would you like me to continue?"

But when I look at her, she's smirking. "Those witches really have done a number on you, haven't they?"

"No one's done anything to me except you. The witches had nothing to do with you killing Drake or you massacring my people."

"Quite the little loyalist, aren't we?" She chuckles, and I want to scream. Jason laughs with her, shaking his head at my nonsense.

"And you—she kidnapped you from your family! How are you going along with all of this?"

"As I've been telling you, Cheyenne, those people are not family. They are a group of Deuxsang that I was placed with at birth. Lamia is my true mother, as she is yours. We are stronger—we are better—because we share DNA with the queen of the vampires. We are the heirs to her dynasty."

I must be in some kind of psychedelic dream right now. Even if what he's saying is literally true, I know in my gut that it's wrong, just wrong. "Her heirs? I'm pretty sure she's not planning on dying anytime soon, seeing as how she's, ya know, immortal. We don't mean anything to her, Jason; we're just puppets in her plan!"

Jason opens his mouth to snap back at me, but Lamia holds her hand up to silence us. "I don't want to hear any arguing. It's Christmas, my dears. A time for joy." She takes both of our hands, but when I try to pull away, she grips my hand harder and jerks me toward her. "Cheyenne, dear, I know this is a lot to take in. And I don't expect you to accept everything now, especially after you've been through so much. But what I do want you to know is that you are home with us. No harm will come to you, and we are very glad that you are safe in our home. All truth will be revealed in time, and don't worry—now that we are together, we have all the time in the world." Her smile is as bright as the star on top of the tree as she releases our hands and leans back, reaching for her glass of blood. "I do think this is the best Christmas I've had in centuries."

Three

I don't know why I slept so well last night. I haven't slept well the past month, but here I am in the most luxurious bed I've ever laid in, surrounded by the monsters of my nightmares, separated from my family, but the moment Lamia and Jason left, I couldn't keep my eyes open. I tried to keep myself awake, to figure out a way out, but my limbs just grew heavier and my head cloudier, and I know I wasn't drugged because I didn't touch any of the food or the blood. That's extremely apparent this morning, with my growling stomach.

When I look over at the alarm clock blinking beside me, I leap out of bed. It's already noon! I've wasted nearly a day sleeping. I could've been getting answers! I could've been trying to contact Eli or Anne or...figuring out a way out of here.

I'm still in Lamia's red sweater as I flit to the door, fully prepared for it to be locked. I hesitate, completely terrified for the truth of my situation. But when I push down on the handle, the door clicks and opens when I pull. But of course, Arlo is waiting for me outside with a pompous grin on his lips.

"Good morning, princess. Ready for lunch with the queen?" I haven't been awake long enough to deal with his attitude. The sight of his face crushed that momentary flicker of hope that I had when the door opened.

"No, I think I'll just go back inside."

"She'll just have me come get you in half an hour. You might as well come now so that I don't have to come barging in." Again with the grin. I want to rip that grin off his face.

"I could refuse to go."

"You could also be thrown into a dungeon with a bunch of bloodthirsty vampires." He pauses for emphasis. "Your choice."

It's possible that he's bluffing. It's more likely that he's not. A dungeon is what I was expecting anyways. So I step across the threshold of my room and follow him down the hallway. "Where are all your siblings?" I ask, eyeing the back of his now shaven head.

"Doing their jobs, like all of us." There's a notable tensing in his back. Like a coil wrapped too tight.

"Lamia separated you? That can't be easy."

"They're fine," he snaps.

"Are you sure about that?"

"Why don't you keep your mouth shut, half-breed? Or I'll figure out how to get that door locked from the outside."

I fall silent, only because there's no point in a one-way conversation. So I follow, admiring the Christmas decorations that deck the halls, resisting every urge I have as I ride in the elevator with him not to knock him out from behind. My brain tells me to do it. My gut tells me to wait. My gut seems to know what it's doing more so than my mixed-up brain right now.

The elevator dings open into the lobby, and Arlo leads me straight through the Christmas rush of people checking out. They don't even look our way. I keep forgetting that Arlo doesn't look like a street rat anymore. He's in a button-up shirt and slacks. His hair is actually washed and combed.

"Can I ask you a question?"

He doesn't respond, continues to walk through the crowded dining room. My stomach grumbles.

"How old were you when Lamia turned you? You don't talk like you're from a different century."

Still, he doesn't speak. Doesn't turn around. Doesn't flinch. And then my opportunity to ask questions disappears as he leads me into a private dining room where Lamia, Jason, and Mirnov are waiting for me. Jason's scarfing down a full breakfast, barely coming up for a breath between bites. And Mirnov and Lamia watch him, Lamia with pride, Mirnov with disgust.

"Ah, there she is!" Lamia stands, pulling Mirnov up with her when he doesn't automatically follow. "Good morning, my dear. How did you sleep?"

I don't say anything, turning to Arlo for some assistance that I know he won't give. Silent resistance has worked in the past, right?

Arlo disappears from my side, and I never thought I'd wish that he were back with me.

"Come take a seat, dear. Your breakfast is on the way."

I sit down even though every limb in my body fights against it. "I'm not hungry." They're all staring at me with looks of severe disappointment, as if they're surprised that I wasn't converted to their point of view in my sleep. Did they believe that a meal I didn't eat and a warm sweater would make up for everything that they've done, that they plan to do?

"Well, you're going to eat, half-breed," Mirnov growls, baring his teeth at me. "Unless you're planning to die of starvation."

I flinch my eyes into a glare. "That's not such a bad idea. Thank you."

His nostrils flare out, and he grips his glass that undoubtedly has blood inside. I can smell it, and I hate that it doesn't make me sick to my stomach. "You're eating. You need your strength for training today."

"Training?" I sputter after taking a sip of water. There's nothing wrong with drinking water, I tell myself. I can't interrogate them if my throat is dry.

"Of course." Lamia smiles. "We have to get you trained for the fight ahead. I'm sure the witches didn't do that for you."

"They did, actually." I stare at her over the rim of my glass, waiting for her response. But her face is a mask of calm and peace. If she's surprised, she's not showing it.

"Oh right, of course, the Cofi family, the bewitched traitors. They would know nothing about how to train you if it weren't for them."

"They weren't bewitched. They just discovered the truth." I can't resist the smell of breakfast anymore and stuff a large bite of chocolate chip pancakes into my mouth. I ignore Jason's smug smile.

"And what do you believe the truth to be?" Lamia leans forward onto her crossed hands, and Mirnov does the same, almost as if he's pulled by strings.

I look to Jason, absently hoping that he'll come to my aid and agree. But what does he know of the outside world, of real truth? He's completely brainwashed. He's not even looking at me, just staring adoringly at Lamia.

"I don't think I need to tell you the truth. You don't have to lie to me anymore," I say quietly and spear another bite of pancake.

"Yes." She smiles gently, and it makes me sick to my stomach. The pancakes feel like rocks now. "You're not a child anymore. You're a clever young woman." Mirnov watches us both carefully as she settles back in her chair, crossing her legs and linking her fingers together. "We did trick the witches into helping us create the Deuxsang. And yes, we were the ones who exterminated the first generation when they proved to be disappointing. The lie was necessary to secure trust and obedience."

"Admit it," Mirnov whispers, leaning closer to me. I back away, terrified by the burn in my throat at smelling the blood on his breath. "You loved us before the witches messed with your mind." His smile looks like the Cheshire cat. His fangs never go away.

"You've terrified me my entire life." I spit in his face, leaning close just for that one moment. "You're the boogie man, the creep who stares for too long with evil in his eyes. And you," I turn to Lamia, "were an unnamable monster. Someone to fear, not love. No one in my family loves you."

"Is that so?" Mirnov asks, just as the private door opens and in walks Lilith, but a Lilith that I've never seen before. She's dressed as she always has, like a socialite with too much money on her hands, but there's something in her face that's all wrong, fear and longing all mixed together. Her steps are slow and determined, but she seems to wobble in her heels, where before she walked like she was stabbing the ground into submission.

Mirnov holds his hand out to her, and she takes it as she sits down beside him. She doesn't look at me, or won't. Her eyes look blurry though. "Good morning, my love." He kisses her cheek gently, and my stomach retches. She smiles back at him, then finally turns to me.

"Good morning, cousin." She reaches for my hand, but I wrench away. "So touchy." Lilith clicks her tongue and shakes her head.

"Cheyenne was just talking to us about how much truth she knows." Lamia turns a slow nod on Lilith, but I can feel the tightness in her words.

"I did my best, ma'am." Lilith's head falls to her chest, and her hand squeezes Mirnov's under the table. But he gives her no response or support. "The witches must have brainwashed her."

"That's a good story, but I believe what happened—and Cheyenne, please agree yes or no to this—is that they gained her trust. Am I correct, my dear?" She turns to me, but words are frozen in my throat. This conversation feels wrong. "No need, I see that that's true. Which, if I remember correctly," Lamia pauses, her words hanging in the air like a haze, "was your job."

Lilith's gulp is audible around the table. Jason has finally stopped eating, glaring at Lilith just as fiercely as Lamia is. "I did, ma'am. But then the witches got her, and they changed her mind. Cheyenne is just so susceptible to influence."

"If that were true, she would have been susceptible to your influence." Then everyone's staring at me. Lamia's head is cocked to one side. Mirnov is smirking, his hand limp in Lilith's, who looks like she wants to murder me, probably thinking she should've done it ages ago. "In failing Cheyenne, Lilith, you have failed me. You are finished."

"What?" Lilith shrieks, and her body starts to shake. "No, please no. Give me another job. I won't fail you. I'll find the witches. Please, Lamia. I swear to you." Her voice trembles, and she grips the edge of the table to keep herself still.

"You know I don't like begging. My decision has been made. Mirnov." Lamia nods, just slightly, and turns to her glass of blood.

My mouth falls open as Mirnov flits to his feet, jerking Lilith out of her chair with a shriek. He drags her by her hair through the private dining room as she holds her head, trying to wriggle away as best she can, but to him, it's like she's not even trying. For a moment, our eyes meet, and I've never seen my cousin look so terrified.

"Wait!" I yell, knocking my chair out from under me. Lamia looks up lazily, and Mirnov stops, turning to face me.

"Do you have something to say, Cheyenne?" Lamia asks, and I can hear the smile in her voice.

"I'll train with you." My voice shakes as I look back at Lilith, crying silently and no longer meeting my gaze. "Just don't kill her."

"Think carefully, Cheyenne," Lilith stares at me like there's no one else in the room, like this is exactly what she wanted all along. "You have an impulse to save Lilith, even though you despise her. Don't try to deny it." I close my mouth, open ready to retort. Where's she going with this? "I see you, Cheyenne. Your heart is in the right place, but it is ill-managed. You want to save people because you are born to be a leader, but being a leader means making hard choices, knowing what must be sacrificed in order to achieve the greater good."

"How will killing Lilith achieve the greater good?" I shout, unable to control the level of my voice.

"What will happen to Lilith if I let her go?" Lamia asks, waiting for my response.

"She could leave," I say. "She could go home."

"You still don't understand, my dear. This was her

home. How would the Deuxsang react if she came strolling back? You have to know they wouldn't welcome her with open arms."

"No, but..."

"But what, Cheyenne? Lilith is mine. She is my responsibility. She cannot return to the Deuxsang whom she betrayed, and she cannot safely remain among the vampires whom she failed. I cannot release her to find her way in the human world, knowing it's only a matter of time before she will be discovered consuming blood. No, as her leader, I shoulder the burden of her fate."

Thoughts whir through my head, clouding my vision. Let her die here, where I know it's happening, could possibly hear it happening—or let her die later, with everyone she betrayed?

"What if you don't kill her at all, and instead let her train with Jason and me? Get her ready."

Lamia's smile broadens. "Lilith is not like you and Jason, Cheyenne."

I narrow my gaze. "No, but she's another trained body fighting for you. Obviously, she'll do anything for you. Might as well use that to your advantage."

Lamia considers a moment, looking between me and Lilith, who's still sniveling on the ground. It almost makes me regret saving her. But not really. "Very well, she can train with you. As long as you understand, my dear, that the consequences of this decision lie solely with you. Whatever happens to Lilith from this moment on is the result of your choice. She is yours now."

Silent tears stream out of Lilith's eyes, but Mirnov has released his hold on her. She curls in on herself and cries, turning her back to us. "Mirnov, take her to her room." I watch the big bad monster rip Lilith to her feet, his fingers digging into her arm as he guides her out of the dining room, but the second the door opens, his arm slides around her waist, and she straightens up after a jab in the side.

Lamia finishes off the blood in her glass and smiles at us. Neither of us really know what to make of what we just saw, though Jason must be more used to it than I am. "Well, finish your breakfasts, my dears. Training starts in an hour."

Four

Training is on top of the hotel's roof, even though the wind is blusteringly cold and vicious this morning. Yes, it is practically afternoon, and the sun is shining, but it's like the sun has lost all of its warmth. Yet here we are. Me, Jason, and Lamia. She still hasn't allowed Mirnov to drink from us, so he's stuck downstairs, hopefully keeping Lilith alive.

"Where's my cousin?" I ask, waiting for Lilith to join us as agreed.

"She needed a rest after all that...excitement." Lamia stands elegantly before us as if the cold isn't touching her at all. Her hair seems to defy the wind as it lies perfectly flat and curled against her head. "She will join us for the next session."

"That is if you don't kill her first."

"I made an agreement with you, Cheyenne." She steps a bit closer to me, looking down to meet my eyes. "I will not go back on my word."

"My experience with your word is that it's a bunch of lies."

For a moment, her façade flickers, and frustration bubbles below the surface. "That was a means to an end." Her voice drops, and the wind carries it to my ears. "You, my dear, are the end." She stares at me for a long, uncomfortable moment, observing her creation then breaks into a smile and spins on her heel, clapping. "Now, then, let's begin! Cheyenne, Jason is already far ahead of you, I believe, as he has been training with me for years."

"Then how come I was able to break through his defenses the other night?"

She stops, apparently forgetting that little detail of the nightmare before Christmas. "Because together, you two make the perfect creation—our saving grace. Neither of you are perfect; you each have strengths that the other lacks. But together, you create something…beautiful." The glint in her eyes sets my nerves on end.

"So what, we just have to stay together in the battle the whole time, or we'll die?" Jason asks, the first time he's spoken since breakfast.

"No, lovely." She smiles sympathetically at him. Would Anne still love him so much if she knew what Jason was like? Brainless, spineless?

"But enough chitchat. Cheyenne, let's see what you can do. Please step apart a bit more." Jason and I move away from each other to opposite ends of the roof. The city has come alive after a quiet Christmas morning. People are alive again with music and conversation. Lights are on in restaurants. And I want nothing more than to be down in my city, with my people, away from this nightmare.

"Cheyenne, I've seen you in action. I'd like to see what your defense system is like." A knot twists in my stomach. Dr. Cofi and I never really got to the defense part of the fighting. We were cut short. "So

Jason, if you will, please try to inflict on Cheyenne. Thank you." She stands in the middle of us, slightly outside of our line of vision, her hands folded in anticipation.

A sadistic smile plays across Jason's lips, as he leans forward just a bit, almost like he's about to ram into me. My whole body tenses as his eyes narrow. I build up the mental block that I've only read about, pulling from all the strength in my body and mind. I can feel the wall, shielding the area that I think he's going to go at—my heart.

And I'm right. The force of his strength hits me, and I'm nearly knocked back. It rams into me, searching for an opening in my mental wall around my heart. His strength is crushing though. I can feel it weighing in on me as he's patient, poking, and prodding. I close my eyes against the force, focusing all my strength on that wall. When it feels like his strength is failing, I gain a little bit of confidence. My wall strengthens. His force lessens, and I take my opportunity and push back.

But that's what he was waiting for. His strength comes back in new force, striking exactly where I thought he would because my wall had crumbled when I focused on action instead of protection. An invisible hand wraps itself around my heart, and I can literally feel fingers puncturing it. I drop to my knees, my mouth gaping open. When I set my left hand down to prop myself up, it fails under the pain rushing down the left side of my body. His grip tightens, and I fall onto my back, gasping like a guppy out of water.

"Enough, Jason." Lamia's voice breaks through the haze of pain clouding my mind. Slowly, the fingers release my heart, and I can feel his power fade from my body. Still, I lie on the cold concrete, feeling the shadow of the pain more than I thought a shadow could cause.

My eyes close, focusing on calming my mind, but I hear the tapping of Lamia's heels growing closer to me. A chill runs through me as her shadow falls over me, and she kneels down, brushing my hair away from my sweating face. I reluctantly open my eyes as she grabs my chin with enough force to get my attention. "We still have some work to do, my dear."

***

Jason is the lucky soul tasked with "accompanying me back to my room." Lamia thinks she's giving me this image of freedom, but it's not working. Jason is silent most of the way back, but he's got a smirk stuck on his mouth, and I want to smack it away.

"Just because you beat me once doesn't mean you're better than me," I say just before we come to my door.

"It does actually. Because if you were better than me than you would've been able to block me." My chest is still sore from where he nearly crushed my heart.

"Maybe you've just been drinking more human blood longer than I have."

And I think that's going to be the end of the conversation when I unlock my door and walk into my room. But he follows me inside and lets the door close behind him. "Um, I don't remember inviting you in?"

"I'm not a vampire, Cheyenne. That rule doesn't apply." He collapses onto my sofa and starts browsing through his phone. He has a phone!

"Where did you get that?" I flit to his side and try to snatch it out of his hand, but he's too fast and sees my movement coming.

"What? It's a phone. Don't you have one?"

"No, I've been on lockdown for six months. Maybe I should belly up and abandon my family because apparently, they reward people for that now." I move away from him to sit on the end of my bed. Being in the same space with him is unnerving. What would Anne think of her brother now?

"My family is here. I didn't abandon anybody." His voice drops an octave, and the smirk of amusement is gone.

"Your sister is my best friend, Jason. And I don't see her anywhere here." The muscle in his jaw twitches and something flashes dark in his blue eyes.

"I don't have a sister. I have a mother, Lamia. I have a family here. I don't even know this girl that you're talking about."

The fight is obvious in his eyes, storming over, almost as if it's compulsion fighting with his memories. But the compulsion is too strong. For the first time since I've been here, I feel sorry for him. What has Lamia done?

"You're sister is insane, by the way. But in the best kind of way." I smile, more to myself than to him. "I didn't really choose to be her friend. We were basically set up on a play date. And then she chose me. I've never had a friend like her before." My chest tightens as I talk about Anne, cause talking leads to remembering—remembering everything that she led me to. If it weren't for her, I wouldn't know who I am. I wouldn't have Eli. I wouldn't have the courage to do what I'm about to do.

"Sounds like you're lucky then...to have friends." He's not looking at me anymore, but he also doesn't look like he wants to punch me either.

"Mommy Lamia doesn't let you pal around with any of the other vampires?"

His glare returns with a new fierceness. "Watch how you talk about her." But that eye contact is all I needed. He wasn't expecting my compulsion, so I easily slip into his brain and root around for the initial compulsion that Lamia put in place years ago. And it's there, all over his mind, and memories, entrenched in all his synapses. So I just start pulling, reaching at the strings that weave into his mind and pull them away, imagining them flying out of his brain altogether.

He puts up a fight once he feels what I'm doing, but it's too late. Lamia's thread is unraveling. I carefully pull away from him, back into my own mind, feeling lucky that the strands of memory that I have are my own and haven't been tampered with the way his mind has been.

I open my eyes and watch his face as he comes into himself again, readjusting to his own mind. His eyes roam back and forth as he travels through his memories—his real memories, scenes that I saw play out. Once a week, he would take little toddler Anne to Cleary Park and push her until she couldn't be seen through the sun. His favorite times were family game nights of Scrabble and Monopoly. And when I was in his mind, once Lamia's vicious compulsion was gone, I could feel overwhelming love. Not from him, but the love he felt from his mother and father and the baby sister who was still too young to remember when he'd been taken away.

Tears leak down his cheeks, and he grips the edges of the couch as if the memories pain him.

"Why would you do that to me?" he gasps, throwing himself forward so that his broad chest rests on his knees. "I was happy."

I crawl over to him so that his eyes are on my level and place my hands on his shoulders as he cries. "But it wasn't real, Jason." He tries to say something, but his cries are too thick in his throat.

"Your family loves you very much. They searched and searched, fought, and fought. Anne can't wait to meet you again."I sit on the couch next to him and let him cry into my shoulder. "How could I forget them?" he manages to choke out.

"It's not your fault." I hold him tighter, wanting to cry with him now. How could I have just stood there and let them kill Drake? What has she done to Lilith? Who is this monster who destroys families like it's nothing? Nausea roils in my stomach as I take a deep breath in and out. Jason presses his fists into his eyes, trying to stop his tears, but now I'm crying too.

I don't know how much time passes before we're both able to calm ourselves enough to sit up and breathe without a shudder running through our bodies. I hate crying. I especially hate crying in front of strangers.

"So, I'm assuming you have a plan on how to get out of here?" He asks, but his voice feels unnatural to my ears, almost as if he's a completely different person than the man who almost crushed my heart a couple of hours ago.

Lamely, I shake my head. I wish I could say that I did. But even if I actually did, I'm not sure I can trust Jason not to squeal to Lamia or Mirnov, not yet. If someone messes with your brain that much, it's not ever going to go away completely. "No, I don't."

"So we're just stuck here with them? Knowing what they're going to do? I can't let that happen."

"You have any ideas since you've been living with them for nearly 20 years?" I don't appreciate the criticism from the guy who only moments ago was preaching Lamia's righteousness.

He stares at the carpet for a good long time—an annoyingly long time. I sit there, twisting my fingers, waiting for Lamia to walk through the door any moment to kill us because she obviously has hidden cameras in here and heard and saw everything I just did. Except time continues to pass, and nothing happens. Jason keeps thinking.

"We could just make a run for it," he finally says, eyeing the door.

"That's a terrible idea." He shoots me a glare but doesn't have a retort. "No, I think you're going to have to pretend."

"I don't know if I can do that." Jason wrings his hands together, "not now that I remember everything. Whenever I see her now, I'm just going to think of everything she took from me. I can't do it, Cheyenne, I can't." His gaze meets mine completely for the first time, and I'm stunned. His eyes are wide, hazy again with fear. Maybe I can trust him.

I squeeze his shoulders, trying not to break his intense stare. "Yes, you can. Because if you don't, then we're stuck here forever. And everyone we love is going to die."

The sound that comes out of his mouth as his head falls to his chest is somewhere between a laugh and a sob. "So no pressure."

I smile weakly and pat his shoulder. "Exactly. Like you said earlier, you're stronger than me."

He goes rigid then, slightly scooting away from me. "I really didn't mean that…I mean, it wasn't me talking…that was— "

"I know, Jason. It's fine. I was kidding."

"Yeah, we're not really used to that around here." Jason sighs and stands, staring shamefaced at the floor. And then silence settles over us, and he's just standing there, and I'm waiting for him to leave because my chest still hurts and I'm exhausted after all that compulsion removal. "So uh..."

"Sorry, do you mind if I just get a bit of rest? I had a run-in with a bit of a heartbreaker earlier, and I haven't quite recovered."

He winces, and I feel bad for making it a joke. "Yeah, I'll get out of your hair."

"Jason, I—"

"I'll see you tomorrow, Cheyenne. Sorry about earlier." And then he disappears out my door, and my head's spinning so fast I can barely see straight. What have I gotten us into?

Five

The night passes slowly in my room. I can hear every chilly wind that slams against my window, and just when I'm about to fall asleep, there's footsteps outside my door. Thoughts of Jason run through my mind on a loop. I don't know how sure I am that he can pull this off, lie to Lamia, not after the years of subconscious torture that she's put him through. What if he cracks under pressure? What happens if she finds out what I did to him? But then another thought occurs: what if she's trying to do the same to me? Despite a ridiculously warm, heavy blanket, the thought sends chills through my bones.

But sleep does eventually come—at least, a semblance of sleep. And again, just as I'm about to let myself sink into unconsciousness, there's a slight twinkling sound, but not from outside my mind. In my head. It's been such a long time since I dreamwalked that I'd almost forgotten what it feels like to be called by someone's dream. I try not to get my hopes up thinking that it's Eli's. Of all the people sleeping in the world right now, it's highly unlikely that it's his. Then again, who else's dream would be calling me?

I walk up to the bulky wooden door where the twinkling sound is coming from and push open the unlocked door. At first, there's nothing. Well, there's just a big, empty beach. The sky angrily swirls above me, churning the ocean water into vicious, crashing waves. I tiptoe to the edge of the shore, gasping when the chilled December water slides over my bare feet.

I barely remember the last time I was at the beach, years ago, when Nana decided it would be a good idea for all of us to take a family trip. The cheapest, closest beach was Virginia Beach—we could get there in a couple of hours and just stay for the day. It was naturally a disaster with all of the younger kids complaining how cold it was. Several of us built sandcastles, then Rove went around running, crashing through them, which led to a giant sand battle, where I ended up with so much dirt in my mouth from screaming that all the parents had decided to pack us up three hours early and rush us home, dripping wet, shivering, with sand packed into our ears.

But this kind of beach—I see why people like it so much, even though I have no idea where I am.

"Having a nice think there, princess." I freeze, thinking Lamia has followed me into someone's dream. Or it's Lamia's dream. But that's not possible. The woman's voice is too low.

I turn, just barely looking over my shoulder to see who's speaking to me, and fear courses through me as the Voodoo Queen of New Orleans flashes a charming smile. "I'm glad ya finally heard me, child. I've been callin you in your dreams for ages now. Well, not ages. A couple nights." Her laugh seems to echo in the ocean water as she floats up next to me, staring out over the vast distance with white eyes. The light from the moon shines through her. I have to remind myself that this is a dream. "Do you not know how to speak in dreams, princess?" When she opens her mouth into a smile, moonlight fills it and shines so bright that I have to look away.

"How am I here? You're a ghost. Ghosts don't dream."

"Says who?" Marie Laveau snaps. "My death is made of dreams. Dreams of a better life."

"Well, then why am I here?" It's hard to look directly at her. She's so different from the last time I saw her in the graveyard—haunted, ghoulish, terrifying.

With a sigh, her feet float up from beneath her, and she's lying flat on the top of the water, moving in and out with the waves. "Because you're the only way life is going to get better. Well...the only way it won't get worse, I should say." Her words come to my ears as if she were standing right next to me, and I watch her, waiting for this dream to slip away.

"What do you expect me to do about it? I'm stuck with them."

Her body snaps up, her glowing eyes boring into me. "Who are you, and what have you done with the little brat who's messed up the whole ecosystem?"

"Excuse me? What is that supposed to mean?"

"I mean it as a compliment, princess." She laughs at my reaction, floating closer to me until we're face to face. "If it weren't for you and the little high priest, a lot more of your people would already be dead."

Reminding me of how many are dead already sends black spots into my eyes, as if I'm permanently marked by them. "You think so?"

"Dahlin, I know so. I know everything, if we want to be technical, I suppose." She twirls around me in one giant loop, singing an eerie song I don't recognize.

"Do you know how to get me out of this hotel then?"

"Be patient, princess." She stops spinning for one moment, to stare at me with those big, bright eyes. "You've been there this long for a reason. Do you know all the things you want to know?"

"What are you talking about?"

"Lamia's confident. She thinks she has you. She's tasted your blood, believes she's started to sway your feeble little Deuxsang brain." I open my mouth to object, but she continues on without a thought of me. "Now's your chance to get answers to the questions you won't get anywhere else. So why aren't you taking advantage of it?"

"Don't you think if I start asking her questions, she'll get suspicious?"

"Not if you phrase them the right way. You're a smart girl, or so the spirits tell me. After tonight, I'm not so sure." She cackles and spins straight up into the air like a torpedo. I blink, and she's next to me again.

"Well, what questions am I supposed to ask if you know everything?"

She stops moving for the first time since I stepped foot into this dream, and her face darkens with the clouds. "You'd do well to remember who you're talking to. The vampire queen might think you're the answer. I do not. If you do not work with me, I will find another way." And she starts spinning again, and humming. And I wish I were anywhere but here. "Do you know where your family is, princess? Do you know what Lamia's plan is? Her full plan? Do you know what they're planning on doing to the witches once they've dispatched with the Deuxsang?" She pauses. "No? Then your time is not done. Don't worry, once you have the answers we need, you can be free."

"Are you telling me that you could get Jason and me out now, but you won't because we don't have all the answers."

"I didn't say anything about Lamia's blood bag. I just said you."

"We're a package deal." I cross my arms and try to look at her, but she's moving so fast that my eyes can't focus.

"Are you now? Since when?" I spot her riding the waves, a little ways out, smiling despite the bite in her tone.

"That doesn't matter. If you're saving me, you have to save both of us. He doesn't deserve to be left behind."

"Very well, princess." She's in front of me again, and all her movement is making me dizzy. "If you get the answers that we need, I'll rescue both of you."

"Who's we?"

"Our time is done here. I'm tired of dreaming. Go to sleep, princess. We'll speak soon." And then I don't have a choice in the matter as she shoves me around the sand and back out the door that I came in. I reappear in my own consciousness for a moment, but can't keep my eyes open for any longer than that. I fall asleep to the memory of her eerie, unnatural humming.

***

"Did your mother let you sleep this long?"

My soul flies out of my body and back in again as I open my eyes to Lamia standing over me. I seize up, gripping the sheets in my fist, prepared for her to kill me. She's smiling, but that means nothing. She always smiles. It could just mean she's excited to drain me.

We stare at each other, me preparing to die, her smiling, until she chuckles to herself, backing away just slightly. "Oh, that's right. Your file did say you weren't a morning person. Should I give you a minute to wake up?"

I continue to stare, my fists not loosening, every nerve in my body prickling inside my skin. "What are you doing in my room?" I manage to cough out, slowly sitting up.

"Telling you to get dressed so that we can go for some beignets."

"You can't eat beignets." I grumble warily, watching her out of the corner of my eye as she wipes dust off the table.

"I can do whatever I want, my dear. Nothing restricts me anymore." Her words have a bitter bite to them, and no part of me wants to get out of this bed and go anywhere with her. "New clothes are on your dresser. Meet me in the lobby in fifteen minutes."

And she flits out the door, and I'm alone. I shiver hard, shaking off the feeling of waking up to her piercing red eyes—a waking nightmare.

But I know that if don't get up right now, she'll be back up here, and this time, the smile will be gone. Or she'll send Arlo in after me. I don't like either of those options. So I crawl my way out of bed, blinking at the bright winter light from the opened curtains. When I pick up the clothes she's left me, I almost consider the consequences of staying in bed. She's dressing me like her, just shorter and without the heels. For a good long minute, I stare at the slacks and button-up. A trench coat is hanging up beside the TV, and I'm shaking my head. Because there's no way. I pull open the drawer to wear the sweater she made me wear for Christmas and the comfortable jeans. But they're gone. What kind of psycho only leaves someone a suit?

I have no choice. I rip through the tangles in my hair and wrench on the suit, nearly gagging at my reflection. I look like Lilith's evil twin, which is horribly ironic. For a long time, I stare at myself in the mirror, and the voodoo queen's conversation runs through my head. I blink, and Jason's distraught face is staring back at me, tears running down his cheeks. His reflection whispers, "I can't do this." I can't either, but I have to. All I can think about is getting out of here, especially now that there's hope. Someone knows where I am, even if it's just a half-crazy ghost with no allegiance to anyone but herself.

Then I'm standing in front of the door, pressing my too-long nails into my fists until crescent-shaped scars are decorating the skin. I breathe in then out before working up the nerve to open the door, expecting Arlo to be waiting for me with a grim smirk. But he's not there. No one's in the hallway at all. This could be my chance. Maybe they're expecting me to run, or try to at least. But we're on the top floor of a huge hotel. The jump out the window wouldn't kill me, but I wouldn't get very far.

I look down to the end of the hall, where the huge window is calling me. Escape is possible. And I just stare, listening to the argument between my gut and my head.

Then I turn my back on the window, on freedom. And I walk away, down the hall, to the elevator that dings open right as I push the button. I expect Jason or Mirnov or maybe even Lilith to be waiting with Lamia downstairs, but it's just her—the queen of evil and destruction. She wears a perfectly white fur coat that makes her look small, but in the most elegant way. As I approach, she situates her rehearsed smile on her lips.

"That suit looks just as lovely on you as I pictured it. You look like a proper young lady."

"You mean a proper minion?" I raise my eyebrow to her, but she just smiles harder.

"I don't have minions, Cheyenne. I have followers who believe in my message and my cause, as I'm sure you will once we have a little chat." She slides her arm around mine and nods to the doorman, who pulls the great doors of the hotel open for us. It takes every muscle in my brain to keep myself from bolting onto Royal Street and disappearing. Except I know that I'll never be able to escape her, not really. So I keep my pace slow and steady, in step with her. My skin prickles being so near to the woman who killed my cousins, who's killed who knows how many other people. I feel like I'm in the presence of manipulation personified.

"How are you finding yourself now? Calmed down a bit?" The calmness in her voice sets my teeth on edge. As if everything that happened on Christmas was nothing to her—just another blip in a moment of her immortal life. What must that be like—to care about nothing and no one but yourself?

We weave in and out of streets, between tourists, heading towards Jackson Square. The tourist crowds get thicker, the music louder. And for just a moment, I'm able to forget who's holding onto my arm and revel in my city, remember the summer, let the shock wash over me as I realize that my life has gone from the best it's ever been to an absolute nightmare in less than a year. The blink of an eye to Lamia.

"Jason seems to be getting on better with you. He told me that he was happy you're finally with us." She stops me just in front of Café du Monde, turning me to face her. I try not to cringe away as she brings her chilled hand up to my temple, brushing a strand of hair out of my face. "We've been waiting so long for you, my dear." Her voice is barely a whisper, carried off quickly by the December wind. I shiver; she smiles. "Come. I can't wait to taste one of these finally. I've heard about them for over a century now."

I keep pace with her as she finds us a table at the fence, looking out into the crowd, our voices covered by the street band covering famous oldies. The smell of chocolate and powdered sugar makes my stomach rumble. She starts to order a café au lait for me, but I cut her off. "Hot chocolate, please."

The tiny waitress bobs her head in answer and scuttles away, throwing a worried glance over her shoulder at Lamia, who just smiles. When she turns her head one way, her eyes look light brown. But then she blinks, and they're red as her permanently stained lips. "I would've thought you a coffee drinker after all those shops you frequented this summer."

My body stiffens. She'd been watching me much longer than I thought. "It's too bitter."

"You acquire the taste I suppose. I've always had a bit of a sweet tooth myself." She winks as if we share a commonality now.

"How would you know that?"

"Everyone's blood is different. You've tasted it,

my dear. The muck that Lilith was feeding you compared to that little taste you had of the witch boy? You can't tell me there wasn't a difference, how much sweeter the witch's blood was."

She's watching my face hungrily, and I can't help that my mouth waters as my memories flashback to that night, the night when everything went wrong.

"You can't lie to me, my dear." She smiles that Cheshire grin and leans back in her seat, tilting her face up to the sun. "And your reaction just proves what I already knew to be true—we are more alike than either of us thought."

"Because it's a scientific fact that everyone's blood is different?" I spit. "That proves nothing."

"No. Because I can tell how much you enjoyed the difference." She laughs, turning a blinding smile on the waitress as she comes up to our table with a pile of beignets and my hot chocolate. The woman twitters in front of us for a moment, eyeing Lamia, trying to smile, but then just stares. "Anything I can help you with, my dear?" Lamia turns slowly to the waitress with her cat-like smile, and her eyes flash red. The waitress goes deathly white, her mouth gaping open, then scurries away as before, as if nothing happened.

"Are you feeling stronger now, with a morning out? I thought it was just what you needed."

"What I need is to be as far away from you as possible."

"You don't know what you need, my dear. You have so much power inside of you. You're going to heal all my children. You're going to save humanity. You're going to heal our home."

She opens her mouth to continue, but I cut her off. "You don't care about humanity or healing the planet." I don't know where this courage is coming from. Maybe it's the sugar in the hot chocolate or the fact that I'm surrounded by humans, and even though she might be able to walk in the daylight, there's nothing she can do to me out here, not without ruining her entire plan. But then Marie Laveau's words and threats run through my brain. "If you want me to trust you, I need the truth."

For a long moment, she stares at me. Her smile is gone, and I already feel like I'll keep my life for a few more hours. Before answering me, she takes a bite of a steaming beignet, and closes her eyes, tilting her head back again. She's doing this on purpose—testing me. I purse my lips and breathe in and out slowly, locking my hands together beneath the table.

"I have lived centuries waiting for the day that I could once again feel the sun. I convert so many because time passed where I felt utterly and completely desolate—all I wanted to do was kill. I needed a family to make me whole. And now I have that family, but I've cursed them to the same fate as me—hiding in the shadows for always, drinking from those lesser than us, hiding in the night, when we should be the ones ruling our home.

"It is true that I care about the environment only so much as that we need it to survive, but I knew the witches worshipped this rock, which made it very easy for me to get them onside at the time. If I was seen as the one saving their precious nature and protecting humans from their own ignorance, they couldn't live with themselves if they didn't help me." She grins, looking off to the side in memory. "So, yes, maybe what I'm doing isn't for the good of humanity. But it is for the good of my family. Everything I do…is for my family. You can understand that, can't you, my dear?" Lamia leans forward, her hands clasped together, with a look of almost desperation.

"My family's done nothing for me." I reply through gritted teeth.

Lamia shakes her head, chiding me with a cluck of her tongue. "Now, now, Cheyenne. That's not true. Your parents have provided for you. Your grandparents loved you. Rove has been everything else to you. Your sister even brought you to this city." She looks at me, and her eyes are glinting, though her face is still. "Despite how your family has treated you, you'd do anything for them."

I nod slowly, unsure, though deep down I know that I would.

"As would I."

She prowls in front of me, brushing her fingers over the line of tombs.

"But what's good for your family means the death of an entire race of people that you created. How can you live with yourself?" I try to keep the disgust from my voice, but she shows no remorse whatsoever.

"Oh, my dear, what have those witches been filling you're head with? We will not be wiping out the Deuxsang." She shakes her head at my confusion.

"Then why--?"

"Cheyenne, I have perfected the Deuxsang gene. Together, you and Jason make the perfect creation. And now that we have perfection, we no longer have a need for the older, flawed generation."

"So you're just going to murder everyone?" I keep my voice even, despite the pounding in my head.

"The new generation of Deuxsang will be strong, placid, happy creatures. They will give us everything we've dreamed of. And it's all thanks to you."

My mind runs a million miles a minute. My vision won't stay straight. "If you've already gotten what you need from me, how do I know you won't kill me too, along with my family?"

Again, she falls silent. I watch her leave a pile of money on the table, pull me up from my chair—almost gently—and lead me out of the crowded café. Then we're flitting, and my vision is blurred, though I don't know if it's from dizziness or tears. The hot chocolate and beignets roil in my stomach.

When we stop, I land on my knees, trying not to heave up my breakfast. Lamia watches me patiently while I compose myself and realize where we are—the tombs, the bare willow trees. I look up at the sign in front of me: Marie Laveau.

"I could very easily kill you, my dear." Lamia prowls in front of the tombs, brushing her fingers over the shadowed tombs. "I could've easily killed your family and your little witch boyfriend. That would've made my family a lot happier." She kneels down in front of me and lifts my chin with one finger. "They are itching for me to kill you and get this whole messy business over with." She tilts my head to one side, then the other, smirking. "But I won't. Because you are special to me—part of my family."

I lean away, picking myself up off the frosted cemetery ground. "Then why am I here?"

She sighs, looking around the lines of tombs slowly and stops on Marie Laveau's tomb with the scattered offerings. She strolls up to the semicircle and kicks away a dirty piece of candy. "Because I wanted you to know that if you betray me, if you turn your back on this family, there will be nothing I can do to save you."

Six

"I knew you'd be slow, just not this slow." Mirnov doesn't pause before he strikes at me again. All I have to do is drop to my stomach, just barely avoiding the swing at my head. "What's your family been teaching you?"

Jason watches a little ways away, arms crossed over his broad chest. I jump back onto my feet, body tensed.

Mirnov circles me, like a snake in the grass, ready to strike. "I don't even know how to start to fix you." He sneers, but there's a disgusting glimmer in his eye.

"I don't need to be fixed." I spit the word at him.

He snorts and backs away from me, rearing up for another strike. "You think too much. Be more like Lilith." If I had a dollar for every time someone's said that to me... He winks at my cousin. "It's basically hot air up there." And he pats her head like she's a puppy, smirking as he walks away.

I glower at him, and thankfully, even though Lilith smiles at him, her nostrils flare when he turns his back. At least she's not completely brainwashed. Then he strikes at her, but his hand slices through air. She dodges slightly to the side milliseconds before his hand moves, and as he pauses, slightly confused as to why he didn't make contact with her face, her fist pummels into his stomach, and he doubles over.

When he straightens up, she's smiling. "I guess a little hot air is a good thing."

Anger flickers beneath Mirnov's smooth features, but he turns his back to me without another word. "Your turn," he says to me.

I steel myself against whatever he has prepared, closing my eyes to clear my mind. I hear his move coming and slip backward just out of his reach. My eyes flash open, and I thrust my hand out at his throat. But he dodges just in time.

From a distance, Jason calls, "Don't think. Feel, listen, watch." And again, I clear my head as we move about in a circular dance. His skin twinges, yelling to strike at me. And I see it coming. See the grabs and stabs. But I move out of the way and get in little jabs here and there. He's growing tired and frustrated, which is working to my advantage.

"Getting tired, grandpa?" I smirk.

A growl rips through his throat, and he flits into a lunge. But even through the blur, I stick my arm out and link it around his neck. He gags, freezing in his flit and struggles in my grasp. I flit myself, pinning one of his arms behind his back, wrench it in the socket. "Give," I hiss in his ear.

"No."

My arm moves at lightning speed as I release his arm, but pound my fist over his still heart. "Then you're dead." And I shove him away. Irregular clapping echoes over the rooftop, and I see Jason try to hide his smile.

Lamia stands at the door to the rooftop, her claps beating in time with her slow steps. "Well done, my dear. Mirnov is my best warrior." He stands off to the side now, nursing his ego with Lilith at his side. "But you took too long to take him down."

And then I'm on the ground, my head slamming into the concrete. She stands over me, her heel hovering over my chest. The rooftop echoes silence.

Lamia's eyes lock onto mine, but then she's smiling and pulling me to my feet before I even know what's happening. She dusts off my jacket, then takes my hand and pulls me to the door behind her. "Come along, Jason. I have something I'd like to show the both of you."

When I look back over my shoulder, Lilith is watching me, and for the first time, it's not with loathing or hatred. She almost looks sorry for me. She opens her mouth as if she's about to say something, something unreadable flickering across her features, but then her mouth closes, and she shudders. Mirnov says something, and her attention is returned to him. Then Jason's blocking my view of them, and I'm being pulled down the stairs by Lamia.

"I've been trying to decide the perfect moment for me to share this with you. But now that I've seen you training, and now that we've had our talk." Her eyes glow when she looks back at me, and her white smile reflects in the darkness of the stairwell. "I know you're ready to hear this. Both of you."

Jason doesn't say anything, but I can feel him behind me, a nervous energy. But he's kept his distance since we had our moment while trying to have more conversations with me at the same time. I think its part of his act—showing Lamia that he's accepted me, that I'm a part of his family now.

My eyes have to adjust to the light once we've reached the top floor of the hotel again. Lamia struts in front of us, thankfully releasing my hand so that I can walk on my own and slow my pace so that Jason and I walk together.

"Mother," he clears his throat, "you've been saying for weeks now that we're going to mobilize." Jason's careful not to look at me. "And yet...?"

Lamia stops in front of her room at the end of the hall, just barely looking over her shoulder at Jason. "We will carry out the plan," her words are as light as a breath, "when I say it's time. Do I make myself clear?" Then she's looking at both of us full-on, and after a glance at each other, we nod. "Lovely, now come. I just can't wait to show you!"

I thought my room was grand and lavish, but Lamia's room ramps that up to a whole other level, a ridiculous level really. Everything is either gold or red or purple, and looking at anything for too long hurts my eyes. What I mistook as a bottle of champagne turns out to be a full bottle of blood, waiting for us, and I surprise myself with how thirsty I am. I haven't felt this kind of thirst since...since I smelled Erik's blood. I don't even have to taste it to know that it's witch blood in that bottle. I just know. My stomach seizes to think whose it might be.

But then my ears are distracted by cooing and gurgling, and lying in a crib is my nephew, Freddie. I flit to his side before Lamia can stop me and lift him into my arms. It's been over a month since I've seen him, but he still seems to recognize me, a tiny little crook of a smile on his chubby face. His blue eyes roam all over the room, stopping one too many times on Lamia.

I cradle his head to my chest, turning on her while trying to maintain my composure. I suck in a quiet breath through my nose before speaking. "What are you doing with my nephew? Where's my sister?"

"Cheyenne, you know very well that Freddie is not Kara's biological child. You discovered our little illusion on your own this past semester—kudos to you." She strolls up to my side, running a bony finger over Freddie's lumpy arm. Jason stares, waiting for an explanation as to why he has to be here for this.

"This precious little boy is the first of his generation—the first perfect creation." My skin crawls at the way Lamia's gazing at him like he's a sweet treat. "So naturally, he can't be your nephew because Kara and Thomas's genes are filth compared to yours and Jason's."

At first, the words pass by my notice. I'm too worried about Freddie being kept in Lamia's room all this time. But then the weight of her words hit me, and I stop bouncing Freddie on my hip. Jason and I meet gazes at the same moment, hitting the realization together.

And she's watching us, like a puppet master watching her play commence. "Yes. Freddie is an exactly perfect combination of your DNAs—your first child, my dears."

"What?!" I nearly drop Freddie, and that just makes me hold him tighter. Then I'm staring at him, and I see it—ginger hair like Jason's, my eyes…

He's…

Mine…

I have a baby…

"This beautiful child is yours. Congratulations, my dears."

Her words sound utterly ridiculous, and I'm now convinced that I must be dreaming. That this is a nightmare. That I'm just worried about Freddie and about what's happening. But I pinch myself and bite the inside of my cheek until it's raw. I'm still here.

Jason and I stare at each other. I can't look at Lamia. I can't look anywhere except at Jason, and it seems the same goes for him. His mouth opens and closes several times, then his gaze flickers to Freddie, then back to me. Then we're both looking at Freddie.

"How…how could you do this?" I try to keep my voice even, but I don't know how much I'm succeeding. Freddie's growing restless in my arms, picking up the tension in my grasp.

"What do you mean?" Lamia asks innocently, and I have to restrain myself from hurling her into the wall.

"You went and made a baby of ours," I look to Jason again for support, but he's gone comatose, "without our permission. You took our DNA... without our consent. Do you not see how completely...?"

"Watch your words, my dear. Remember who you're speaking to." Her tone is hushed, calming, just to keep Freddie calm in the rising panic. But I can feel the unspoken threat. "You had no choice in the matter. My entire operation—centuries of effort have led to you two. And you were ultimately meant to create this beautiful, perfect child." I nearly wretch when Freddie reaches for her. She moves to take him out of my arms, but I back away, close to Jason.

"How did you even do it?"

"Your Ascension ceremonies. Mirnov could taste the difference in your blood, the extra bit of everything. And he brought samples to me for testing."

"So you've had our blood for this long, and just now made Freddie? Why?" I don't know how I'm forming coherent questions. All I'm thinking inside is I'm a mom I'm a mom I'm a mom how the hell am I a mom.

"Yes, I had to be sure I had the right girl. Jason's blood—I could tell immediately. It was that potent. Yours, I wasn't too sure. So we watched you grow, created the illusion in your family's mind about Kara's pregnancy. And if you turned out to be the right girl, we had a fetus ready for your family."

"Only to rip him away from us?" I yell. My skin feels like it's tightening around my bones.

"The time for change is now. You don't fully believe in my cause. I understand that." Lamia looks at me, but she's speaking to Jason too. "You don't want to fight for me." Then she looks down at Freddie in my arms, whose head is crooked back looking at the intricacies laced into the ceiling. "Now, you're fighting for him. You're fighting for us, to keep him alive. Because if we fail, then your precious boy falls with us."

Her words settle in around me, forming an abyss between Jason and me. Jason nearly falls onto the bed, just barely keeping himself from sliding onto the floor.

Lamia's gaze pierces between us, slicing through the silence like a shriek. "I'll give you all some family time, a moment to process everything, and make up your minds about how you intend to move forward. Come find me for tea when you're ready, my dears." She places a kiss on all three of our cheeks before flitting out of the room.

The moment she's gone, I set to pacing the length of the suite, holding Freddie too tight for comfort, but he amuses himself by playing with my hair. "Jason, I need you to say something, please." I stop in front of him. He opens his mouth but promptly shuts it when his eyes glaze over. So I pace again. "We have a kid. This is…he's our baby."

I stop, looking to him once again, waiting for anything. I can't be the only one talking.

He opens his mouth, but no sound comes out.

"We have to get out of here. We have to get Freddie out of here. This is bad. So bad. I didn't realize that she'd already done this. I thought this was just the plan. But she already put the plan into motion."

"Cheyenne, Cheyenne, stop." Jason jumps to his feet, and for the first time, really looks at Freddie. "Can I hold him?"

I can't honestly say that my eyeballs double in size. I think it's more like quadruple, but I don't know if that's biologically possible. But I can't exactly say no, so, carefully, I pass my nephew… my son…Freddie to Jason, slightly relieved of the weight. I watch them carefully as I pour myself a glass of blood because at this point, I don't care whose it is. All I know is that it will make me feel better. So I down one glass, then two, I'm on my third when Jason stops me.

"You're going to go into a blood frenzy if you drink that fast."

I bite my words back but listen to his advice, stepping away from the table.

"You're right. We have to get out of here. Lamia can't have access to him, to us even."

"Does it matter if she has access to us? She probably has our DNA on store somewhere to make a whole army of Cheyenne-Jason monster babies."

"Cheyenne, shut up and pull yourself together!" He shouts. It's the first time he's shouted at me, and Freddie starts to whimper and reaches for me. I immediately take him from Jason, turning my back on him.

"I'll contact the Voodoo Queen tonight. I'll tell her we're ready."

"I'm sorry, you'll contact who?" He asks, coming up behind me. I sway Freddie side to side, shushing his increasingly loud cries.

"Marie Laveau, she appeared to me the other night when I was dreamwalking. Said she needed me to get information out of Lamia about what her plan was. Now I've done that. Now I'm in custody of half the plan basically. So…we need to get out of here. She can help us get out of here."

"What's she going to do, just poof into a hotel full of vampires and poof the three of us out? No way."

"It's called warping. And no, I don't think she can do that—she's not a witch. Plus, she's dead."

Jason turns me around, staring at me like I've just told the biggest lie ever to be thought of. "I'm sorry…a dead voodoo queen is going to save us from an army of vampires? I don't think so." He shakes his head then downs his first glass of blood, staring off into space as he allows the warm liquid to settle him.

"I don't know what she's going to do. That's why I'm going to contact her. But until then, we have to act like we're on board with this. Like we are all in on her plan. Or else she won't give us access to Freddie at all, and we won't be able to get him out when she comes for us."

Again, he looks at me like I'm the biggest moron on the planet. "Cheyenne...she's a ghost. The only way she's coming for us is for a nice haunting."

I try not to roll my eyes. "She's not exactly your normal ghost. I mean, if she can still dream, doesn't that set her apart?"

"Are you sure she's not just messing with you?"

"What reason does she have to do that?" And finally I've stumped him. He stares at me, waiting for a response to come to him, but it doesn't and he just stares. Freddie's big eyes wander between the two of us, and he gurgles as if this is the most normal moment in the world. I hate that this is what normal is for him.

"So we go with my plan—act like we're on board. I'll contact Marie Laveau. And we're getting out of here, as soon as possible, and getting to our families and the witches."

It's like my words are a punch in the gut to him. Every surety washes from his face and again, he falls back onto the gigantic bed. "I don't know if I'm ready for that..."

"Ready for what? To finally be free from her? Of course you are. You're a freaking father."

His eyes flash up at me, and the words feel wrong in my mouth. He's silent for a long moment, staring down at the floor. "Seeing my family again. It's been so long, Cheyenne. I don't even know how many years have passed since Lamia took me. I don't think I can do it."

I feel like the biggest jerk on the planet, my stomach dropping down to my toes. For a minute, we just sit there, with Freddie gurgling between us, then I walk him back over to his crib and set him down. When I look back at Jason, the heels of his hands are pressed into his eyes. I sit down next to him, carefully, but this bed is so firm, it doesn't even feel my weight. I've never been good at comforting people—Anne has told me this on multiple occasions. But I slide my arm around his broad shoulders and lean into him.

"Your family is going to be so excited to see you. They've never stopped loving you."

His voice is thick with tears, though he won't let me actually see his face. "Yeah, but they don't know what I've done. They don't know how complicit I've been in all of this."

"None of that is your fault. Lamia is the most powerful vampire in history. A teenage Deuxsang who has barely been affirmed is no match against her, even if she did specifically create us. She compelled you to think and act the way you were thinking. But now that your mind is clear, you're doing the right thing. And that's all that matters, and that's all they're going to care about."

He still won't look up at me, and his shoulders shake once, twice. Then he's the one leaning into me, and I'm holding him as I cry, and I promise myself that I will never tell anyone about this moment—especially Eli.

After awhile, Jason's calm enough to meet Lamia. He washes away the redness and puffiness in his face with some cold water. I gulp down another glass of blood for some extra courage then lift Freddie back up out of his crib. He stares at me like I'm the center of the universe, and then I'm the one ready to break down. How could she be such a monster? But I can't because this sweet baby is staring at me, and Jason is waiting at the door for me, and that monster is waiting for us to tell her that we are on her side, ready to support her until victory or death, whichever comes first.

We walk down the hall, Freddie on my hip, watching the empty hallway behind me. The elevator ride down to the restaurant lobby is silent, but for one moment, Jason takes my hand in his and squeezes. But when the doors open, we're inches apart and stride in step through the lobby and dining room, to Lamia's private room, where she's waiting with a champagne flute of blood in her hand. She watches us walk, and it gives me a thought. I drop my hand again, keeping a firm arm around Freddie, and reach for Jason's hand. I feel him seize up, but then he realizes my plan when Lamia's face changes into a smile. His fingers link between mine, and then we're standing in front of her.

"Well, it seems you two have made your decision then?" She raises an eyebrow, looking between the three of us.

"We have," I say, making my voice stronger than I feel. "You know you've always had Jason. And you're right, I don't want to fight for you. But you saw it in me as soon as you brought me, that I'd do anything for my family. I'll do whatever it takes to protect Freddie. I will fight." I squeeze Jason's hand for Lamia's benefit. "We will fight. Together." The words feel tight in my throat as her smile grows.

"Excellent. Now, the work truly begins."

Seven

Back in my room, even though it's still early in the evening, I close my eyes, trying to force that state of half unconsciousness on myself. In the dream state, I stand in a room of dim darkness, waiting for Marie Laveau to call to me as she did the first time a couple of weeks ago. But silence fills the room around me.

Then I hear it, the soft jazz, the rattle of the snare, and the runs of the saxophone. And then a door appears, a simple door, and I have a feeling that it's not Marie Laveau's dream that I'm about to walk into. Then I'm running, sprinting, flitting. I land against the door, my hand falling on the knob and wrenching it open.

I find him in a jazz club, sitting alone, watching instruments play themselves into a wonderful melody. He stares straight ahead, his curls highlighted by the stage lights, and I want to drop to my knees right then. He senses the disturbance in his dream wave and turns slowly over his shoulder. Then he's on his feet, in front of me. He stands there, his hands hovering on either side of my face before he pulls me into him. I link my hands around his shoulders, pulling myself deeper into the kiss that I've been waiting for, dreaming of. He squeezes me tight until he has to come up for air. But he stays as close as possible, staring down at me as if I'm not real. The silence between us is filled with the soft jazz music, and I'm afraid to break it with words. So I just pull him into me again, resting my head against his shoulder, digging my fingers into his shirt.

"Is this actually you?" he whispers into my hair. I can feel his lips and shiver.

"Yeah." I realize that I'm crying into his shirt and pull myself even closer to him.

"Why have you taken so long?"

"I don't' know... your dreams haven't found me." When I look back up at him, I can't help kissing him. The fact that I'm here means that he's still alive, and that thought makes me weak in the knees. "Where are you?"

"Grand Isle, just off the coast—another safe house of mom's."

"I'm going to be out of here soon. I'll find you."

"What are you talking about?"

"I've been in contact with—"

"She's been talking to me, little priest." A slight cackle bounces around the music hall. "Oh wow, the acoustics are just lovely in here, Elijah. Very nice choice of venue."

"How did you get in here?" I ask, thoroughly pissed off that she's interrupting my time with Eli when I've only just gotten here.

"Did you really think the bounds of the dreamscape could hold me, princess? I'm dead!" She cackles again and floats up to the ceiling with a twist and a twirl. Then with a graceful spin, she lands in front of us, her chin hovering over her dark hands. "Now, what have you gotten for me, princess? Enough to get you out of that luxury five-star hotel they've got you chained up in?"

"You've known where she's been this entire time and didn't think to inform my mom?" Eli shouts, his voice echoing back at us.

"Of course not, little priest." Her eyes roll back in her head before refocusing on me. "If I'd done that, you would've tried to save her, and we wouldn't now have the information that we're about to learn. Now would we?" Her glowing gaze focuses on him for an intimidating minute before turning back to me.

"Lamia is planning on starting over everything. She wants to rule the world."

"What are you saying?" Eli says, trying to follow along.

"Now that she has Jason and me, the perfect combination of DNA that gets her the power to walk in the sun, enhanced abilities and strength, she doesn't need the older 'flawed' generation of Deuxsang. And she doesn't need the witches anymore. She's perfected the formula. So now she can just…copy it." I debate on whether to tell Eli about Freddie, but Marie Laveau is watching me too closely, and this is not a conversation that I want to have with him and her. "Now that Jason and I have convinced her that we fully support her, she's ready to move forward with the plan."

"Which will be happening when?" Marie Laveau

asks.

"She won't say. We've asked several times, but she's keeping it under lock and key."

"That's not good enough, princess." Her eyes blaze in front of me, and she spins around us in frustration. "We have to know when it's happening. I'm afraid you haven't kept up your end of the deal."

"Yes, I have. You wanted information about Lamia's plan. I have that. I know who she wants to wipe out and who she doesn't. I know what she wants. Just because I don't know the precise moment she's going to strike..."

Her cackle cuts me off. "That IS the information I need. What does the rest of it matter without that tiny tidbit?" She giggles and floats away from us. "Give it another week."

"No." Eli and I say at the same time.

"You can't just leave her there."

"It's not just me I'm worried about."

"Yes, of course, little martyr. We know you care about all living creatures, great and small."

The urge to smack her rushes through me, but I can only imagine how badly that would go over. Plus, my hand would probably just pass right through her. "I don't know how long Jason can keep up this game of pretending. And...she has my nephew, Freddie. I can't sleep knowing that he's in her room. She could be drinking from him for all I know."

For the first time in the dream, there's complete silence. Marie Laveau is still watching me carefully, and from her lack of a response, I know she knows. She hums low, barely a sound at all. Her gaze rotates between Eli and me, and I wish with every fiber of my being that she won't say anything in front of him. And she doesn't. "Alright, princess. We'll get you out of the Monteleone. Just keep your head above water until then. And protect that baby."

Her humming grows louder, then she switches her gaze to Eli. "I'll be seeing you soon, little priest." Both of us scrunch our faces at that term, but she's gone before we have the chance to question her.

Silence stretches between us for a long moment, for ten of Eli's breaths. "We're going to get you out of there. I promise." His hand easily finds the back of my neck, applying a comforting pressure, enough to keep the tears away.

"How long have I been gone?"

"Two weeks," he whispers.

"I feel like Christmas was forever ago." He makes a sound of agreement, stroking my cheekbone with his thumb, and then I finally look up at him. "I need to tell you something else. I didn't want to say it with her here… but… I don't know how to say this…"

"What, Cheyenne? Whatever it is, you can tell me." He looks down on me with those beautiful green eyes, and I wish more than anything that I wasn't about to hurt him.

"Lamia has already put her plan into motion. She has mine and Jason's DNA, and with it, she has created the perfect Deuxsang. Eli, Freddie isn't my nephew. He's my son. Mine and Jason's." I bring my hand to my mouth and hold in a sob. Eli pulls me into his lap, holding my head against his chest that rises faster now. "Eli, when did the world get like this?"

He's silent again, and I almost look up to make sure that he's still there. But then his breath falls on the back of my neck, and he says, "The world's always been this way. It's just our turn to deal with it." The tears come in a steady stream now, washing over my hands and onto his shirt. "We're gonna deal with this."

I let my tears run out before lifting my head. "I think we can do it. I don't know how, but I think we can. I know what they want now. We have Jason now."

"You sure you can trust Jason? I know you want to, but..."

"Eli, he's basically been brainwashed for the past however many years. I was able to clear out Lamia's compulsion over him."

He smoothes my ruffled hair. "How are you going to get Freddie away from her?"

"I don't know yet. I don't even know if she's keeping anyone else."

Eli's jaw stiffens. "We lost some people after Lamia pulled you and Jason away. Ms. Rose is real weak now. Mason hasn't left her bedside, and Anne's not great either. She feels guilty that you're gone, that Jason is still gone, that your cousin..." I wince, but try to keep it in, encourage him to keep going. "She'll be glad to know you're okay. And her brother too."

"What happened after we left?" I'm not sure if I want to know the answer, but I'm asking anyway. I have to know.

He hesitates, trying to piece together how to tell me everything. Is it more gruesome than I've allowed myself to imagine? "Nothing's really happened. Your mom and Rove are with us. I tried to get your grandparents and Marilyn, but some vampires flitted them away before I could grab them. I'm sorry."

"But they're still alive, though, as far as you know?"

"As far as I know. We lost people though. I don't know how many Deuxsang, a lot of witches… Mom's not really in a good place. She's kind of locked herself away from everyone. Not even Andrew can coax her out."

It's all my fault. All the death, the plan going wrong—if I hadn't frozen, if she hadn't trapped me, I would've been able to fight them, for my family. So many wouldn't have died. I would actually be holding Eli right now, instead of his dream self.

"Eli, I'm going to fix all this. I know it's my fault all those people died—"

"That's not true, Cheyenne." I press my fingers gently to his lips, thankful for his assurances, but knowing he's wrong.

"It is. It was my plan that got them all killed. It was me freezing, allowing Lamia to do that to me.

I swear, I'll do all I can to fix this, to make it up to your people, and to mine."

"I'm just glad you're alive," Eli whispers again and leans into me with a real kiss, the type of kiss that I've been dreaming about for weeks. I don't think he can pull me any closer, his arms circling tight around me, and I hold him, twisting my fingers in the curls at the base of his head, digging my nails into his shoulder. God, I missed him. I missed him so much that this hurts. To see him, to touch him, hurts. I didn't know if this would ever happen again.

And then as soon as I was there, I'm gone, and I wake up in a cold sweat, staring up at the ceiling of my room in the Monteleone. I don't know how long it is before the tears stop.

"Jason, we're getting out of here." He walks a pace faster than me down our hallway. Lamia called us to a meeting on the rooftop, and he's still in the habit of rushing to meet her every beck and call.

"When?" He flits around, and I nearly stumble into him.

"I'm not sure. They didn't say when they were going to come..."

His eyes flicker into a narrow slice. "Who are they?"

I bite down hard on my lip because I know he's not going to like what I'm about to tell him. I don't even know if he'll believe me. "Marie Laveau and the witches."

His face contorts into a mask of confusion. "Have you completely lost your mind?"

"No, she wants to help us. I don't exactly know why." I frown at the ground, asking myself the question for the first time.

"Are you sure you didn't dream all of this up?"

I open my mouth to retort, but stop myself. "I mean...technically yes, it was a dream. But I was dreamwalking so it wasn't my dream. But none of that matters. She's real. I've met her ghost before, and yes, she might be a ghost, but she can still mess with the mortal world."

He's staring at me now, mouth slightly parted, and I know I've lost him. "So what you're telling me is we're never getting out of here. Fantastic." His jaw works itself into stone as he takes a deep breath in through his nostrils. "Thanks for getting my hopes up, Cheyenne."

"Jason, I'm not making this stuff up. The witches are coming for us. They know where we are now, and they have a plan. Just trust me."

"I trust you. I don't trust them," he says over his shoulder.

"Your family does."

Again, he stops.

"Your sister definitely does. Your mom spied for them while I was locked in Clandestine. She infiltrated the Ascending and reported back to us, even though none of us knew it until right before Christmas. So if they can trust them, if I trust them, why can't you?"

He sighs, and his broad shoulders sag. "It's not that I don't want to, Cheyenne."

"Then what is it?"

He turns slowly, eyes not quite meeting mine. "Despite how much I don't like it, I was raised by the most powerful vampire in history. Everything I know, even the stuff she didn't force into my head, I know because of her. So I'm sorry, Cheyenne. I'll believe it when I see it."

Then we're practically flitting up the rooftop stairs to where Lamia and Mirnov are waiting for us. It takes me a minute to notice Lilith standing off in the corner, burrowed into a fur coat against the sharp bitterness of the December wind.

"Here they are, the prodigal children." Lamia's smile seems to reflect off of pools of water on the roof.

In a flash, Jason reverts to his old self and returns Lamia's smile, rushing up to her for a hug. I steel myself against the self-loathing and do the same. She looks almost shocked when I accept her hug, and it's kind of satisfying.

"Well, you two look well-rested. Have you been enjoying each other's company?"

"Of course, Mother. What did you need from us?"

She watches us for a moment, a long moment, her red eyes flickering between Jason and me, and her smile dissipates. "Well, I thought it was time for another lesson. Cheyenne is stronger, and she might actually be able to handle you now." Lamia winks at me, and I repress the shiver that's fighting to work its way down my body. "Alright, you know what to do."

Jason and I exchange a worried look. He's trying to tell me something, but whatever he's trying to warn me about is not coming through just from his eyes. We move apart to nearly opposite sides of the roof. Mirnov stands between us.

"This time, Jason is defending. Cheyenne, you're on the attack. Knock him to the ground," he growls then moves out of our way.

Jason nods to me, just a slight movement of his head. He better not be about to let me win. We're going to have problems. In synchronicity, we adjust our stances, mirroring each other's movements, feet shoulder-width apart, back tense, ready for the strike.

I take in a deep breath, focusing on Jason's eyes. I can already feel his wall building. But before I can start building up my infliction, Lamia steps between us. "This practice is all good and fun, but the time for practice is over. When you're fighting in the war, you won't be standing and staring at each other." She gestures us both closer with a curl of her index fingers.

I look up at him, and he looks across at me. We both take several steps forward until Lamia takes both of our hands and pulls us to stand next to each other. "When you are fighting, you have to be aware of every nerve in your body, of every other nerve around you—every movement, hesitation, breath, death, victory. Who's killing the most? Who's the weakest? You have to think about all this during the fight. And then you have to fight, and you have to use your mind. A moment's hesitation and you're ashes. Do you understand me?"

We both nod. I guess I hadn't thought about it before. Some part of my brain knew that it would come to this—fighting, war. People have already died for this. But I never thought about the actual act of fighting. What if I fail? What if I hesitate and…?

"Cheyenne, are you ready?" Lamia's cold hand rests on my shoulder, and when I meet her eyes, I want to scream and run. I want to grab Freddie, sprint out the front doors of the Monteleone, and never look back. I want to wake up.

But I'm never going to wake up from this. I'm staring at my reality, and right now, this nightmare is about to teach me how to survive. So I grit my teeth and nod, barely sparing a look over at Jason, who's staring down into a rippling puddle.

"Alright, my dear, ladies first. You throw the first punch." She steps away from us, and I'm left standing shoulder to shoulder with Jason. His breath hitches in his chest, but he won't look up at me.

Lilith steps forward. "Mother, I see the point you're trying to make, but this doesn't feel realistic. They can't fight if they have no anger toward each other."

For a minute, I think Lamia is going to rip Lilith's perfect head off her shoulders. But then she sighs and smiles. "You're right, my dear. Cheyenne and Jason have grown too close over the last few days. But you two," she looks between me and my cousin with a conspiratorial grin, "have a fair amount of hatred for one another, yes?"

We don't look at each other, and we don't say anything.

Lamia takes my hand, pulling me away from the group, and leans down to whisper in my ear. "Now's your chance for revenge, Cheyenne. She betrayed you, used you, has always hated you. She gave you up to me, got your cousin killed." I hide my tightened fists behind my back as she continues to whisper Lilith's atrocities at me.

My throat restricts, and my gaze flickers over to Lilith from beneath my lashes. I've wanted to punch her for as long as I can remember. Maybe now's my chance… ?

The door to the rooftop slams open, and we all jump, looking up at the new arrival. Arlo stands with two of his younger siblings behind him. "Mother, we have a problem."

Lamia flits to him, stirring a burst of cold air around Lilith and me. I take a step away from her.

"The witch priestess is downstairs. She's requesting a meeting with you." His voice travels over to us, though Lamia is arcing herself around him so that we won't hear anything.

"How many of them are down there?"

"From what we can see? About ten," Arlo says. "I told them to leave, but they seem to have a death wish."

Lamia's gaze flicks over her shoulder at me, then at Jason. "Mirnov, come here." He's by her side in a moment—the obedient puppy. "Show them to the private dining room. Only two are allowed in. The others must wait in the lobby." She turns back to Arlo. "Four of your siblings will guard them."

"You three," she nods to Jason, me, and Lilith. "Back to your rooms immediately. Lock the doors, and you will not come out until I come for you. Am I clear?" Her voice carries across the roof and nips at our skin. We all three nod. "Arlo, take them to their rooms."

"Yes, Mother." She spares one last glance back at us before flitting down the stairs with Mirnov on her heels.

"Let's go, half-breeds." Arlo jerks his head toward the door. Lilith moves first, and Jason quickly follows.

"What's going on?" I ask Arlo, stopping at the top of the stairs.

His blazing eyes meet mine, and it's like the first time I ever noticed him and his siblings, dirty on the street, watching me. "Witches are here. I'm getting you to safety." His words are slow, and his gaze doesn't break. "Go to Mother's room. Jason too."

"But she said to go to our rooms..."

"She meant for you to go to her room." His voice is low, almost impossible to hear. "Hurry. Both of you." And he pushes me at the stairs. Two parts of my brain scream at each other, and they're both in an argument with my gut. Is this a trick? They have to be plotting something. But Arlo...he seemed—

I shake my head, shooing away the thoughts, and focus on catching up with Jason. I grab onto his shirt right before he unlocks his door, just two down from mine. Arlo's right behind me, waiting for us to follow him.

"We're supposed to go to Lamia's room, Jason."

"No, she said our rooms."

"You misunderstood her, half-breed." Jason looks back at Arlo with a glare. "You're to go to her room and protect the baby." Again, he meets my gaze, and my gut starts fighting with reason and history. Everything points to this being a trap. But deep in my gut, I feel like I have to trust him.

"Let's go, Jason."

Arlo sets off before us at a slight jog, and I grab Jason's hand to pull him along behind me. I can feel his resistance, and I don't know if it's a remnant compulsion, or his newfound wariness of vampires. But he follows, stumbling after me.

Arlo fits the skeleton key into Lamia's door at the end of the hallway, and the three of us slip into the door, which he locks behind us. But I come to a halt. Freddie's in his crib, on his back, staring straight up at Marie Laveau's ghost floating above him. I listen for his cries but instead hear giggles.

"Momma, what are you doing?" My head jerks over to Arlo, whose clean-cut accent has dissolved into a thick southern drawl. A New Orleans drawl. "Don't scare the baby, or they'll all come running here."

Arlo walks over to Marie Laveau as she floats upright and lands soundlessly on her feet. I look over at Jason. His jaw is nearly touching his chest.

"I'm sorry, did you just call her Momma?" I take a step forward.

"Yes, princess, Arlo here is my eldest. But we don't have time to get into all this. Regina can only distract Lamia so long before the cunning old succubus realizes what's happening."

But we're all frozen on the spot. At least, Jason

and I are. "Have I said something wrong?" Marie's familiar cackle echoes in my ears as she turns to Arlo with the question.

"Wake up." Arlo stomps in front of me and snaps his fingers in Jason's face. "Get the kid, and go!" He jerks his thumb over his shoulder at Freddie, who's sitting up now, smiling at all of us. "Now!" He growls, frustrated at our frozen bodies.

But three sharp raps on the door break our paralysis. I flit to Freddie's crib, lifting him into my arms just as his bottom lip trembles. "Sh sh sh it's okay, Freddie. It's okay." I hold him close to me, keeping a wide berth between myself and Marie Laveau. Jason stands close to me, ready to attack, as Arlo slowly opens the door. I nearly cry with relief when Lucas's face is on the other side. He strides into the room, assessing everything, and is followed by another witch who I don't recognize.

"Lucas!" I yell, running over to him and throwing my free arm around his neck. "You're here. Where's Eli?"

After an uncomfortable moment, he unhooks my arm from around him. "Mom wouldn't let him come. He's waiting for you on Grand Isle. We have to get out of here now."

"What's happening downstairs?" I ask.

Without answering, he takes my hand, ready to warp us to wherever they've been hiding out, but when the new girl holds her hand out to Jason, he just stares.

"Jason, we have to go. Take her hand." I hold

Freddie tighter as I watch Jason's face argue with itself, twisting itself into painful contortions. He drops to his knees, holding his head at his temples.

"Ahhhh, I can't, Cheyenne. Just go."

I hand Freddie to Lucas, who holds him out at arms length. I drop to my knees beside Jason. "Listen to me. I know she's in your head, but you can't let her stop you. This is our chance to go."

He yells again, crushing his head into his chest. "I can't, I can't," he mumbles, curling in on himself. I circle my arm around his shoulders, ignoring the raised eyebrow from Lucas.

"Jason," I whisper roughly. "Jason, look at me." But he cringes, holding tighter to his head. I pull his arms down with a struggle, exerting all my strength, and then grab his head to look at me. The second he meets my eyes, I say, "You can leave. She has no power over you. We're leaving now."

Slowly, his body relaxes, and his eyes stay locked on mine.

"What's going on here?" Every part of me seizes as Lilith's sharp voice hits my ears.

I stand, pulling Jason up with me, and there's my cousin, standing in the open doorway. How the hell did she get a key to Lilith's room? Mirnov, of course.

I tense as she takes a step into the room, letting the door close behind her. "I hope you're not as stupid as you look, cousin, stealing from the queen of vampires, and trying to escape with a bunch of witches and a creepy ghost."

Moving in a mirroring dance, Lilith steps farther

into the room, and Lucas and the witch girl move closer to us.

I take Freddie from Lucas and turn him so that Lilith has to look at him. "Don't do this, Lilith. For once in your life, do the right thing."

"I'm not the one abandoning our family, cousin."

"I'm fighting for our family. You're just a selfish—"

"Oh really?" She laughs. "You do know that Lamia has our family, don't you? Not the witches?"

I turn to Lucas then. I realize that I'd never actually asked where my family was. He shakes his head, looking ashamed. "The vampires got to most of them before we could. Rove followed us. But that's it."

Part of my will withers away. Can I just leave my family, to save myself and Jason?

"Cheyenne, we can come back for them. But we have to go now." Lucas is holding onto my free arm, but I shrug him away and look back at Arlo.

"Do you know where my family is?" I ask, my voice dropping an octave.

He shrugs and mumbles something but cringes away when Marie Laveau raises her hand as if she's going to pop him on the back of the head. "I don't know, okay? Lamia doesn't tell us anything, just what we need to know to get a job done. I don't know anything about your family." Marie's hand lowers, and Arlo sighs.

"Well, my son, then you're job is to find out and report to me," Marie says, smiling as if she's proud of herself. But then her face falls, and her dull ghostly glow shines. "Get out of here now, you fools." And she disappears.

We all freeze as a wall of footsteps comes from the hallway. "Lilith, please."

My cousin still stands a distance away from us and, in a breath, flits to the door, sliding the chain in on the extra lock. The door slams open, catching at the end of the chain. Lilith is thrown forward. "End this, cousin." Then she shoves herself back against the door, trying to hold it as a force slams on it from the other side.

But I don't see what happens next, but I can guess. Lucas's hand is on my shoulder, my arms around Freddie, and we're pulled into the familiar nothingness of warping, Lamia's words reverberating in my mind: Whatever happens to Lilith is the result of your choice.

***

When we hit solid ground, Lucas grabs the back of my shirt to stop me from pitching both Freddie and me into the ground. I gasp in a breath of fresh air and shake at the taste of salt on my tongue. Are we back in the bayou? But it's too dark to see anything now. I look over at Jason, who has his face pressed into the grass. I nudge him with my foot, urging him to his feet.

Live oaks and palm trees surround a house on stilts, staring down at us with a single porch light. A van is parked beneath where the house rests in the air. It almost hurts—seeing all this normal.

"Come on. They're all waiting." Lucas gets us all moving.

The girl helps Jason to his feet, but he leaps away from her. "Sorry," she holds her hands up. "Just trying to help." Then she follows Lucas up the wooden stairs.

"Can you stop being so jumpy?" I whisper-hiss at him. "These people are helping us. We're free."

He looks up at the beach house, at the encasing trees, all around us. I have no idea where we are. But it's better than the hotel. "This just looks like another prison to me." Then he sighs and trudges up the sandy stairs.

He's wrong. This isn't a prison. This is freedom.

But then we're in a room surrounded by everyone I've imagined dead over the past couple of weeks—Mason, Dr. Cofi, Regina, Niki, Hugo, Rove, Anne, Ms. Rose. Slowly, they all look up from their conversations and stare at us. Lucas crosses the room to hug his mom, then turns back to us.

Anne stands up slowly from her seat by Mason, looking at the three of us. "You are alive," she whispers, taking a hesitant step toward us. I don't know who she's talking about—me or Jason—because she's looking at both of us. All three of us. She takes a step closer, then another, until she's standing in front of us.

This doesn't feel like Anne. What's happened to my bouncy best friend? Her hand reaches out to touch me, and I hold my hand out to her. Then our nails are digging into each other's skin, and we ignore the pain. "I'm so glad you're alive," she whispers again, and then she bursts into tears, her head falling onto my shoulder.

Everybody watches as I start crying too, and we're hugging each other, with Freddie still hitched on my hip. "I'm glad you're alive too." I hug her closer, then pull away. "But I want you to...re-meet someone." I turn us to face Jason, who looks the most uncomfortable I've ever seen him, apart from when Lamia told us about Freddie.

"Jason, you remember your sister?"

Across from us, Jason is trying to smile, but it's coming off as a painful grimace. He finally manages a, "Hi."

Anne struggles for a moment, trying to find the words she's been planning her entire life. She starts to hold out her hand for a handshake, but scratches that idea, and ends up throwing her arms around him and bursting into a new batch of tears. His body seizes, but she just hugs him tighter, as she always does to me when I refuse a hug from her. But then he softens, and slowly, his arms circle around her like a giant bear, and her face buries in his chest. They're both shaking as his face rests on top of her head, and I can see the tears dripping off his cheeks.

"Hi," Anne finally croaks, but it's muffled in Jason's shirt. I smile, surprised at the tears in my eyes and look over at the rest of the room.

I catalog each face in front of me that isn't dead until I realize that Eli isn't among them.

Nine

I hug everyone silently, holding on a bit longer to Rove cause I can't believe he's alive and not trapped with the rest of our family. Ms. Rose takes Freddie from me, giving my arm a break from holding him up.

I jump as the door to the left of me swings open, and Mr. and Mrs. Lacroix freeze. Jason looks up from where he's still hugging Anne, and I see the slight tremble run through him.

"Jason," Mrs. Lacroix whispers, lifting a shaking hand to her lips. Jason's smile is tight but genuine as he nods. And then she's falling over herself to flit to his side, and he's nearly knocked off his feet as she slams into him. Her cries echo to the sea. "Baby, I'm so sorry."

It takes him a moment, but he slowly returns his mom's hug. And then he's crumbling, and he sags into her, digging his fingers into her back. "I'm sorry," he whispers, sucking in a large gulp of air, and lets out a huge cry that shocks us all.

Mr. Lacroix slowly makes his way across the room, his hands shoved in his slacks' pockets. Red lines creep across his eyes, but he keeps blinking as he watches the scene in front of him. I know all of us are crying as well.

"Son," Mr. Lacroix says, placing his hand on Jason's shaking shoulder. "Welcome home." His voice trembles, and they're all hugging and crying. I feel like I'm violating their privacy, watching this family moment. But there's nowhere to go.

After a long while, Jason pulls away, wiping at his puffy eyes and snotty nose. "I have to...I have to apologize."

"Why, darling?" Mrs. Lacroix cups his cheek in her tiny hand. "None of this was your fault. Please, just forget everything."

"I-I can't. I just...I know that Lamia was controlling me. But I was still complicit. And part of me still wants to be back there, and I'm just..." He looks out at everyone in the room, "I'm sorry for everything that I helped to cause." He rubs his eyes roughly.

"No one blames you, son," Mr. Lacroix says. "No one at all." We all mumble our agreement.

Niki appears from the kitchen carrying bottles of blood, handing one to Jason and me. Everyone waits patiently for us to finish as Niki hands us another one. Two still isn't enough to quench the thirst, but I'm already feeling lightheaded and shouldn't drink anymore right now. I hate myself a little bit for craving the human blood over the dull blood of whatever animal is in this bottle.

"Okay, Cheyenne," Regina finally says as I'm savoring the last drops. "You need to tell us what happened. What they did to you in there, where you were, how you got out, how you got here—

everything from the beginning. "

"First, I want to know where Eli is."

"He's out meeting a family who is joining the fight." Dr. Cofi breaks in. "He should be back any minute now."

It takes everything in me not to go find him immediately, but these people want answers. I don't have a lot, but I have more than they do. So I tell them what I can remember from the early days after Christmas Eve, how they took care of us, gave us freedom. The lessons, the outings, the family dinners. That they have my family locked up somewhere they haven't even shared with the vampire kids. Then I come to Freddie, looking down at the baby who's growing irritable and hungry.

"They apparently took Jason's and my DNA to create Freddie, the perfect combination that they've been searching for. And they're going to make more..."

"So wait—you and my brother have a baby together?" Of course, that's what Anne focuses on.

"Technically yes. But he's still Kara's. We had no say in the matter, and I won't that away from her." If she's still alive, that is...

Anne still looks uncomfortable, as does everyone else if I'm being honest. Welcome to my life. "But they're planning to make more."

"Did she allow any of the other vampires to drink from you?" Dr. Cofi asks.

"None," Jason says for the first time. "She only ever drank from us that one time and never anyone else, not even Mirnov."

"Why keep you around then?" Regina's pacing now, the way Eli does when he thinks. "If she has the DNA she needs, if she's drank from the two of you, why didn't she just kill you?"

"Not really sure," I shrug, trying to bite back my sarcasm. "I'll remember to ask her next time I see her— " All the adult eyes in the room narrow at me, and I bite down the rest of the words. But then I stop altogether.

I hear creaking footsteps on the stairs and turn around to Eli. When he spots me, it's like a slap to the face. He closes the distance between us, wrapping me in warm arms that I'd thought I'd never feel again. I pull against him, my fingers digging into his back as I uselessly try to hold back tears. He pulls away, his hands running over my face, my hair, my shoulders, and arms, making sure that I'm here and I'm real. This isn't a dream. Then he kisses me in front of everyone. I hear a couple of gasps, but I couldn't care less. I throw my hands around his neck and lean into him. It's stupid how much I missed him.

"I can't believe you're here," he whispers against my lips, and I smile.

"I can't believe we're both here. I thought you all were dead."

"How...?" His thumb brushes under my eye, wiping away the residual tears.

Several clearings of throats pull us apart, just barely, and we turn to the rest of the group. I'm slightly embarrassed to admit that I completely forgot they were there. "Cheyenne was just explaining that to us before you so kindly interrupted, Eli." Regina gives him a pointed glare, and a slight look of disappointment, but Dr. Cofi, Niki, and Ms. Rose are grinning like fools. Niki nudges Hugo in the gut, winking up at him.

"Did Lamia see you as you were warping?"

"I don't think so. But she definitely knows. Lilith blocked the door right as we were leaving." Everyone stops at the mention of Lilith's name, and I just shrug. "I guess she's not a completely horrible monster. But I do have actual information. Lamia started to trust me. I guess it was believable enough to her that I would fight for the vampires for Freddie's sake."

"We know the plan, Cheyenne—" Regina starts, but I cut her off.

"No, you don't. She's not planning on killing the humans. She needs the humans. She is, however, planning on killing all of the Deuxsang and the witches. And I think they're going to start moving soon."

The room is silent, and I hug Eli tighter. I can't believe he's here.

"That's all you have?" Regina asks.

"Mom!" Both Eli and Lucas say at the same time.

"What? She's been with them for weeks, and all she got is that? We could've figured that out on our own."

"Mom, cut it out." Eli pulls me closer to him protectively, but I pull away, looking at Regina head on.

"I found out about Freddie and what Lamia's plan is for the future. What have you done?"

Regina stands, her nails digging into her palm. "I'd thank you not to talk to me that way. Not after I just sent a rescue party for you into a vampire cave, risking my people's lives. Again."

"And I'm very thankful for that, for you. But you have no idea what I've been through." Her gaze wavers and she has no retort. "So now what's the plan?" I look to Eli, who seems on edge as he glares at his mother.

"I don't know yet. I need time to process all this," Regina says.

"Well, we know the first step," I say, and her head snaps to attention.

"Please, let's hear it, Cheyenne."

I wince away from the bite in her words but try to hold her gaze. "Find out where Lamia is keeping the rest of my family. They don't deserve to be locked up like animals."

"And what do you propose we do after that? Just go storming into an army of vampires?" I'm getting a bit annoyed at Regina's sarcasm. She's supposed to be the leader here. What's her deal?

"We've done it before." My voice is smaller than I want it to be.

"And look how that turned out." She rolls her eyes and turns away, pacing the length of the room. "Dozens of witches and Deuxsang lost their lives following you on Christmas Eve. Your cousin is dead. Men and women that I have known all of my life are dead. I'd think good and hard before you start recommending plans to us again."

My stomach clenches as I finally have a death toll. But how many are dozens? I knew people died because of me, but not how many. And now faces from that night flash behind my eyelids.

"I was wrong, and I'm so, so sorry." My voice cracks more than I wish it would. "But I can't take back the past, and we have to do something now."

"I'm done listening to you. Go get some rest." She waves her hand at me dismissively, and anger flares up my throat.

"No, Regina." Everyone looks up when I use her name. "If you won't listen to my plan, then give me yours. We don't have time just to sit and wait."

She pauses, hesitating with her words, holding my gaze. "I just need time to think." And with that, she storms out of the room, followed reluctantly by Dr. Cofi. When he passes me, he rests a warm hand on my shoulder with a squeeze.

"We'll get it figured, Cheyenne. I'm glad you're back."

Ten

The rest of us are left in the basement without any of the adults, even Niki, who tries very hard not to consider herself an adult, takes Freddie to find him some formula at the grocery store. The Lacroixs try to get Jason to go with them, but Anne insists that he stay with us. So now here we all are, sitting in the den in silence, staring at one another then at the floor.

Eli hasn't dropped my hand all this time, and no one is saying anything. I don't know how to say anything. I've told them what happened, what's been happening. "So..." I finally break the silence. "Where are we?"

The tense silence breaks as they laugh, just slightly. "We're on Grand Isle, and it's about an hour below the city. Teeny tiny," Eli says, scooting closer to me on the couch. "The perfect place to hideout." I smile back.

"What has been going on here, then?"

Everyone looks around the room at each other, deciding who's going to talk. "Well," Eli starts, "really a whole lot of nothing. Well, we've been training. Mom's been working with me, and Dr. Cofi with Rove and Anne."

"What's your ability, Anne?" Jason asks.

Her mouth tightens, embarrassed, though I've told her time and again that she shouldn't be. "I'm just a dreamwalker."

Jason smiles at her reassuringly. "You shouldn't be ashamed of that. Cheyenne's dreamwalking is the reason that we're here now." He nods to me, and I smile back, taking Anne's hand in mine.

"What's yours then?" Mason asks, desperately wanting to be part of the conversation.

"Ah, I have all four, like Cheyenne." Jason yawns, and then I'm yawning, and the rest of them stare at us.

But Anne looks like she's about to bust. "Jason…I have to ask," Anne says, looking down at the floor. "What was it like—all this time with her?" I knew she wouldn't be able to resist asking him for long.

"Um…" He drops his gaze, then flickers his eyes over to me. "It was…"

"Anne," Eli cuts in, "why don't you show Jason where mine and Mason's room is? He can bunk with us."

Anne's holding her words in now. I'm afraid she's going to bite right through her cheek. But Mason's hand wraps around hers.

"Come on, babe. Eli obviously wants some alone time with the hostage."

"Mason!" Anne whacks him on the chest, but a smile cracks through her frown. And even though Eli's glaring at his best friend, he's not denying it. So Mason pulls Anne off the couch, which inevitably pulls Jason off the couch since she hasn't let go of his arm. But as she's dragging him away, he looks back at me desperately. The big strong man, the answer to everything, the cure, needs me. But he doesn't say anything as Anne pulls him through the door. And then Eli and I are alone, for the first time in so long.

We sit in silence for a moment, just taking in the realness of it, of being in the same room, of it not being a dream. Then he says, just barely, "Want to go for a walk?"

***

Apparently, Regina isn't as strict here about us going out unsupervised. Or he didn't tell her, and she's too upset to notice anything going on. For all she knows, we're all still in the house trying to navigate the murky waters of our current reality. But instead, Eli and I are walking down the sands of Grand Isle. There are no lights along the beach, which I find infinitely more amazing because I've never known the moon to be so bright or big.

We walk and listen, gentle waves hitting the shore, crabs skittering around our feet, fish dipping in and out of the water. His fingers don't unlock from mine as we keep step with each other. His thumb rubs patterns into my palm, following my heart and lifeline, and I don't know if it's the evening chill or him that's giving me goosebumps.

"So how many safe houses does your mom have?"

He snorts, and I thank my stronger senses that

I'm able to see his amused profile in the glowing darkness. "You've been trapped with vampires for weeks, and that's the first thing you choose to say to me?"

I purse my lips to hide my smile. "I'm sorry, let me just go through my mental files and pull out a Shakespeare monologue then. Will that make you happy?"

He laughs and pulls me to a stop. We're both staring at each other, but I think he's staring harder—only because he's not as strong as me. "You being here, you being alive—that's what's making me happy." He brings his hands up to my face, brushing his thumbs across my cheeks. "I thought..."

"I know." I rest my hands on his arms, pulling myself against his chest just to listen to him breathe, to feel the rise and fall of his body. "I did too."

Eli's arms wrap around me, running his fingers through my hair, and it's the first feeling of safety that I've had in a long time, even though I'm out here in the open, even though I've let all my defenses down and anyone could come at any moment, they won't. Not here, not now. Not with him.

"You know your mother's gone crazy right?" I mumble into his chest.

He tenses beneath me, but then relaxes with a sigh. "She's under a lot of stress," he says into the top of my head.

"She's not listening to reason."

Then he pulls away, leaning down so that we're eye to eye. "She will, Cheyenne. It's just a lot to process. But I promise we're still behind you one hundred percent."

"The right move is to free my family and end this." I drop his hands ever so slightly and walk to the edge of the water, staring out at the endless nothing, not feeling the bitter cold water when it touches my toes. "I'm thankful we got Freddie out of there, but it doesn't stop her. She has the DNA she needs. She can make more of her perfect doll."

"How do you feel about," he clears his throat, "all that?"

I sigh, knowing that he'd hone in on the fact that Freddie is technically my child. "Eli..."

"I mean, it's weird, Cheyenne. You can't say it's not weird."

"Of course it's weird! I don't quite know how to..."

"Have you and Jason...?"

I spin around, holding my hands out to balance me. "Have we what? You think because I was locked up with him that we got together?"

He doesn't say it, but I know that's what he was thinking. "Well, I saw the way he looked at you when Anne pulled him away. I just..."

"Eli." I take his hands and pull him against me. "We were all each other had in there. But that's it."

He sighs, resting his forehead gently against mine. "But that's not it, is it? You have a baby with him."

"No." I wrench away, that rock settling in my stomach again. "I didn't have a baby with him. A baby was created from my DNA and his. We were not involved at all."

"Yeah, but that baby links you two in a way that I…"

"Stop it, Eli!" My words hit the waves and bounce back at us. "Yes, it's incredibly weird, and I'm still freaking out. I don't know who I am to him or who he is to me. But that shouldn't affect us at all. Please, don't let it get between us." The last of my words are a whisper. His footsteps behind me are nearly silent, but I can still hear them. I don't know how. I feel weaker than I've ever felt. Then his arms wrap around me, resting his chin on my shoulder, and I relax into him.

"I'm sorry. I'll get over it. I promise. I know you didn't ask for this." He presses a warm kiss into my cheek, and I shiver, snuggling closer to him. And we just stand like that for a while, wrapped in each other's arms, staring at the ocean and the moon and wishing this all away. Everything except each other.

Except my brain won't stop working.

"So please tell me you at least have a plan? You've mobilized the witches and Deuxsang, and they're ready to fight. And we can end all of this." My mind flashes back to Lilith's last words, and I get a little pang in my chest.

"I'm working on it, Cheyenne. It's complicated, and people are, well, complicated. I know you're worried about the Deuxsang and your family, but we have our people to think about too."

"I know that," I whisper to the wind. "I know

I'm selfish--"

"Stop it. If it were me in your position, I'd be thinking exactly the same way. If that monster had my parents, my brother, Mason, I wouldn't want to wait either."

"The problem is," I turn around to face him, "I don't even know where she's keeping them. They could be in the hotel. They could be in freaking New York City already, back at the headquarters. Lamia could be keeping them at Clandestine for all I know. I just..."

"Hey, calm down." Eli pulls me into his chest, and again I'm crying. Why can't I stop crying? "We're going to figure this out."

"I don't need promises, Eli, I need action. And I need it now. So please stop— "

We both freeze as fast footsteps approach. We step away from each other, both poised to fight whatever's coming at us until I see the long red hair. Anne. "God, don't sneak up on us like that!" Eli yells.

"Were you going to attack me?" She snorts. "How dare you? Pay more attention, Ashford."

I smirk at his eye roll, reaching for his hand in the darkness. "Who's with Jason?"

"Mason and Rove, which I'm sure he'll hate me for leaving him with those two weirdos... Anyways, Ms. Rose is asking to see you, so I figured I'd come break up the lovefest. Now that everyone's alive, you have plenty of time for all that." Eli's blush is strong enough for the both of us, and it makes me smile.

"Yeah, I want to talk to her too." To no surprise, Anne comes between us, detaching my hand from Eli's so that she can link her arm through mine.

"Excuse me!" Eli says, slightly annoyed but too amused to let it get to him.

"You had your time. I want to see my best friend, thank you very much." So she pulls me ahead of Eli, even though we're still in close enough range that he can hear us, see us, warn us if anything's coming. Which, hopefully, on this island of seclusion, it won't. Although if they were able to find us in the swamps, who says they won't be able to find us here?

Anne and I walk in silence for a while. "Anne, are you okay?" I finally ask.

I can see her smile in the moonlight. "Of course you're asking if I'm okay after you've just escaped from a psychopathic vampire's lair." I try to ignore the flashback. "But no, I guess if I'm being honest, I'm not fine. I don't know what to think about all of this—Jason, my parents, what you told us about Freddie. But mainly Jason. I don't know what to do about him. How do I talk to him?"

I almost laugh, but keep it to myself. "Anne, I've never known you to have trouble talking to anyone. You have no filter, which in this instance might very well work in your favor, yeah?"

"Hey, I have plenty of filter, thank you very much. I could've said a lot worse back there with Eli—"

"I can still hear you." His voice comes out of nowhere in the darkness of the beach.

"I know you can!" she calls back.

"Just start talking to him, Anne. Even if he doesn't talk back right away, he will. You're too wonderful not to love. Lamia's been compelling him for years. He just needs time to adjust. Besides, I know he missed you." I pause to let those words sink in. "He's damaged goods. We all just have to give him time."

"I know that—logically. But selfishly, I just want him to be my brother again."

"Like I said, just start talking." She nods her head slowly, though I can tell she's not convinced. "I talked about you, you know, while we were locked up together."

Her head springs up, eyes glistening with tears. "You did? What did you say?"

"All the terrible parts about you." I laugh when she punches me in the arm. "I'm just kidding, jeez. I told him how wonderful you are, how much you've missed him, how much I love you. And I think that's part of what got through to him. Memories of his old life, his real life. Maybe just remind him of all that?"

Again she nods, then rests her head on my shoulder as we keep walking, passing countless houses on stilts until we come to the one at the end of the lane.

Eleven

Morning shines through the shaded windows as Anne and I approach Ms. Rose's room. Eli left us to go check on the rest of the guys, giving my hand a squeeze of encouragement before he left. Anne knocks gently on the closed door but doesn't wait for Ms. Rose's cheery voice to call us in. The room is nearly dark except for twinkling star lights stapled across the low ceiling, illuminating Ms. Rose's sleeping form, propped up on a pile of pillows.

She looks impossibly small. Like an overgrown fairy. Pieces of her hair have fallen out in chunks, and her skin is even more sunken in. I finally notice Mason sitting in the corner lounge chair, half-asleep.

"He doesn't leave her side often," Anne whispers.

I nod in understanding, even though I don't really want to understand. I don't want to have to think about death, not right now. Anne pulls me over to the side of the bed to sit. My stomach seizes at the prominent veins running up and down Ms. Rose's hands and arms, at the yellowish tint to her skin. Anne takes her frail hand in hers, rubbing gentle circles with her thumb.

"Ms. Rose," she whispers again. Mason wakes at Anne's voice, sitting up straight in his chair, looking first at his mom to make sure she's still breathing. We all watch her chest. Anne smoothes her patchy hair away from her face. "Cheyenne's here, Ms. Rose. She's missed you."

Just barely, Ms. Rose opens her eyes, slowly looking around the room. She lands on me, and a small smile makes its way onto her lips. I can't even imagine how much strength that takes, just that small action.

Anne gestures for me to scoot over and take her place by Ms. Rose's ear, taking her hand in mine. "Hi, how are you feeling?"

She opens her mouth as if it's full of cotton. Mason jumps to his feet with a glass of water, holding the straw up to her lips. She drinks slowly, before releasing the straw from her lips and nodding just barely to let Mason know she's done.

Her voice sounds like there's a little frog stuck in her throat. "Hi, sweet girl." Her smile reaches her eyes, and it seems impossible. "I'm so glad you're here." She turns her hand upside down so that she can grasp mine. Her nails are long and painted as they squeeze around my palm. "How are you? Did...did they hurt you, sweetie?"

"No, they didn't!' I say a little bit too loudly so that Anne nudges me and shakes her head. "How are you?"

"Don't worry about me, sweet girl. We all knew this was coming."

My eyes sting with tears. That's the last thing she needs right now. Out of my peripherals, I see

Anne walk around the bed and pull Mason out of the room, somewhat reluctantly. She closes the door behind them, and I give silent thanks for my intuitive best friend.

"But you're not supposed to die." I know I sound like a child, but I can't help it. In a world where everything's gone wrong, why couldn't she stay, right?

"Cheyenne, everyone dies. I accepted this a long time ago, even if Mason hasn't."

"You don't have to die. We can find a cure for you. Maybe..."

"Sweet girl...it's too late for that. And I don't want to talk about it anymore. I want you to tell me what's going on in the outside world. The rest of them are trying to shield me." Her throat grows scratchy and then breaks into a terrible coughing fit. I flit around the bed for her water, lifting the straw to her lips. She smiles when she's finished and breathes out heavily, leaning back into her throne of pillows.

"They're not telling you because it's pretty terrible." I laugh, bitterly.

"It's better than the nothing that's inside of this room. Please, Cheyenne."

I bite the inside of my cheeks, wiping at my scornful tears that slip down my cheeks. Then I go into the whole story, leaving nothing out because apart from Eli, she's the only person I trust with everything. "And now Regina is ignoring everything that I say to her. See, this is why we need you here. You're the voice of reason. You tell her when she's being difficult when the rest of us can't."

"I'll talk to her when she comes to visit." She chuckles but immediately breaks into a wince. "Regina's just strategizing in her head, doing what she thinks is best."

"Yeah, but she's not always right. Less and less in fact."

"So show her."

"Me?" I stop, looking up from our locked hands. "Why do I have to be the one to do it?"

"Because sweet girl," she closes her eyes for a moment and takes a deep breath, "this is your show now. You know deep in your gut that you're the only one who can truly lead this revolution. You've seen all the sides, know all the reasons, have the right amount of empathy. No one else understands it like you do." Her words are getting quieter.

"I can't...lead a revolution, Ms. Rose. What idiot is going to follow me?"

"This idiot already is." My head whips around at the sound of Eli's voice. "At the risk of sounding cheesy, I'll follow you into the valley of death, even if that valley is the ritziest hotel in all of New Orleans." He walks next to me and presses a kiss onto the top of my head. "Now come on, we're going to get breakfast." He pulls me to my feet then leans down to kiss Ms. Rose's cheek.

"Now? Don't we need to have a meeting?"

"No, we need food first. The best meetings always happen when food is involved."

"Ms. Rose, will you be okay?"

She smiles her sweet smile and squeezes my hand. "Of course, sweetie. And I'll talk to Regina." She winks at the two of us as Eli pulls me out of the room and hands me a jacket.

"Eli, I really don't see how this is a good use of time..."

Anne, Mason, Rove, and Jason are waiting for us by the front door all standing at an awkward distance from one another. When Jason sees me, he stands a little straighter and smiles. Eli tenses. Rove snorts, and I smack his shoulder.

"Cheyenne, relax. You'll love Yum's." Anne slings her arms over my shoulder, obviously trying to avoid the way that Jason is so much more comfortable around me than he is her. And I'm trying to ignore the rise in testosterone around us.

It's my first time walking around the island, and I'm surprised to think that at the very bottom of America, it's a wildly beautiful place. Huge live oak trees cover most of the ground, hanging over stilted houses. People in golf carts are wearing t-shirts whizz past us on the narrow concrete roads, waving and smiling as they go by.

"This place is amazing. How did you find it?" I turn back to Eli, sliding out from under Anne's arm. And Jason just watches me.

"Ah, it's actually your old bodyguard's—Hugo."

"What?" I stop, and everyone stops with me. "He was working for Lilith. So really he was working for Lamia."

"Kind of," Anne smiles, sharing a knowing

glance with Eli.

"He was working for them, yeah. But apparently, his affections for Auntie Niki outweigh any loyalty he might've had towards your cousin." And he snorts, shaking his head.

"Can you blame him? Niki's hot as..."

Eli cuts Rove off. "Can we not talk about my aunt's hotness?" Rove smirks, looking off to the side, but thankfully keeps his mouth shut.

"How can you know that for sure?" I ask. "He might just be sending information back to Lamia..."

"If he were, don't you think they'd be here by now, dragging you away in chains?" Eli brushes the hair out of my eyes and smiles. "Don't worry, you can trust him. Besides," we start walking again, "didn't you always like him?"

"Yeah, apart from all those times he kept me locked up in a dorm room and did absolutely nothing to help me," I grumble, and Eli smiles.

Jason looks at me briefly over his shoulder. "He wasn't supposed to keep you locked up." His words are barely audible. "He was supposed to be training you."

"How do you know that?" Mason asks, hackles raised.

"Cause I knew whatever Lamia chose to share with me. The plan for Cheyenne—I was always part of that." Jason meets all of our gazes without blinking, then turns away back up the road. I know his presence is setting everyone on edge, but we're just going to have to deal with a little discomfort for a while to move beyond this.

I nudge Anne. "Why don't you go talk to him?"

She hesitates, and I can see the fight in her eyes. She usually's so sure in everything she says and does—the total opposite of me. But now she's looking to me for answers. But then she nods and leaves Mason back with us. We watch as they stand a distance away from one another, the air between them a solid wall of the years spent apart.

"I don't trust the guy, Cheyenne. How do we know he's not just going to go running back to that bloodsucker?" Mason glares at Jason's back, and I understand why. Anne's already been hurt so much by this whole situation. I don't want to see her hurt any more than he does.

"I get it. But I swear Jason's fine. He's been brainwashed all these years and was ready to leave once he was able to think clearly."

"You're only saying that cause he's your baby daddy."

"Mason!" I shout the same time Eli smacks him over the back of the head.

"What's wrong with you, man?"

Mason weaves away before Eli can smack him again. "Well, he is."

"Freddie isn't our baby." I walk a little faster, ready for a change of subject. I can feel Eli's piercing gaze on my shoulders, but I really don't want to talk about this.

Rove snorts from behind him, and I resist the urge to whip around and clock him in the neck.

"Sure he is. Jason's DNA plus your DNA equals Freddie. No denying it, munchkin."

"Rove, drop it." Eli's voice drops, and for once, I hear the danger in it, the power. It almost makes me stop. But then we're turning onto the main road, and I smell breakfast food. My stomach growls rumble through my body, and it feels like ages since I've eaten real food, even though the thirst never really goes away anymore.

Anne and Jason are already seated inside a pale pink building. No one else is inside other than an old couple with Hawaiian shirts. We all order a Cajun breakfast with an early order of beignets. When they come out, faster than I expect them to, I flashback to my talk with Lamia at Café du Monde. I betrayed her family, but so far, a few days have passed, and nothing's happened. Maybe it was all empty threats. Or perhaps she's biding her time. Or maybe she's already killed my entire family. I look up at Rove, and it's like he knows what I'm thinking. Or it's possible he thinks about it all the time like I do.

"So I officially bring to order this first meeting of the only sane members left in this community. Welcome to Yum's, the best and only breakfast restaurant on the island. Now, how are we going to fix the world's problems?" Eli's smiling, but his chest is tight, and his words are forced, staggered. I take his hand under the table and feel him relax.

"I can't fix anything until I get some coffee," Mason mumbles.

Jason side-eyes him, and I catch the slightest eye

roll. "You're also a human, so you can't really fix anything."

"Hey man..." Mason grips the table, and Rove leans back with an amused smile.

Eli leans forward to cut the tension. "Guys, cool it. We're here to fix the old problems, not start new ones. We have enough as is."

Jason looks at me to come to his defense, but I turn away. He throws his arms over his chest and slouches back in his chair like a child. I am surrounded by children.

"Good. Moving on. So Cheyenne, what all did you learn from Lamia?"

Jason eyes me from his pouting but doesn't stop me from telling them everything I know. I get déjà vu except for Café du Monde was loud and claustrophobic. They're silent as they listen to me; all I can hear in the background is the cook singing some old blues song. I tell them about what Ms. Rose said—how I'm supposed to lead this revolution. Only I think this is wrong. I don't think it's just supposed to be me. Madame Laveau keeps calling Eli 'little priest.' And I think she's onto something.

"You think I'm going to be High Priest?" He nearly laughs, but no one else is.

"It makes sense," Rove agrees, looking serious for once in his life. "Your mom's the High Priestess now, so it would naturally fall to you."

"Or one of my brothers. And besides, that's way in the future."

"It doesn't have to be..." I say, quietly.

"What are you trying to say, Cheyenne?" He drops my hand and leans away from me.

"I'm saying..." I know I have to be careful here, "that your mom has been playing things a little bit too safe. It's like she's avoiding all the problems rather than trying to figure out ways to solve them."

"That's not true." His voice is quiet, unnerving.

"She's not wrong, man."

"Shut up, Mason."

"I've only been here a couple of days, and I can see that," Jason says. "I haven't seen her since we got here, and here you are leading a meeting trying to solve things."

"I can solve problems without becoming High Priest and stealing my mother's role."

"Yeah, but they follow the High Priest, Eli. They don't follow the High Priestess's kid who's girlfriend caused this mess."

Eli sits back in his chair, rubbing his hands over his face roughly. "I can't just...lead the witches. I can't do that."

I lean forward, pulling his hands away from his face. It's just him and me. "You're not going to be doing it alone. We're doing this together. And I think we can do it. Because if we don't, everyone's going to die." And then I smile and break into a laugh because this is all just so utterly ridiculous. This is the stuff I read about in books. This is the stuff that happens to other people. Or not at all. But here we are, four half-breeds, one witch, and one human trying to figure out how to stop a bunch of world-hungry vampires from killing all that we've ever known.

And then we're all laughing, and some of the cooks peek their heads around the corner to see about all the racket as the waitress brings us our food and coffees. "Alright, kiddos, let's leave saving the world until after I devour this entire meal." Rove grins down at his food, and then there's silence and no more talk of teenagers becoming heroes.

Twelve

Back at the house, I'm barely given any time to breathe before Dr. Cofi ushers Anne and me outside for a training session. No rest for the weary. Niki and, to my surprise, Hugo are waiting for us. It's also surprising how happy I am to see that he's alive, even though I knew it. But really, it's different knowing and seeing, isn't it? I've never prescribed in that whole "believing is seeing." Not in matters of life and death.

Hugo drops his head as I approach, with a slight smile. "Cheyenne, I…"

"I'm glad you're alive."

He lifts his head, trying to hide his surprise, but not well. Then he holds out his hand, and I shake it. It's the most contact we've ever had. "I'm glad you're alive too, Cheyenne."

"Alright, lovely, we're glad everyone's alive. But we won't be in the future if we don't do some training now." Dr. Cofi claps his hands once like he used to in my lessons. It's even more annoying now.

"Where's Regina?" I ask.

"She's out." We're all staring at Dr. Cofi, but he doesn't meet anyone's eyes. Niki crosses her arms, and I can see her fighting off words. I know we're thinking the same thing. "But she'll do lessons with the boys later. Besides, they've been training all this time that you've been gone."

"I've been training too." I snap, though I get a sick feeling in my stomach for being the slightest bit appreciative of something Lamia did for me.

"Really?" Dr. Cofi's ears perk up like a rabbit. "She trained you."

"Yeah, and Jason. She thought we were all part of her family and completely believed that we'd fight for her when the war came."

"That's so screwed up," Anne mutters under her breath.

"Yeah, tell me about it."

"Well, then I guess that's not all that surprising. Anyways, let's get started. Cheyenne, you can show us what you've learned." Dr. Cofi steps out of the way, and Hugo steps up to be my opponent.

"Well, we did a lot of physical training, and I was getting better at that. But I have a theory about something—Do you mind if I go get Eli?"

They all look at me, speechless. "I thought this was supposed to the Deuxsang only club." Anne laughs. "Can't have just one thing to ourselves."

I smile and start walking back to the house. "Just train with Anne. I'll be right back." Then I turn and flit inside, upstairs to the bedroom that the boys have been sharing. I don't knock, which I probably should've, because I walk into a room of shirtless guys, and the room smells ripe. "Holy mother of..." I pinch my nose closed, standing in the doorway. "What died in here?"

"Shut up, Cheyenne." Mason throws a dirty shirt at me that I dodge. Jason's sitting in the corner of his bunk bed with a book in his hands. I didn't know he liked to read.

I try not to let my eyes linger on Eli's bare chest. "Can you come downstairs with me. I'm training, and I want to try something." My words come out slightly staggered, and if I could blush, I'd be blushing super hard.

Mason snorts from his bed, his guitar in his lap. "We're not a meat market, Cheyenne. Stop objectifying us."

My lips pinch closed as I throw the dirty shirt back in his face. "Based on the smell, this definitely is a meat market." I catch a hint of a smile from Jason as I flit back downstairs, ignoring the tightness in my chest. Eli's next to me a few moments later. I start to walk away to lead him outside, but he grabs my arm and spins me into his chest. Then his mouth opens to mine, and he's pressing me against him, and I'm getting dizzy. I latch onto him, and then we're against the wall, and I can't get enough. My body's on fire, and I don't even notice my fangs dropping. His hands tangle in my hair as I pull him against me, pressing myself between him and the wall.

We pull apart at the sound of footsteps on the stairs, and as if nothing happened, walk outside hand in hand. I know my lips are red and swollen, and my hair is a mess, but I'm hoping that no one will notice. Or if they do notice, to keep it to themselves.

"Now what's your experiment, Cheyenne?" Dr.

Cofi asks as we return to the beach that acts as this house's backyard.

"Before I was taken back to Clandestine, Eli and I realized something. I was never able to practice any of my abilities before I met him. I was barely able to flit. But once we got together, it was like he released all the abilities. And then when he was trying to lift the house in the swamp, he was only able to do it when I was there with him..."

"Huh," Dr. Cofi crosses his arms, his eyes narrow as he considers us and the hypothesis. "You believe that you make each other stronger?"

I look at Eli, and he looks at me. We nod together.

"Alright, well go for it." Dr. Cofi gestures to Niki, whose smirk is a little bit too smug for me. I don't know if I need to be holding Eli's hand, but I'm going to try—plus, I want to. I interlock our fingers and instantly feel calmer. Strength runs through me, more than normal, even after a drink of blood.

As Niki walks toward us, I picture each tendon, each ligament, and cartilage, and watch in my mind as her kneecap slides to the left, gasping at Niki's screech when it actually happens. She drops to her good knee, grinding her fingers into the dirt.

"Now back, Cheyenne."

I move the kneecap back into place easily, and Niki sighs with relief, hopping over into Hugo's arms. When I look back at Dr. Cofi, he's staring at us, staring at our hands, but mostly at me.

"What's wrong?" I ask.

"Nothing. I just don't get why..." His words taper off into silence, then he shakes his head, almost pulling himself out of a trance. "This is interesting, and definitely works to our benefit, but you have to be strong on your own, Cheyenne. You won't always be able to be holding hands or even be together, especially in a fight. We'll practice with the two of you, but you'll have to work on your own as well." I nod, Eli nods, then Dr. Cofi nods. He pushes up his glasses again and walks back into the house.

From the distance between us, Niki says, "That freaking hurt, Cheyenne." Beside me, Eli snorts and squeezes my hand.

"Sorry," I call back, but secretly smiling to myself, though I shouldn't be.

***

Regina has been in isolation all this time, avoiding us when we walk into rooms, going out for long walks to "think," but she still maintains a strict rule of separate rooms for the guys and girls by 11 o'clock. It's now 11:30, and Eli and Mason and Rove were promptly kicked out of Anne's and my room. I regret that I haven't gotten time to talk to Rove alone. I want to know how he was the only one of the family who wasn't taken, and how come he's been so quiet. This isn't like him at all.

But I can't ask him now. Anne's been writing in her notebook all night, not really speaking to any of us as we ignored all the pain and destruction going on around us. Niki was kind enough to salvage my art supplies from my dorm room before the world imploded. So now I'm drawing while Anne writes, her head bent over her notebook, pencil poised between her fingers.

"If you would kindly stop drawing me, I'd very much appreciate it."

"You're in a mood." I drop my chalk, hoping in return she'll drop her pencil to look at me. But she doesn't.

"I'm not in a mood, Cheyenne, I'm just not in the mood to be drawn when I look like a slob." I don't know what she's talking about. She looks beautiful all the time, to the point that it's annoying. And of course she doesn't see it, no matter how many times Mason or I tell her, which also drives me nuts. She should acknowledge how amazing she is.

"But this is you in your natural state. Why shouldn't I capture it?"

"Because!" She slams her pencil down in her notebook to the point that it makes a thumping sound. "I'm not exactly writing about anything happy, alright?" Her eyes are bloodshot and puffy. I climb off my bed and into hers to wrap my arms around her.

"What's going on?" I try to steal a glance at her notebook, but her handwriting is in scribbly cursive that's nearly impossible to read. "Did you and Mason have a fight? He seemed kind of distant too."

"No." She sighs, resting her head on top of mine. "He's just worried about Ms. Rose. And I am too, of course I am. But it's this whole Jason thing. He's still not talking to us, even me. It's like he shuts down whenever we come into the room, and I don't know what to do about it. Should I ask my parents to leave? Is that maybe triggering him? Or is it me? Am I the problem? I don't know, C, and it's driving me crazy." I squeeze her arm when a teardrop falls on my head. "I finally have my brother back." Her voice is thick with tears as she fights for the right words. "But that man is not my brother. Lamia's taken him in more ways than one."

I'm silent for a long time because I don't know how to fix this, how to mend their relationship, and put back together a broken man. None of us can imagine what Jason's gone through, what kind of psychological torture that's brought him to where he is. "Anne, I know this is ridiculously hard. Like, stuff we shouldn't even have to be thinking about hard. But Jason is himself…he just doesn't know how to be around you yet. All these years, Lamia has been his family. You just have to show him how much you love him—that you're his true family." She nods through the tears, agreeing with me, even though she doesn't want to. "Maybe we can get Regina to sanction an outing. Get him out of the house, away from all the witches, your parents. He can just see you, spend time with you and our friends. Finally push Lamia's illusions and compulsion out of his head."

"You really think we can crack him?" She looks up at me with watery eyes, squeezing her pencil tightly in her palm.

"One hundred percent. I think we can do anything, but I definitely think we can do this. It's just a weird situation."

"Maybe we can go to the club—or Mason can find an open mic night. I know he and Eli miss playing with the rest of the guys."

"Has Mason heard from them at all?"

"Not really." Anne shakes her head, and she looks pissed. "They kind of gave him an ultimatum after he and Eli kept bailing on gigs because of...extenuating circumstances. So now they're just a duo I guess."

"How's that going to work—just drums and guitar?"

She shrugs. "Not my problem."

I laugh and pull her into a hug. "He's always going to be your problem, weirdo. No matter how much you deny it."

"That is the annoying truth," she mumbles into my hair. "Alright, get off my bed. I'm tired." But she holds onto me a little longer.

Thirteen

I'm barely able to fall asleep in the first place, but all the sounds around me—footsteps, wind, waves, everything—keep waking me up. I flip this way and that in my small bed, but my mind keeps flashing back to the hotel, to Lamia's threats. I have nightmares of my family locked in a basement somewhere, being slowly drained of life by Mirnov.

I press fists against my eyes, trying to force sleep on myself, but it's pointless. It just creates even more distracting stars behind my lids. At the rush of wind, I open them again and nearly scream but can't for the hand pressed against my mouth. I shove myself back against the wall, searching the darkened room for a pair of eyes to focus on. Then Arlo comes into focus.

"She's ready to see you again." He grabs my wrist, and then we're flitting. I have no idea where we're going or who we're going to. It could be Marie Laveau. It could be Lamia.

When I open my eyes again, The Voodoo Queen's ghost stares at me. She's wearing the exact same outfit, though now her head wrap is gone, and her long hair floats eerily behind her, not touching her back at all. She doesn't look happy though, not that she's ever looked joyful when I've interacted with her.

I look around me, shivers running through my bones. I'm inside a tomb. No living creature should ever be inside a tomb, and there's a reason for it. Tombs are where death lives, and death and sorrow are prominent inside this hole.

"Evening, princess." She glowers down at me, taking in my oversized t-shirt for pajamas. I curl my legs under my body to cover myself some, but I still feel naked in front of her. That's when I realize I'm sitting on top of her casket and leap to my feet. "Have you been working hard over on Grand Isle?"

"We're still getting things figured out. There's a lot of moving pieces."

She scoffs and floats closer to me. "Why is Regina still the High Priestess and not your little lover boy? Haven't I told you he's the one that should be leading the witches?"

"You haven't actually told me anything. But I'm working on it. Eli's reluctant, and Regina is isolating herself." I lean away from her as she hovers in front of my face, her neck craning at unnatural angles. She pauses to give Arlo a ghostly kiss on the cheek.

"Oh, little girl, that's the perfect time. Where's our leader when we need her?" She cackles quietly, and I shiver. "If she's not there to defend herself, then the game is already checkmate."

"I can't just remove someone from the role they were born into."

"Have you never picked up a history book?" Her cackle gets higher pitched as she floats up in her room, twirling like a child in a field of flowers.

"Take her down, or you lose my dears. That clear, little girl?" In a flash, she's sitting next to me, her sown legs crossed to mirror mine, grinning from ear to earringed ear.

"Yes, of course. But who exactly are these 'dears' of yours?" I look back at Arlo, who's stonefaced.

"Arlo hasn't told you?" She giggles but it sounds more like a cry. "All those little kid vampires you saw running around. The little mangy mutts, Lamia calls them—they're my babies."

"Your kids?" I ask a slight horror dawning on me.

"Yep, and that cretin took them one by one—drained their precious lives and replaced their souls with demons." She looks forlornly at Arlo, bowing his head. She touches his face. "It's not your fault, baby."

I shake my head, trying to work my way through this. "But why would she do that? Who were you to her?"

"I was the one person who could've stopped her—who saw her for who and what she was. I sniffed right through her wicked plan, but before I could get to the High Priestess, she started taking my babies." And then her voice is a terrible shriek, a cry, as she whips up violently to the ceiling, slamming her ghostly form against the stone. "And I was broken."

Her cries echo in the tomb until all that's left is silence. "I'm so sorry, ma'am. I had no idea."

"No one does. And we're going to keep it that

way—to protect them from the witches who might see my children harmed. They're here to help you. You'd do best to do the same for them." She eyes me as she floats slowly down from the ceiling.

"If you have nothing for me..."

"I just have one question for you before I go."

"And what's that?"

"Why me?" I ask quietly, lowering my eyes from hers.

Her head snaps over her shoulder, her dark face an image of consideration. She floats over to me and takes my hand in hers, running her fingers over the lines in my palms. "You see this line here?" She traces one that goes straight up my hand. "Most people think that's the breaking of your love line. Not true, of course—everyone's love line is a little broken. That, princess, is your power line, and yes, you have power in you. More than most. Enough to challenge Regina, for sure." Then she moves her hands up to my head, pressing gently against my skull, hovering over my temples. "Are you getting enough blood?"

"I'm getting what they give me."

"Get more. That family of yours got you stronger than you could handle, and now you're suffering for it. Also," she whips around, browsing her jars before pulling out a little bag of powder and dropping it in my hand. "Mix this in with your blood every evening. I think it's just the pep you need." She smiles at her own generosity before opening the tomb door the same way she did before. "Takedown Regina, princess," she hovers close in front of me, her chilled breath pricking at my skin unnaturally, "before I lose my patience and you lose my support."

I purse my lips together and nod, afraid of what I'll say if I open my mouth. Arlo steps up and grabs my wrist. Marie wiggles her fingers in a goodbye before we disappear into a flit, and I'm lying back on my tiny bed next to Anne, who's ignorantly snoring away. The little baggie of powder, whatever it is, is still in my hand. I sniff it, but it has no discernible smell.

I shuffle quietly downstairs, keeping my footsteps as light as possible, and sneak down to the basement, where I know Dr. Cofi keeps his supply of blood for us. When I find the back kitchen, Dr. Cofi is there in plaid pajama pants and a ratty shirt, no glasses, and no sleep in his eyes. "Dr. Cofi, are you okay?"

He jumps when I speak, staring at me a moment before responding. "Cheyenne, what are you doing awake?"

I slip Marie's pouch behind my back. "I asked you first."

"Just can't sleep. Regina's having a hard time right now." Guilt instantly starts gnawing at me. How much is he going to hate me if I do what Marie Laveau wants, even if she says it is fate? Dr. Cofi doesn't seem like one to believe in fate.

"I couldn't sleep either. I was hoping to get a bottle of blood."

"Cheyenne, it's early...not the time."

"Please, Dr. Cofi? I've been feeling so weak since I've been back..."

I see him sigh as he reaches into the fridge and hands it to me, though I can see the reluctance in his grip. ""Alright. Just one bottle. Good night, Cheyenne."

"Night, Dr. Cofi." I slip out of the kitchen and bound up the stairs to the bathroom across the hall from my room. I open my bottle and dump half the contents of Marie's powder into it, though the urge to drink it all first is annoying. I swish it around, making sure the powder mixes in before chugging the entire thing. I lean against the counter, staring at the dark mirror as the blood burns through me, and my throat begs for more. My eyes seem brighter, my body stronger. But at what price?

Fourteen

Another day of nothing passes: doing nothing, talking about nothing, acting on nothing. Regina has still yet to show her face, and more and more, I'm starting not to feel so guilty about knocking her off her throne, despite everything she's done for me, like saving my life on a couple of occasions. But she obviously can't handle this. Despite an entire lifetime of knowing the truth, she's still not prepared. None of them really are, I think. They don't truly understand the plan. But I think I do now, and I'm not going to sit by and let it happen.

The house is mostly empty, except for Jason. I walk the house slowly, memorizing the rooms I've been in before and taking in the ones I haven't. This whole house is a wonderful illusion that Niki has cast. On the outside, it looks like every other house on stilts, blending in perfectly to the surroundings. But on the inside, it fits all of us with room to spare. There's a library, a gigantic kitchen, a beach view sunroom—everything that's totally unnecessary for a safe house. But I'm not going to complain.

I find Rove reading in the sunroom, though really he's half asleep. I'm not sure I've ever seen him finish a book in his life. War and Peace is halfway draped over his face as his hand loses strength. I watch, letting it fall until it smacks him in the face, and he nearly jumps to his feet with something between a growl and a scream.

"Enjoying your light reading?" I snort, relaxing into the chair beside him.

He gives me a stink eye, rubbing the bridge of his nose where the binding of the book rammed him. "I was just preparing for the oncoming insanity that is our lives...which you started."

"Shut up, Rove, this isn't all my fault." I think he's kidding, but these days I can't be so sure. He's different, quieter. I don't think I've heard him say more than ten words the entire time we've been here.

"I know. It's half your fault."

I choose to ignore him cause I know this will only lead to a fight. That's what always happens when he's in these moods.

"Well, don't you get your panties in a twist."

"My boxers are just fine, thanks."

"What's your problem, Rove?"

He slams the book down between us. "Maybe the fact that the rest of my family is probably being sucked dry by a bunch of psycho vampires, and I'm sitting here in a beach view room reading my life away while our fearless leader sulks in her room."

I wait a minute, checking to make sure there's nothing left of his tirade. He turns to look at me for my rebuttal. "So, let's do something about it."

"Excuse me?"

"Let's take over."

"Great, two weeks with the vampires, and you think you're General Munchkin." He starts to stand from his chair, but I pull him back down.

"No, listen to me, Rove." I glance over my chair to make sure no one else is in the room with us and listen for footsteps outside. "You can't tell anyone this, but the Voodoo Queen had a price for rescuing me."

"Did she want more candy? 'Cause the stuff that people leave there is rotten and nasty."

I roll my eyes. "No, she made me promise to end Regina's reign as High Priestess."

Rove raises an eyebrow, putting two and two together. "This again?" Rove shakes his head. " Eli's not about to shove his mom off her pedestal. You heard him."

"That's not what I'm saying. He won't be doing any of the shoving. She'll step down without his influence. We're already on the same page about what needs to happen with the vampires, and the only thing standing in the way is his devotion to his mom."

"Cheyenne, you're starting to sound like...evil."

His words sting, but I have to stay strong if I'm going to stand a chance against the real evil. "Are you with me?"

" I don't think Eli's going to go along with this."

"I think he will."

"Well, you know him better than I do, I guess. Even though we have been sharing a room for the past three weeks. That has made me privy to some pretty dark secrets, dear cousin."

"You're not going to tempt me with your stupid slumber party stories, dummy."

He almost cracks a smile, and I get a glimpse of

the Rove that I've grown up with, the Rove I need to make me smile when the world seems impossible to handle, and right now the world is beyond impossible to handle. My nightmares have become a reality.

Fifteen

Dr. Cofi insists that Jason train with me, despite the complaints of his parents, who say that he needs time to rest and adjust. But today he's standing next to me on the beach with a small audience behind us. From the house, I see Regina looking out at us from the sunroom, arms crossed in front of her chest. I haven't spoken to her in the week that I've been here. I don't know how I'm supposed to convince her to step down if she won't even step into the same room as me.

I turn away from the window and try to focus on what Dr. Cofi is saying.

"Okay, Jason, so have you ever exercised any of your abilities before?"

Jason snorts and gives an annoying smirk. "Yeah, Lamia has trained me from day one."

"Don't be a jerk, Jason," Anne says. I shoot her a glare and shake my head once. I can practically hear her grinding her teeth at me.

Jason's head twitches to the side, trying to ignore Anne. "She was prepping me to be one of her soldiers—just as good as the other vampires."

"That's impossible," Hugo says. "You can't be as good as the vampires."

"Based on how much blood she was feeding me,

and being trained by Mirnov and Lamia herself—yeah, it is possible."

Everyone stares at Jason; Dr. Cofi and Hugo look at each other, trying to come up with a logical response, but there is none.

"If you don't believe me, Cheyenne and I could go against one another. She's my most worthy opponent."

From the side, Rove snorts. "You think the Munchkin is your best opponent? They must not have trained you that well, man."

"Thanks for the support, Rove," I mutter, giving him a side glare.

Again, silence as Dr. Cofi and Hugo look between us. "Alright then," Dr. Cofi sighs. "Two meters apart. Let's do this."

"You can do this, Jason." Anne moves to pat him on the shoulder, but hesitates and drops her hand then steps away, biting her lip. I stand beside her, checking to make sure we're okay. She grabs my hands as Jason steps away from us. Eli and Rove are on the other side of him, watching carefully, but Eli looks up for just a moment to smile at me, that little crooked smile that I missed, that I almost lost. I want to run to him then and tell him to take control. But now's not the moment. Maybe Rove will plant a bug in his ear while they're having all their slumber parties.

"Let's see what you can do, my man." Dr. Cofi claps Jason on the back then steps away to give us room. I hate that a little bit of fear shoots through me, but fear is good. Fear is healthy. Fear should make me see clearly. Because unlike these morons, I know what Jason can do.

And then he's rushing at me, and I can feel the force of his infliction racing ahead of him for me. I build up my wall barely in time to block a pain headed straight for my back and dodge his barreling body in just enough time. Like a bull, he skids to a stop and whips around, ready for round two. But it gives me my chance, as he starts to flit, I work my compulsion through his protection, and he slows to a stop just in front of me, eyes dazed over. Carefully, I transfer from the compulsion to an illusion—one of he and Anne, joking around the way Rove and I do, the way it's supposed to be.

But then he's fighting me, shattering the illusion and pushing it out of his head. And before I can build up my defenses again, or even think to move, he has me pinned against the sand, hands on either side of my jaw, ready to snap my neck.

"And you're dead."

He meets my gaze and holds it, and I find I can't move, can't look away. Then slowly, the claps start, and he un-straddles me, falling back into the sand to calm down. I avoid looking at him as I stand and walk back over to my friends.

Eli meets me halfway, checking my face to see if he hurt me. "Are you alright?" His words are hushed as he glares over my shoulder.

"Yeah, of course. He didn't actually do anything."

"He tried to!" I flinch as his voice rises.

"No, he was just showing what he could do. And really, I think that was mild for him." I glance over my shoulder at Dr. Cofi and Hugo talking to him. When I look back, Anne's staring at her brother, partly in fear, partly in awe. I know what she's thinking—I'm just a lousy dreamwalker. I wish I could make her see differently.

Slowly, the rest of them join us, Jason holding his chin up proudly. I want to smack it off of him. He thinks he's superior to us, and while he might've had more training, that doesn't mean anything. Not in the long run.

"So...now that we've had our entertainment for the day, anyone want a cup of tea?" Dr. Cofi smiles, trying to cut the tension in the circle, but everyone is stonefaced and not amused.

"I think I could definitely go for a good chai right now." Rove breaks the silence and heads back to the house before he can hear my laugh.

***

Eli, Rove, and Mason have gone off to the one supermarket on the island, and everyone else has dispersed. Anne and I are in a room overlooking the water, and I'd give anything to dive headfirst into it right now and swim away. It seems like nothing I'm doing to set this plan into motion is working. And everyone's so tense.

Freddie sits between my legs, giggling at Anne's funny faces and trying to grab her tongue when she sticks it out at him. I smile at his giggles and rest my head back against the pillow, reveling in the momentary silence.

"So that was quite the show Jason put on," Anne says quietly.

Silence over. I lift my head, but she's not looking at me, still down at Freddie. "Well, he's been trained by vampires for a long time. You had to expect he'd be strong."

She pauses for a moment before answering. "Not really, I always had nightmares that they were keeping him locked up in some basement, sucking the life out of him. I think that's what my parents thought too."

"Well, I can assure you that wasn't the case. The opposite in fact."

"Really?" Her voice is small, and I realize that I haven't really told her about my time with Lamia.

I nod, sitting up straighter. "Yeah, she has this warped sense of family and a fear of being alone. She treated him like a prince. He had his own penthouse suite in the hotel and more food and blood than I could ever eat. He wasn't tortured, Anne."

"I'm not sure if that makes me feel better or worse." She sighs, picking Freddie up and holding him close against her, nuzzling against his chubby cheeks. "Why would he ever want to leave that?"

"Because he woke up."

"He still seems like a jerk vampire to me." And I smile because she's right. He has an annoying superiority complex right now, and I think everyone's getting tired of it. I'm just waiting for one of us to snap.

Then the door to the sunroom bursts open, and Jason comes flitting through, slamming the doors closed behind him. He looks up, startled, at us. "Sorry. I was trying to get away from Mom and Dad. They keep pestering me with questions, and Mom keeps crying." He glances down at Freddie, suddenly slightly more uncomfortable. "Mind if I hide out in here with you?"

We both shrug, but I can't find the words to say anything. I haven't been alone with the two of them, and this feels like an increasingly infringing moment. He sits down next to Anne and reaches for Freddie, who smiles at the sight of him.

"It's weird, he's my son, but I haven't spent much time with him. Lamia always kept him to herself." Jason bounces Freddie on his knees, and I feel my throat constrict.

"He's not really your son," Anne says.

"Well, he's ours." He looks up at me and smiles his charming smile that I'm sure could win a million people over, but considering the circumstances, it makes my stomach lurch.

"No," I say shortly. "We share DNA with him. But he is not our child."

"Our genetics made him, so technically speaking, yes, he is." Jason's eyes narrow, and Anne scoots closer to me.

"Technically speaking, Lamia's genetics made all the vampires and therefore all of us. So we're all related if you're going to go with that logic."

"Calm down, Cheyenne." He huffs, looking down at Freddie, falling asleep in his arms. "It's not like I'm proposing to you or anything."

"Hey, you'd be lucky to land Cheyenne." Anne's brow is knit into a deep frown, but then her face instantly changes. "Oh my god, so Freddie is my nephew! OH, my god, it's like we're sisters, C!" And she squeals a little bit, waking Freddie, who begins to whine.

"No, it's not..." I jump to my feet and back away from them. And like I have every moment since I discovered the truth, I curse Lamia for doing this to me, for stealing from me. "Freddie is Kara's baby. And that's that."

"Yeah, well I don't see them anywhere around here." Jason stands too. Then Anne's on her feet, and you could cut the tension with a knife.

"That's because your precious vampire mommy probably has them stashed in a basement somewhere, torturing them, if she hasn't already killed my entire family!"

"Cheyenne, calm down." Anne holds her hand out to me, but I jerk away.

The door opens, and Eli and Mason walk back in with bags of groceries. "What's going on in here?" Eli asks, looking between me and Jason holding Freddie. His face blanches a little bit, but he stands strong.

"Cheyenne's just wigged out that we made a baby together." Jason grins, meeting Eli's icy gaze.

"We did not make a baby together!" I yell desperately, and then Freddie is crying, his face red with tears and screams.

Mason rushes up, taking the baby from Jason and backs out of the room to quiet him.

"Cheyenne, you can't deny that Freddie is ours!" Jason takes a step closer to me while Eli takes a step closer to him.

"I think you need to cool it, man. Cheyenne doesn't want to talk about it." Eli grabs his shoulder, but in the blink of an eye, he is slung onto his back, the air knocked out of him.

"Don't touch me," Jason growls.

Eli's eyes narrow. He looks once at me; then, I feel the stir of a breeze. Stronger, stronger, and then Jason is wrapped up in a tunnel of air. He slams at it, trying to push through. But Eli, up on his knees now, holds him in tight.

"Eli, let him go!" Anne yells. But Eli only focuses more, his face getting red with concentration. Pictures shake on the walls, and the furniture is slowly moving about the room. I drop to my knees and crawl over to him, placing my hand on his arm. Wrong move. The wind just gets stronger and squeezes tighter against Jason.

"Eli, stop. I'm fine." He looks at me for a long moment to convince himself, then slowly, the wind dies down, disappearing completely. Anne rushes to her brother as he collapses to the carpet.

"Jason, are you okay?" she asks, carefully resting a hand on his back. This time, he doesn't shake her off.

"Yeah," he says through a tight throat, "I'm fine."

I'm expecting him to be mad, furious, but when he finally looks up, the look on his face is...impressed.

Then Rove saunters into the room with his newest book, whistling at the damage. "Well, what in the hell happened in here?"

"I think..." I say slowly, "that we all need a day out."

Anne shakes her head. "I don't know, C. The city is gearing up for Mardi Gras. It might be a little too wild to go out."

"That'll be perfect. We can just blend into the craziness, right?"

"But what if we lose him?" Rove asks, nodding at Jason. "He'll go straight back to those psychos, and we won't stand a chance."

"No, I won't!" Jason says, offended.

Mason's back now with a sleeping Freddie. "I still don't trust you, man." His glare is a little pathetic, as he tries to be intimidating. I hide my smile.

"Mason, knock it off." Anne snaps.

"Fine, Cheyenne," Eli says. "We'll go out. But Jason isn't leaving our sight, and all of us are going. I think Niki or Andrew should come too."

I shake my head. "No, this is for us. A day without them—to just be us for a day before everything goes to hell."

"Mom's not going to let us go out without someone."

"So convince her." I say the words too slowly, and I hear how rude I sound. But I can't help it. I'm over this. We have agency. We're all strong and know how to take care of ourselves. We can go out into the city for the day without the world ending.

Silence echoes in the room, and everyone glances between Eli and me. Eli won't look away from me, surprised and a little annoyed. "Fine, I'll go talk to them."

"I'll go with you." I start to follow him out of the room, but he holds his hand up to stop me.

"No, I don't think that's the best idea."

"And why not?" I cross my arms over my chest and bite the inside of my cheek to keep from saying anything more.

"Because you're not really in control right now, and if you want them to go along with your plan, you probably won't help convince them." He doesn't give me the chance to defend myself; he just runs up the stairs and away from my glare. Rove leaves to go do whatever it is he does. Mason takes Freddie to go check on Ms. Rose, holding his hand out to Anne, but she just smiles up at him.

"I'll be there in a minute."

Mason starts to walk past me without a word, but then he thinks better of it, stops, and turns to wrap me in a one-armed hug. I'm still for a moment, but eventually give in and hug him back. "I'm sorry... about everything." He hugs me tighter then drops his arm and leaves.

Then it's just me, Anne, and Jason again, and I

put up my shields. At the moment, I don't want to be anywhere near them. Jason starts to say something, then sighs and leaves the room.

"You didn't have to be so rude to him, you know?" Anne finally says, and red fills my eyes.

"Listen, Anne, I know he's your brother and everything, but..."

"Exactly, he's my brother. Not yours."

"What are you talking about?" I say, my anger peaking.

"Ever since you got back, you've been acting like he's your brother, like you know everything about him. And it drives me nuts. Like you think you know how I should handle everything and cope. Well, you don't know everything, Cheyenne!"

"Of course I don't know everything, but I know a little bit more about him than you do!"

"How dare you?" she shrieks.

"Anne! I was locked up with him! I saw what Lamia put into his head. I was the one who helped him get it out by telling him about you! I'm not trying to be his sister." I huff, my body shaking. "Want to trade places with me? 'Cause please—" I gesture out for her to take over my body, "do it. I'm tired of being me." I fall back into a chair. "The job is open for applications."

"I'm sorry, C." I stumble at her words, definitely not what I was expecting. "It's just that every time Jason looks to you first, or asks you questions, or..."

"I'm not trying to steal your place, Anne. You have to know that."

She smiles just a bit. "It just makes me so angry, and I'm taking it out on you and Mason and my parents, though my parents actually deserve it. This is half their fault anyways."

I can't match her smile. All of my energy has drained out of me. "I'm sorry, Anne. I don't know how to make it better."

We're cut off when Eli walks back through the door, followed by Regina and Dr. Cofi. "You all can go on your little outing. You'll have five hours and no more. We'll drive you into the city and pick you up. You call if something feels off. And you'll stay together no matter what." Regina doesn't look any of us in the eye, just holds her chin up high. "We'll go tomorrow at 10 am." I look to Eli with a small smile, but he just frowns back and turns to his mom, concern clouding his face.

Sixteen

I've never sat in such uncomfortable silence in all my life, packed into the minivan, stuffed between Anne and Eli, the latter of whom refuses to look at me and won't speak to me since Regina agreed to take us to the city. Dr. Cofi and Niki are up front because Regina insisted on staying home with Rose and the Lacroixs to guard the safe house and take care of Freddie. A while ago, Niki cranked up the music nearly as high as it would go to block out the silence, but it's not really working, just making it more apparent that everyone's staring out their own designated window. Or in my case, between Dr. Cofi and Niki's heads.

A two-hour car ride in silence is maybe one of the worst possible ways to spend a morning. I pull out one of the books that Niki brought to the house for me, thankful for the distraction, but it's hard to get into the reading with Eli drumming his fingers against his knee and Anne wriggling in the seat next to me. I drop one hand from my book to stop Eli's fidgeting, pressing his hand against his knee.

He looks up at me, and for a moment, I catch a glimpse of fear in his face. His hand is still beneath mine, so I wrap my fingers around his palm, not dropping my gaze from his. I'm afraid he's going to pull away, rip his hand out from mine, but he doesn't—he just sighs, leaning his head back against the seat to look out the window, and turns his palm up so that our fingers interlock. I drop my book in my lap and rest my head against his shoulder.

***

"Cheyenne, wake up." Eli's voice rouses me from the deepest sleep I've gotten in months. I lift my head from his shoulder, blinking awake. We're in the center of the Quarter, in the parking lot just beyond Café du Monde. We all pile out of the car, standing in a tight group because the parking lot is so packed. I didn't realize how many people would be here before Mardi Gras even started. From here, I can see decorations being hung from balconies—giant masks hooked to railings, beads, and wreaths decorating doors. For the first time in a while, I feel alive, like this city has always made me feel. I take a deep breath in, looking around and ignoring whatever Dr. Cofi is saying right now.

"Cheyenne, did you hear what I said?" He steps up in front of me, snapping to get my attention.

"Yeah, meet back here in four hours. What'll you be doing?" I look to Niki because I can't see it being worth their time to drive all the way back only to have to immediately turn around.

"Doing some recon. Going to check out the hotel." At first I think they're going to do something, I don't know, fun. But based on the look they exchange, they definitely have an agenda today, and nothing that I want to be a part of but should probably ask about.

"And you didn't think to include us?" I ask, narrowing my eyes.

"This doesn't concern you today. For the next four hours, you all are normal teenagers enjoying the city at its peak time. Now, everyone has their phones, yeah?"

All six of us nod. "Get out of here then." Dr. Cofi attempts a smile, but it's completely transparent. So is Niki's, and I thought she'd be more supportive of this.

Eli leads us away, and I know exactly where he's headed. Despite the tourist trap of it, despite the fact that the lines are ridiculous, he loves Café du Monde. We discreetly situate it so that Jason's walking in the middle of the group, with Anne and Mason on either side of him.

Oddly enough, the line at the cafe isn't completely ridiculous. We're seated quickly at a corner table where we pull in extra chairs to fit everybody. A five-piece jazz band is set up on the sidewalk playing "A Wonderful Life" and interacting with as many tourists as they can to get tips. I know it's cheesy, but I love them, and they sound great. Both Eli and Mason quickly lose themselves in the music, though they're probably critiquing every little mistake that I can't hear. Anne is persistent with her small talk with Jason, desperate to get to know her big brother. And Rove just watches all of us, though really he's looking out into the crowd. So am I. We're all still a little tense.

Anne's watching Jason with a fierce intensity. He's taking in everything, his head unable to stay still. Just barely visible, his foot is tapping beneath the table. "Jason, did Lamia ever bring you into the city while you were with her?"

"Not this one. We lived in Manhattan. This place is another world..."

"Did you, um, like New York?" Anne's hand is fidgeting in Mason's grasp as he tries to calm her down. I know she's restricting herself from saying anything that she actually wants to say. That seems to be all of us these days.

"Yeah, it was alright. Really loud, but not this kind of loud." Then he turns himself back to the street band.

"Do you like music?" Eli asks, leaning forward onto his elbows.

"Love it." His lips quirk up into a smile, and Anne looks like the world just cracked open. She pulls Mason out of his seat, then Eli and rushes them through the maze of tables. Jason hasn't even noticed that they're gone, but Rove looks back at me, confused. I think I know what she's doing.

A minute later, the music comes crashing to a stop, and Jason snaps out of his daze. "What happened?" Then he looks at the band and sees Anne, Mason, and Eli replacing three of the band members. "What are they doing?"

"Just wait," I say, and Rove smiles in response. This is what I wanted.

And then the music strikes up again, and it's almost better than it was, more powerful. Anne's scratchy voice breaks through the chatter of customers, and it's like the first time hearing her all over again. It always surprises me, the powerhouse voice that comes out of that tiny body. I turn to watch Jason's face, and it's like he's an entirely different person. His face lights up, and he leans forward in his seat.

Over his shoulder, he says, "You didn't tell me my sister could sing!"

I laugh and catch Eli's eye, reveling in the déjà vu of him winking while playing the drums, me in the audience, enjoying it but waiting for them to be done so I can be part of the group again. But in this moment, I don't mind at all. If it makes Anne happy, if it breaks through to Jason a little bit, I don't mind waiting just a little bit.

***

Eli and I walk in front of the group, our interlocked hands swinging between us, and I just can't shake that sense of déjà vu. I also can't stop smiling, and my cheeks are starting to hurt. Jason and Anne haven't shut up about music since they finally gave the original band back their show, and Rove and Mason—who knows what they're talking about.

"You're awful happy." Eli squeezes my hand once before moving his arm around my shoulders so that we're walking together, our bodies moving as one.

"Anne's happy. We're back in the city. I got to watch you play music. It's like the summer never ended." I say this, even though I know it's not true, even though the nightmares of the past six months haunt me. But for a moment, for a couple hours, I can forget about all of that. I think. I feel Eli's lips in his little smile as he kisses the side of my head. But that happiness only lasts for so long.

Eli stops short when he realizes where we are—at the entrance to the Hotel Monteleone. His head whips toward me. "What are we doing here, Cheyenne? Did you lead us here?"

I open my mouth, but am cut off by a trio of vampires storming out the front door. One of whom just so happens to be my favorite person, Mirnov.

He takes stock of us with an eerie smile. "Well, well, well. I didn't think you were this stupid, Miss Lane, to walk right back into our arms. I guess I was wrong."

Eli's arm has dropped from my shoulders, and he stands slightly in front of me now. I look back over my shoulder at Jason, warning him to stay where he is. Anne grabs his hand, and he thankfully doesn't pull himself away.

"Lamia too embarrassed to come get us herself since we were able to escape so easily?" I spit in Mirnov's direction.

He smirks, narrowing his eyes. "You're even more idiotic than I thought." His laugh is bitter and hits me like ice. He takes a step forward, and we all take a step back. I say silent thanks that Jason's not running into Mirnov's arms. "The only reason you're out is because she let you out."

"You're lying!" Eli's hand wraps around mine. Don't warp, I think. He can't warp all of us out of here.

"You stupid half-breed."

I lock into Mirnov's eyes and feel the compulsion rise in me. "Turn around now, and forget you saw us." Though the compulsion flows out, Mirnov stops it easily.

"You didn't really think that would work, did you?" He laughs, and I hate how much that wounds my pride. I can't let him affect me. I take Eli's hand in mine, squeezing tight, and focus again. The electricity buzzes from my toes as he and the other vampires come closer.

Wind rises around us, creating a vacuum with an opening just for Mirnov and me. The electricity rises in me, surging up and out in a direct line to him, the monster who's always been watching me. And for a moment, nothing happens, and I'm afraid my theory has been wrong this entire time. The vampires beat at the wind tunnel, but they just get blown backward into the street.

Mirnov resists me with everything he has, but I keep focus, and slowly he breaks down. His red glare slackens, but he's still fighting it. My compulsion searches for holes in his wall, and I nearly sigh as I slip in. He's mine. His body relaxes, and his mind is mine.

I take a step forward, pulling Eli with me. "When

is Lamia planning to attack?"

"Fat Tuesday," he murmurs, eyes glazed over. "When chaos reigns, and you'll never see it coming."

"Where are you keeping my family?" I growl to retain my control.

His smile makes me retch. "The basement of the hotel, of course."

"Does she know where we are?" I ask.

He's struggling against me. "No, but she will now." He stands, despite my best attempts to keep him on his knees. And he turns to go, but then there's a roar from behind me, and Jason pushes between Eli and me, snatching Eli's wooden stake, and knocks Mirnov to the ground. Before I can stop him, he pierces the stake into the right side of Mirnov's back. There's a horrible shriek from him, and then he slowly crumbles to dust.

I stare down, mouth gaping open. But Eli jerks me to attention as the two vampires rush at us. Eli throws a wall of wind at one as Rove rushes at the other. Jason is on his feet immediately, helping Rove. I pull my own stake out, and at just the right moment, Eli opens the wall enough for me to slip through and stab the vampire in the chest. Again, dust flies around us. When I look back, the other vampire is gone too. Rove is bleeding slightly at his neck where the vampires must've tried to bite him.

"Is everyone okay?" I ask, looking back at Anne and Mason, then to Rove and Jason. Everyone nods.

I turn back to Eli, releasing his hand, but reach for him as he falls backward, his body sagging with his exhaustion. I put his arm around my shoulders to support him, while Mason slides under his other side.

"That was awesome, man. You're like some kind of wind god."

Eli sighs, and I think it's supposed to be a laugh. "That's not the coolest thing to be." But he's smiling despite it.

"So what do we do now?" Anne asks. I notice that she's holding onto Jason's arm, smiling proudly. So she's not going to like what I'm about to suggest.

"We go into the hotel and get my family out." I look to Rove for support, but he's hesitating.

"Have you lost your mind?" Mason yells then winces at the volume of his own voice, checking over his shoulder for a vampire army coming at us.

"No, we have the information, we're already in the city--"

"With Eli weakened from what we just did and absolutely no backup!"

"I'm fine," Eli says, releasing us to stand on his own. "I agree with Cheyenne. We're here, and what if we go back and they decide to move their location? Now's our chance."

"Okay, what if we call Dr. Cofi and Niki for backup at least?" Mason suggests, moving to Jason's other side like a wall.

"No," Eli and I both say. "They're just going to call my mom, and there's no way she'll let us do this. We're going to have to go alone. Well, not all of us." He looks at Anne and Mason. "I think you guys should stay back."

"We're not just going to leave you to walk into a suicide mission!" Anne's head whips her head back and forth between the two of us and then again at Rove, who just shrugs. He's just along for the ride.

"Anne, I don't want anything to happen to the two of you. Go find Dr. Cofi and Niki, tell them what we're doing..."

"So we can get yelled at? And what about Jason! He can't go back in there."

"I'm fine. I want this to be over." Jason shuts everybody up, and I smile.

"Alright, so it's agreed. Eli, Rove, Jason, and I will go to the house, and you guys will go find Dr. Cofi." I look around at my group of friends, trying to ignore the glare from Anne.

"Our four hours are almost up. What are we supposed to tell them? That you went on a suicide mission, and they'll just be taking home the two of us now?"

"That we're idiots." Rove smiles, cracking the tension in the group, giving everyone a much-needed laugh. But then the silence settles, and nerves wrack up.

"Okay, we need to get going before Lamia notices that Mirnov's gone. Eli do you think you can warp both of us?" But he's shaking his head before I even finish the question. "That's okay, we'll just flit. Alright, you guys go back to the meeting place, and we'll meet you back in Grand Isle."

Anne steps up to me, finally releasing Jason, and

hugs me tight. "You know I hate you a little bit right now?"

"I know," I mumble into her shoulder. "I hate me too."

"Please don't die. Or I'll hate you even more." We both laugh, but I nod, hugging Mason goodbye too.

I look back at my friends one last time and take Eli's hand. Rove comes to my other side, with Jason on the end, and nods once. "Let's get our family back."

Seventeen

Jason, Rove, and I cast illusions over ourselves so we won't be recognized by the hotel staff, and Eli quickly disappears beside me, but his hand is still wrapped around mine. The doormen, looking at us curiously, pulls the giant doors open, and we walk quickly through the lobby with our heads down.

"Do you know where the basement is?" I whisper to Jason, He nods quickly and diverts us toward the dining room, but I pull him to a stop. "What if she's in there? She'll be able to see past our illusion." He curses, looking around to see if any of the other vampires are around.

"Eli, can you make Cheyenne and Jason invisible?" Rove asks.

"What about you?" I hiss.

"She's not looking for me, Cheyenne. She's looking for you and Jason."

I bite my lip, considering. It'll be suspicious, just one man walking through the private dining room. "I'll make myself into a waiter. She won't think anything of it."

"Fine, alright then. Let's go."

Jason takes Eli's other hand, and I watch as he disappears. Next to me, Rove's clothes turn into a Hotel Monteleone waiter's uniform, and then he's pushing the door open. Everything in me seizes as I expect for Lamia to be on the other side, casually drinking her champagne flute of blood. But she's nowhere to be found. There's just a couple of other waiters setting up, supposedly for her lunch. Apparently, she'd missed eating human food.

They look up at Rove, give him a nod of familiarity, then turn back to their jobs. We move swiftly through the private dining room until we're safely on the other side and in the kitchen, which is slamming with movement and yelling and smells. Jason directs to a back door, but at the top of a set of stairs, we stop. There's no light, nothing at the end of the tunnel.

"Well, come on then." And I tug on Eli's hand, pulling him down the stairs. Rove shuts the door behind us, and all light is gone. I flit us down the stairs, and the moment we step foot on the floor, Eli removes the invisibility, and a motion sensor light flickers on.

There's no rustle of life inside, and the four of us are just standing there, staring. They could come out at any minute. We could be waiting patiently for our death to come out to meet us. But no one does. Where are they?

"So do we have a game plan or...?" Rove asks, pumping his hands into fists to keep from shaking. I don't think I've ever seen my cousin this scared in all our lives.

The main hallway veers off in three different directions. I look down each one, trying to listen to my gut. Come on, Cheyenne. Where are they? I can feel all the guys staring at me, waiting for my decision.

"So...are we splitting up?" Rove asks.

"No!" Both Eli and I whisper yell

Finally, I take a step toward the left hallway and try not to flinch when the light flicks on. I can't just keep standing outside, fearing the inevitable. The boys follow at my heels, down, down, down. And then there's a door.

All four of us stop in unison, and I can feel Eli's heart racing enough to make up for all of our still ones. He grabs the back of my shirt as I grab the doorknob and twist it open. I'm expecting the entire vampire army to be waiting on the other side, fangs bared and ready to strike. But it's empty. And it's not a room, but another hallway. I break into a flit down the hallway, my fear rising. What if we just walked into a labyrinth? Rove shrieks just a bit when the door slams shut behind us.

The three of them are struggling to catch up with me as I race for the door. They scramble to a halt behind me, nearly knocking me off my feet. But I can't make myself move for fear of what's behind that door. The corpses of my drained family?

I flinch when Eli takes my hand. When I look back, he nods me forward, as does Rove and Jason. We can do this. So we walk down the narrow hallway, and I'm holding onto both hands beside me because if I don't, I know that my knees are going to give out.

"It's probably nothing, Cheyenne," Rove whispers. But I know that's not true. Whatever's behind that door is something that I've been looking for but probably don't want to find.

"There you are, my dear. I thought you'd never come home." We all spin around at the sound of Lamia's smooth voice. "Well, go ahead, open the door. You've gotten this far." We all take a step closer together, and Eli's reactive defense goes up—a wall of wind blocking us off from her. And she just laughs and slices her hand through the wind like warm butter. Eli gasps, falling back against me. "I expected more from you, little priest." Her eyes flash between a glare and deep consideration. "Go on, Cheyenne. Open it."

"Where's my family?"

"I think you know the answer to that."

"You didn't answer the question."

"That's because I don't want to. You are old enough to know that you don't have to do everything that everyone asks. We can do exactly what we want."

"I don't remember wanting any of this," I say through gritted teeth. Rove pinches me, warning me to watch myself.

"You do. You just don't know it yet. That's the other part of growing up—figuring out what we want for ourselves and learning to tune out the voices that would sway us from the true path." She steps closer to us, her hands linked behind her back. We back closer to the door. I can hear crying on the other side. "You have all these voices in your head, Cheyenne, trying to sway you, when you know exactly where you should be." She reaches out, but lets her hand drop before it reaches my face. "Here, with your true family. You can bring whoever you'd like with you, even your little priest. I'm sure we could find a place for him here." She looks Eli over once, smirking. "If it'll make you happy."

"Stop!" I yell. I hear all those voices she's talking about now, telling me what to do—what my dad would do, what Regina or Niki or Anne or Jason or Ms. Rose would say to do. I can't hear myself now. What I want to do. With my free hand, I find the door handle. "You're not helping. You want me to make up my own mind? Then be quiet."

"Cheyenne," Rove hisses, grabbing my arm now.

Lamia doesn't look stunned, just amused, like I'm finally falling into line after all these years. But she doesn't say anything else, just tilts her head to the side, smiling at me. What is it with these ancient women and tilting their heads like that? Granted, Marie Laveau can almost turn hers upside down, but still.

"And my sweet boy, Jason."

"Don't talk to me," he growls, backing closer to me. I grab a fistful of his shirt in my hand. "Your compulsion is gone. I'm no longer your slave."

"You were never my slave, darling. You were my son. You know that."

Next to me, Eli can feel my hand on the door, and I gently tug on the arm that Rove has a grip on, trying to warn him of what I'm trying to do. But I'm not waiting on a formal agreement. Without warning, as silently as I can, I wrench the door open and shove Rove and Eli in behind me, pulling Jason backward, and force the door closed. I hold it shut with my back pressed against it. And there they all are—my family, nearly emaciated, weak, barely able to hold their heads up on their own. Even the ones that weren't here on Christmas Eve are here now. They slightly lift their heads when they hear the door slam shut, and a light flashes in their eyes when they see us, not vampires who have apparently been feeding on them based on their bite marks.

"Cheyenne," Kara whispers, stumbling to her feet. She trips over to me, her bony hands resting on either side of my face, before collapsing into me in tears. I keep waiting for someone to slam against the other side of the door and break it down. But there's just silence, disconcerting, unwavering silence.

"It's okay. We're going to get you out of here." I look to Eli, then to Rove, who wear matching faces of horror. I stroke her head. Jason looks like he's about to wretch. At least I know he didn't have any idea that this was going on.

The room rests in an eerie silence as I try to figure out what to do. Rove's run over to his parents, collapsed into a circle of tears and hugs. But everyone else has stayed where they are, silent, waiting. "Eli, do you think you can warp a couple of them back to Grand Isle?" I turn to him, still holding my mom, who has an iron grip around my neck. "And say a prayer to the Voodoo Queen."

"What? Why?"

"'Cause she'll help us."

"Why would she ever help us? Mom said that she hated the witches of New Orleans."

"She supports you."

"What's that supposed to mean?"

I wasn't supposed to say that. Dang it. His eyes blaze against my face, but we don't have time for this.

"Please, can we talk about this later? Just do it for now, and I'll explain everything." I can tell he wants to argue more, or at least wants more information, but he hates seeing everyone suffer as much as I do. This room is eating at the both of us. He walks first to Marilyn, who won't look up, taking her hand in his then offers his other hand to one of my aunts.

"I'll be right back." He looks at me again, that fierce, bold look that reassures me that the Voodoo Queen is right. He's ready to be the High Priest, even if he doesn't know it yet.

Eighteen

The room is silent except for my Kara's sniffling. I can't help running my eyes around my family over and over again, counting everyone, making sure there's no one missing. Each time I look in my dad's direction, he turns away, refusing to make eye contact. Slowly Gramps stands from his resting spot against the back wall. Rove jumps to his feet to help him walk over to me. Kara backs away so that he can hug me, and it's in that moment that I revert to my thirteen-year-old self, after my Ascension, with Gramps sitting at my bedside. All that fear comes rushing back, encircling me, and I want to break down and cry in his arms. I don't want to do this anymore. I can't do this anymore.

He backs away, his giant palms circling my face. "I'm so sorry, kid." Tears blur his eyes, and again, it makes me want to cry and turn my back on these problems. Let someone else deal with this.

"Where's Nana?" I look over his shoulder, waiting for her to be shuffling up next to him. Then I realize that I've been counting wrong this whole time. He shakes his head and clears his throat to keep from choking up.

"She didn't make it long after we were taken." My knees give out beneath me, and I would've gone crashing to the cold floor if Gramps hadn't caught me. I pull myself out of his arms and turn to the door, my vision blurring with red. That's the second member of my family that Lamia has killed—the third that she's stolen. But everyone anticipates what I'm about to do. Rove steps in front of me, and Gramps grabs my arm. Even in his weakened state, he's still strong enough to hold me back.

"Don't be a moron, Cheyenne. You can't take her on by yourself. We'll get her back for this."

And then Eli reappears where he was standing just a few minutes ago. "Who are we getting back?"

I turn away as my eyes fill with tears. Eli takes a step toward me, holding out his hand, but I knock him away. "Not now. Did you talk to Madame Laveau?"

"Yes, she was surprisingly excited to hear from me." He shakes his head, trying to decide for himself if that's a good thing or not.

"Did she say anything about helping us?"

"She said she'll send someone with some poultices for Marilyn and your aunt. And she said when I came back, they would be waiting to come back with me. Do you know what you've gotten us into?" He's right next to me now and has hold of my hand. "You know she's dangerous."

"I know. But she's also the only one who can help us. Take Gramps please."

"How come he gets to go first?" He's half serious, but a Rove-smirk plays at the corner of his lips. I want to punch him and hug him at the same time.

Eli looks between us as he takes my Gramps' hands. Then they twist into thin air and are gone.

I pace the room in the time he's gone, trying to ignore the whimpers of my little cousins, and the thought at how much we're going to get yelled at when we get back to Grand Isle. But there's one annoying thought that won't leave me alone—why aren't they trying to break down the door? Why isn't Lamia doing anything to stop us? Rove's thinking the same thing. He keeps eyeing the door, mainly the knob, waiting for it to move, even though Jason's been guarding it. The curiosity finally becomes too much, and I flit over to the door and move Jason aside. I press my ear against the cold metal, listening for movement on the other side, but there's nothing. But when I try the knob, it's stuck, won't budge at all. Rove's been watching me this whole time and shoves me away, trying the door for himself.

"Well, good job, Cheyenne. We're now trapped in the dungeon of hell. I wonder what circle we're on? Seven or nine?" His mouth pinches as he throws his hardest punches against the metal, coming back with a bloodied fist.

"That's not going to do us any good." I stop his fist and push him away from the door. "You're just going to draw attention."

"Pretty sure they already know we're here," Rove spits at me then turns his back. He's never turned his back on me.

A tension knot in my back releases when Eli appears with Regina and Lucas. Her glare is fiery and terrible, but she doesn't say anything, just grabs two of my family members and warps out of this hellhole. Eli doesn't even look at me as he takes the hands of two of my little cousins, but they look back at me, their lips quivering.

"It's okay, guys. He's our friend. He's magical." I try to smile, but I'm not sure how convincing it is. And then they're gone. And for the first time, I notice Thomas sitting at the back of the room. The urge to rip his neck out is overpowering, to the point where I grab onto the door to keep me from doing just that. The longer I look at him, the stronger the urge is. Look at what you've done! I want to yell. Are you satisfied, finally? But I don't say any of that. Because the witches are back and wordlessly grabbing the hands of my family until all that's left is me, Jason, Kara, and Thomas. There's nothing standing between us now.

***

"So how does it feel, Thomas?"

He finally looks up from the blank spot on the wall that he was staring at to look above my head, not at my eyes. "How does what feel?"

Jason moves to my side, sensing the fight I'm about to pick. And I don't want to fight, not really. I'm so extremely tired of fighting. None of them understand. But I need answers from him. "How does it feel knowing that you did all this? Helped the vampires, helped them imprison your family? How does it feel knowing that you put all your faith into someone who was betraying you the entire time? How does it feel—knowing that a psychopathic vampire was taking care of your son?" I ignore the sobs coming from Kara. Jason is right next to me now, his hand on my shoulder.

"You don't know what you're talking about, Cheyenne," he mutters, barely audible above the silence.

"Oh, so you did all these things knowingly? Is that what you're saying?"

"No. I—" His already weak voice trails off, and I hate the small stab of sympathy that I feel for him. He's not the brute that I knew. This is a defeated man. A broken man. "I didn't want any of this." His head falls to his chest. For a moment, I think he's crying, but there's no way. The Thomas I know doesn't cry. He doesn't have it in him. But I don't get the answers I want. Eli, Regina, and Lucas reappear.

"Alright, that's everyone." He's exhausted, pale, with dark circles under his eyes. I should've been going with him this entire time, helping him channel some strength.

"Is Madame Laveau helping?" I walk to him, and he nearly props up against me to stand straight. His breaths are ragged. "Eli, you can't do this anymore. You need rest."

"I can get us to Grand Isle. Let's go." He takes my hand and gestures for Jason to join us. The moment our hands our linked, I feel him perk up just a bit, a touch of color returning to his cheeks. I take one last look at the locked door, expecting an army of vampires to come busting through, but nothing happens. Everything is silent. And even though we managed to rescue my family, I feel like I completely failed. The room disappears then, and the familiar nausea hits my stomach, but I feel like it's a warp through honey, like we're moving slower than we ever have. I try to turn my head to look at Eli, but it's pointless to try to move. And then I hit solid earth, but not where we'd planned.

Nineteen

When I open my eyes, I have to shield them from the rain pouring out of the sky. I roll over onto my side and realize we're lying on the sand. Eli's next to me, completely still, eyes closed. I crawl over to him, smacking his cheek to wake him up, but he's out cold. Jason groans on the other side of him, rolling his neck back and forth.

"Where the hell did he take us?" Jason looks through the haze of rain, trying to pinpoint where we are.

"Come on, E, wake up," I whisper next to his ear. We're definitely on Grand Isle. I can see the other side of the island, even through the rain, but we're definitely on the wrong side of it. There's the few restaurants on the island around us, and the houses are closer together. We have to get down to the other end.

"Help me get him up." We pull Eli to his feet, looping his arms over our shoulders to keep him steady, but his head lolls onto his chest. "I don't think we can flit together. You're faster than I am."

"You can say that again."

"Can you not right now?" I yell over the rain. "Go ahead and warn them that we're coming." He helps me adjust Eli's weight so that I can flit the both of us to the safe house and then takes off into the blur of rain.

"We're almost home," I wrap one arm around his torso and hold onto his opposite hand, squeezing it tightly, hoping it'll wake him up. But he doesn't budge, just becomes heavier the more soaked we get. So I take off after Jason but pulling Eli's dead weight significantly slows me down. I feel more like I'm sprinting rather than flitting, and it's dragging me down. But the house is in sight. The lights are on, and Regina's waiting in the doorway with a dripping wet Jason, his head hung against his chest. We get to the bottom of the stairs before I stumble and nearly drop Eli. Anne and Mason race out to meet us and help me get him up the stairs.

Regina ignores me completely, just looks at Mason. "Take him to your room. Get him in dry clothes and wrap him in blankets. I'll be in with food later." It's only as I hand him off to Rove that I realize he's shivering, and his lips are blue. I can't even really feel how cold it is, but Regina too is wrapped up in a heavy jacket and a scarf

As soon as Mason and Rove disappear upstairs, she turns on me, backing me into the wall. "How dare you pull such a stupid stunt? You endangered everybody! Eli nearly killed himself trying to help you! My son!"

"He only did what you should've been doing this entire time—helping those who need it! Instead, you've been hiding out in your hole..."

"Don't you talk to me that way. I've been doing

what is best for my people. You have no idea…"

"Except a bunch of untrained teenagers just rescued my entire family without your help. If it were up to you, Jason and I would still be trapped in that hotel. And if it were really up to you, you would've let me die on Thanksgiving."

"You're right. I would have. Because my responsibility is for my family." The echo of Lamia's words sends chills down my spine, and I'm finally looking at Regina in a different light. "The only reason you're here right now is because my son loves you." Loves me? "But I swear on my ancestors and all the magic in my being, that if you ever put my son in harm's way again, I will end you." Before I can rebuke her, she warps away, disappearing back into her hole.

***

Dr. Cofi and Niki are already downstairs, handing out bottles of blood to my family. I come into the room carrying Freddie, ignoring the rest of my family, and walk straight over to Kara. When she sees him, her knees buckle beneath her, and she drops to the ground in sobs, reaching her hands out for him. Thomas turns, mouth parted. He starts to reach for him, but I pull away, kneeling down in front of Kara.

"I'm sorry about everything, sis. I promise he's fine and healthy. We've been taking care of him."

Her hands shake as she takes him from my arms. He squirms as her giant teardrops fall onto his cheeks. "Thank you," she whispers and kisses my cheek with rough, torn lips. And then she holds Freddie close, rocking and shaking.

I back away, sparing my worst glare for Thomas and my dad. Dr. Cofi and Niki are watching Kara carefully, but I know she won't do anything to hurt that baby.

"Cheyenne, what's going on?" Marilyn finally asks. "Where are we?"

I take her in, the warble in her voice, and the tears that seem to perpetually hover in the corners of her eyes. She misses Drake. "We're at a safe house on Grand Isle, protected by the witches." A united grumble runs through my family, but I cut them off with a glare. "If it weren't for the witches, I'd be dead. You all would be dead. And Lamia would already be taking over the world. So I'd try to say thank you if I were you." The grumbling stops, and they look up at me from beneath their lashes, as if they're one person thinking and doing the same thing.

"So what's next?" Gramps asks. I look up, expecting to see Nana beside him, as she always is, but she's just a memory now. And I falter, the words sticking in my throat. I can see her there, her hand linked with his, smiling encouragement at me—encouragement that I don't deserve.

Dr. Cofi and Niki are standing on either side of me now, like a shield from my family's accusatory glares. "A lot has happened in this city while you all were still in Virginia," Dr. Cofi starts, taking on his professor voice. "Cheyenne has discovered her abilities, not just one but all four. And the vampires are aware of this. They now know that she is the key that they've been looking for. Her blood, combined with Jason Lacroix's blood gives them not only increased strength in all aspects, but also the ability to walk in the sun, the power that they've been searching for centuries.

"They are under the belief that humans are going to destroy our planet, so they have taken it upon themselves to take the power from them, to rule in a way that they think is more sustainable."

"That's not actually true..." I cut him off.

"What's not actually true?" Dr. Cofi asks, turning slowly to look at me.

"The whole sustainability bit. That was just a lie that she told to the witches to convince them to work with her. Lamia couldn't care less about the environment. She just wants to wipe out the Deuxsang and witches and start fresh with her new, perfected hybrid."

Everyone's staring at me, especially Dr. Cofi. That's probably something I should've told them before this.

"Well, I guess that changes things a bit. Nevertheless, we were just experiments, all leading up to Jason and Cheyenne, and now Freddie." Everyone tenses at the mention of Freddie's name.

"What does Freddie have to do with this?" My dad asks, speaking up for the first time since we got into the house.

"The vampires combined Cheyenne's and Jason's

DNA to create Freddie."

"What are you talking about?" Dad leaps to his feet, the empty bottle of blood crushing in his fist. "He's Kara's son."

Dr. Cofi looks to me, and we both realize that this is the first time they're hearing about the illusion, apart from Kara, whose head looks like it's about to fall off her neck. I'm sure Lamia told her everything. "Well, Mr. Lane, the Deuxsang, like the vampires, are biologically incapable of procreating. The vampires, for centuries now, have been casting illusions to make us believe we go through pregnancies, give us memories, but they are always there at the births, bringing a baby that they've cultivated to be 'born,'" he raises his fingers into air quotes, "and make us believe the pregnancy was real. Kara never actually carried Freddie. But despite that," Dr. Cofi turns to Kara with all the kindness and sympathy he can muster, "he is still your child. No one can take that away from you."

"No one except the vampires," she cries through heavy tears of shame. It's instinct for me to flit to her side, pulling her against me as she sobs. Thomas should be the one doing this, but of course he's standing awkwardly in the corner, arms crossed over his chest and staring at nothing and nobody. I should've just left him there in that basement room to continue suffering from everything that he caused.

"And that's what we have to stop," Niki interjects herself, hand on popped out hip. "Plus I know that I definitely don't want to die." She looks around the room, waiting for someone to disagree with her. Which, of course, just so happens to be my dad.

"What makes you think you can defeat the vampires?" He asks in that haughty voice that he always used on me when he thought I was being ridiculous.

Dr. Cofi narrows his eyes to slits at my dad through his glasses. "We have the witches on our side, more and more of the Deuxsang are learning the truth and joining us."

Niki's hip pops out even farther, her head bobbing forward. "You saying you don't want to pledge to us after all you been through?" My father, the impenetrable man who is always right, flinches under her glare, and I almost laugh. "Your daughter just rescued you from a very slow, very painful death. Are you actually questioning us right now?" Her voice has raised a few pitches, and she's almost laughing.

"Of course we're with you." My mom stands up then, looking back at me and Kara, who's still crying. "I'm ready for this to end. We all are." My dad's mouth opens and closes in shock, but one look from my mom, and he's silenced. "Just tell us what we need to do."

Twenty

I leave my family with Dr. Cofi and Niki, explaining our lack of a plan. I really don't know what they're explaining, probably actually just getting information—information that we all need. How they were treated differently than Jason and I. What happened to my Nana. But the question keeps nagging in my mind—why did Lamia just lock us in that room when she knew we had a witch with us who could easily warp out? She knew exactly what she was doing, allowing us to escape. Which makes me wonder if Mirnov had been telling the truth. What if she's always one step ahead of us?

A lightning strike of fear bursts through my chest and runs down my body. I flit up the last few stairs to Eli's room, not bothering to knock. Regina's sitting at the head of his bed, brushing his curls out of his sweaty face. When she looks up at me, her face is already fixed into a glare.

I think she might kill me if I sit on the edge of the bed, no matter how bad I want to touch him, just to make sure he's okay. What if Lamia did something to him, something I couldn't see? What if this isn't just exhaustion? "He agreed to help. It was both of us."

"No!" She cuts me off. "You made him help you,

made him warp all of your family out of that god-forsaken house. You all could've died in there."

"We should've died in there. Or at least been trapped." My voice is small, and despite the fury directed at me, I sit down, resting a hand on Eli's still leg.

"What are you talking about?"

"Lamia was there, she talked to us, called Eli 'little priest.'" I shake my head at the memory, at the way she looked at him. Regina's face pales. "Then when we went in the room, she just let it happen. Just locked the door. Didn't try to stop us from warping everyone out. But she had to know we were doing it." Regina's sharp gaze falls from my face, her eyes roaming back and forth, taking in all the information, considering.

"Why would she just let you go?" she whispers, more to herself than to me. "Unless she's confident enough that she'll get you back soon."

"That's why we have to get to her first."

"You can't just go after the vampires without a plan. Again."

This time, I do jump to my feet and can't help myself from shouting. "You've been 'planning' for a month now. The only reason Jason and I are free right now is because of me. The only reason my family is free is because of me, Rove, Jason, and your son! We are teenagers, but we did it. We've stood up to Lamia, and what have you done? Locked yourself away. I am tired of fighting, but I am even more tired of you doing nothing!"

I sit back onto the bed, wincing when Eli groans and turns onto his side, his back facing us. Once he settles down again, I look his mother straight in the eyes.

"Regina, I think… I think it's time for you to step down as High Priestess."

She goes stock still, a deer caught in the headlights but worse. Her words come out slippery and slow. "Excuse me?"

"You've done great things, and I am forever indebted to you for saving me. But something has changed in you. You've lost the confidence and power you had when I first met you. It's like you're afraid to mess up like your ancestors did."

"You have no right to talk about my ancestors." She leaps to her feet, her finger stabbing into my face. I stand, backing against the door. "You're just a child," she nearly spits, but I can hear a wavering in her voice. "You know nothing about leading people, about making choices that affect others, about holding lives in your hands, about having blood on your hands."

"I don't. But I don't really have any choice in the matter, do I? No one else is leading the Deuxsang. And Eli can lead the witches. They will follow him because he's your son. He's the future of the witches, and you know it."

A large, implacable silence fills the room. "He's too young." She barely makes a sound, just stares down at Eli, brushing his curls over and over again. "He's not ready for this life." For the first time, I see how broken she is, how incredibly exhausted. "It weighs on you, like nothing else in the world. And he's my boy—my kind, loving boy." I watch almost in slow motion as a tear falls onto his cheek from hers.

"He can do this. We're all here for him. I... I need him, and I'm not going to let anything happen to him."

I can tell she's holding back a scoff, but instead she nods, sucking her lips into her mouth. "I know that you'll try, Cheyenne. But there's no changing fate, no matter how hard we try."

She stares down at him for a long time, so long that I think she's going to change her mind. But then she suddenly straightens up, staring at the blank wall. "I'll call the covens. We'll do the ceremony as soon as we can." But instead of walking out of the room like a normal person, she warps away, leaving a giant empty space where she stood before, and I'm starting to worry if I just made a very big mistake.

Another week has gone by, with nothing happening other than planning this stupid ceremony. My life has been about nothing but these traditions, and it's getting very old. Do I see the point of my Ascension...kind of. But this? A bunch of witches gathering just so that they can see their new High Priest. Couldn't we just send out a letter with his picture in it? That would make things go a lot faster.

Eli's squirming in front of the mirror, wearing a gold button-up shirt with a black tie snug around his neck. He keeps fooling with it, straightening it over and over again, messing with his curls, and sighing. I look up from where I'm drawing on his bed.

"What's wrong?"

"This stupid ceremony—all these people having to come just to hear me say, 'Yes, I'll be your High Priest. Happy?' I don't even know if I want to be the high priest, you know? I don't know why my mom is forcing this on me so soon."

"I think you're ready." My lip is the victim of this lie-by-exclusion. Regina didn't say anything to him about me convincing her to step down, but he has to know.

He sighs again and throws himself onto the bed, his head landing in my lap. I brush his curls back as those green eyes pierce me. "Thank you." He kisses the inside of my palm and my stomach squirms. "But why now? In the middle of the biggest crisis we've been through in centuries? Why not after? After makes much more sense."

"Maybe because you've already been doing a lot of this on your own. You astral-projected to your ancestor; you figured out what my family was doing to me; you got me out of Clandestine. And you've been getting stronger— "

He smiles gently, twisting his fingers through mine. "That's just because you're here with me, making me stronger."

"That goes both ways." I squeeze his fingers in mine. "But I'm serious. You're ready for this. I believe in you. We all do, or all this pomp and circumstance wouldn't be happening."

"I wish I could tell my mom that none of this is necessary." He closes his eyes, snuggling closer to me, and again, I'm questioning everything. Is he still too sweet to be able to do this?

"It's stupid. I of all people know how stupid ceremonies are. But they're just something we have to get through. Besides, it'll show all your people how awesome you are."

"Only if you're standing up there with me."

"I highly doubt that's allowed. You don't want your first show as High Priest to be that you're choosing the Deuxsang over the witches."

"I'm not. This all started because of us. I'm not going to let an entire species, who we helped to create, be erased. They need to see us united, that you're here for them too."

"Why me?"

He looks at me like I'm being a moron, which is familiar. "' Cause you are the Deuxsang leader. After Lilith's betrayal, they're going to be looking to you. A lot of them already know your face or have met you somehow. Or they've heard about the girl who's the key to the vampire's salvation."

"I don't want to be the vampire's salvation."

Eli holds my hand against his heart. "You won't be. You'll be their ending."

I smile at that, and he smiles back at me. And for a moment, we sit in peaceful silence, even though this lie is starting to eat at me. And then I have a thought. "What if we invite the Deuxsang to the ceremony? That'll definitely show unity, don't you think? All of us in the same space, the two of us together."

He considers for a long time, his face a wall of sincerity and seriousness. "I think that's a perfect idea, two races who have no need to hate each other finally together. You're brilliant." He leaps up to plant a warm kiss on my mouth, his hand pulling the back of my neck closer to him.

"I'll go tell Mom and Dr. Cofi." He starts to scoot off the bed, but I hold onto his hand.

"Eli, wait." I bite my lip again, piercing a hole into the delicate skin. "I need to tell you something." I don't want to. Do I need to? Regina didn't say anything, so why should I?

"Okay." He sits back on the bed, facing me. I start to wave him off, say never mind, but I won't be able to live with myself if I do. If we're going to do this together, I have to tell him.

"I helped convince your mom to step down. Marie Laveau made it a condition of helping us. I don't know why she asked me to, but..."

"But you just went along with it?"

"I wasn't going to at first! I just agreed so that she'd help free us. But, even before now, your mom was hesitating on decisions too much, and you know it."

"That doesn't give you the right!" He drops my hand and leans away from me.

"We have to be on the offensive. We can't just wait for the vampires to come to take us all away. And if we followed your mom, that's what would happen."

"You don't know that." A rough little breeze rushes through the room, and I know he's getting revved up. "She's a great leader."

"I know she's a great leader. She's kept all of you safe and secret all these years. But, Eli, she's tired. And the time for hiding is over. It was her time to step down. And you—you're ready. You know you're ready."

"What makes you think you know what's best for me and my people?"

"She didn't fight me on it!" I jump off the bed and pace the room, pushing through the strong wind now, my hair whipping around me. "She knows it's your time. Madame Laveau knows it's your time. We all believe in you. This is more about you than it is about her. Please, believe me." I finally stop, sitting on the bed opposite Eli's.

He's just staring at me now, and I hate it. I hate when he just stares because I know he's having big thoughts in that brain of his, thoughts that probably don't reflect positively on me right now. "I believe you, Cheyenne. I just... I'll go tell Mom your idea." Then he slips out of the room without a look back at me, and the air is still, and my chest hurts.

***

I'm still not sure if Regina ever actually agreed to my idea, but it's happening nonetheless. Dr. Cofi sent out a message through his secret network to let all the Deuxsang in the New Orleans area know where, when, and why we are meeting. Hopefully, they come. I don't know how to implore them to come other than their lives depending on it. But Dr. Cofi didn't want to send a message like that. I guess he was right.

I stand with my back to the house now, waiting for Eli to call me in to leave. It should be any minute now. The sun is falling over the ocean, casting the most vibrant winter colors I've seen since I've been here. When I hear footsteps crunching on the sand, I turn, expecting Eli. But Jason is the one walking up to me. Anne and Mason are hovering behind him—his bodyguards—but keeping a respectful distance.

"So your boyfriend's about to become a king, huh?"

"High Priest," I say to the wind.

"I think he'll do well. " I turn, surprised. It's not that he's shown an obvious hatred for Eli, but he hasn't exactly tried to befriend him either.

"Thanks. I do too."

"But you do know that means she's going to target him now, right? He's the one thing standing between her getting exactly what she wants."

"And what is that?"

"Us."

He's right, and I know it. By making him High Priest, he's the highest-ranking witch, the closest thing to me, the biggest thing I have to lose. And she knows it. The thought makes me sick. Maybe this was all a big mistake.

I turn my back on the ocean and flit back to the house, not checking to see if Anne, Mason, and Jason are following me. I can feel Anne try to grab me as I pass, but she hasn't quite mastered the mid-flit stop. Thankfully. Everyone else is gathered, even my family, newly restored and looking as healthy as they ever have. I don't know what Madame Laveau gives us to help restore, but it is pure magic. Some familiar witch faces have gathered to help transport everyone to the cemetery. And of course we have to do this stupid ceremony in Cemetery No. 1. Why we couldn't do it in any of the other countless cemeteries is beyond me, but I'm picking my battles. I already won a big one after all.

Eli's standing at the center of the room, waiting for me, even though he very obviously still hasn't forgiven me for knocking his mom off her throne. All eyes are on me as I cross the living room and take Eli's limp hand. I try one more time to apologize to him, though I've been doing nothing but since I told him the truth. "I'm sorry, E. I just thought it's what would be best."

"You could've talked to me about it first." His voice is cold, but not as cold as it was earlier.

"I know, you're right. I should have. I just... I didn't. I don't have an excuse, I'm sorry." I'm whispering, and I can't believe I'm saying this in front of everyone. But I need him to not be mad at me before we do this together. Because we are together in this.

He pulls me into his side and presses his lips against my head. "You have to let me in. I need you. And I need to be able to trust you." I nod against his chest, tightening my arm around his waist. We both look out at the group staring at us, waiting, rather impatiently, based on their expressions. "Let's do this." Just as the witches in the room grab onto the Deuxsang, there are two loud knocks at the door. Regina and Dr. Cofi turn to each other, and I can feel the heartbeats in the room race.

"Everyone get into living room." Niki and Hugo usher us all into the other room and close the door. We all wait in silence, the humans and witches holding their breath, as Regina and Dr. Cofi answer the door.

There's a slight gasp. "Hello, Regina. You didn't really think I'd miss my son's High Priest ceremony, now did you?"

Eli's eyes double in size as he pushes past Hugo and through the door. I follow close behind. In the doorway stands Erik and his older twin, Mr. Ashford, every bit as big, booming, and annoying as I pictured him to be. He smiles a slithery smile around the room and stops when he notices Eli and me.

"Ah, there he is." He pounds through the hallway and ruffles Eli's curls. "And this must be your little half-breed who's caused the world to go straight to hell." He stops, considering me. I look around him at Erik, who's straight-faced.

"Dad, why are you here?"

"Like I said, I wasn't going to miss this, Elijah. You're my son after all. You didn't really think you could do this without my permission, did you?" He turns on Regina, and Dr. Cofi steps up beside her, trying to stand as tall as he can.

"I don't need anything from you, Matthew." She sneers. "I'm the High Priestess, passing off my duties to my son."

"Well, what about Lucas?" He looks over to his oldest son, who stands with his head bowed in the doorway. "He's our oldest."

"I don't want to be High Priest," he mutters, shielding the scarred side of his face from his father. "This is what Eli was meant to do."

"Of course you'd say that, you coward."

"Hey!" both Eli and I shout.

His eyes blaze as he turns to face us. "You two have something to say."

"Yeah," I step up to Mr. Ashford, even though he's twice my height. "You're talking to your High Priest, you'd do well to show some respect. Now," I take Eli's hand, "we have a ceremony to get to. See you there." Thankfully, Eli takes the cue and warps us away.

Twenty One

The world has a sense of humor. As soon as everyone appears in Cemetery No. 1, the sky opens to let out a gentle drizzle of rain. My vision returns to me slowly, and I'm staring into a sea of disgruntled faces, bodies fidgeting under the cover of hundreds of umbrellas. Eli and I stand at the forefront of his family's tomb. I look at Regina, standing off to the side of us, but she's staring up at the sky, her hands open to the rain. Can't she make this stop? It hasn't rained like this the entire time that I've lived here. Granted, I was trapped underground for most of it.

Eli's hand is linked around mine, and I'm losing feeling in my fingers. I squeeze back as best I can and give a nod of encouragement. The Deuxsang and the witches look equally as unhappy to be here. Hopefully what we're about to say will fix that. Hopefully.

"Welcome!" His hand is sweaty in mine, and he keeps clearing his throat as he stares out at the endlessly upset faces. "My name is Elijah Ashford, and this is Cheyenne Lane." He looks back at me, and the nerves are rolling off of him as the rain falls in turrets. He turns back to the crowd, opens his mouth, and closes it again. Regina, with Mr. Ashford next to her, hesitates a moment before walking in front of us, every bit the High Priestess that she was when I first met her—dangerous, commanding, and beautiful.

"We've gathered today to initiate our new High Priest. It is time for me to step down, and my son to take my place." She holds her chin high, peering through the rain that keeps getting heavier and heavier. I can barely see individual faces now. I wait for there to be an argument among the witches, those who are ready to fight for Regina to stay exactly where she is. But no one objects. I think she's waiting for it too, the way she hovers in her space, staring. But she doesn't let herself deflate as she sucks a breath in to project over the rain.

"Witches, please gather close so that we can start the ceremony." She turns around, reaching back for Eli. I give his hand one last squeeze before we release each other, and he takes his mother's hand instead. I look up at the rain, wishing I could feel the cold in this moment. Wishing I could feel anything other than the deep sense of wrong settling in my stomach. Dr. Cofi and Niki are on either side of me. Niki wraps her arm around my shoulders, and a reassuring smile rests on her lips. But it's not really that reassuring. Not at all. The sun has sunk below the cemetery now, and we're only illuminated by the moon and candles that a few fire witches keep ablaze.

Regina, Lucas, Erik, and Mr. Ashford surround Eli in a circle. Regina stands to the west, Lucas to the north, Erik to the south, and Mr. Ashford to the east. So...he must be an air witch, just like Eli. That seems to be the only thing they have in common. Lucas has a bag full of the materials they've been prepping for a week. I don't know if any of it is actually necessary, or just for the sake of tradition. He hands a small flask filled with water to his mom and a huge bundle of sage to Mr. Ashford. To Erik, he gives a large, red candle, and for himself, he holds a bag of salt. Regina takes a breath, ready to start the ceremony, when lightning crackles through the sky, striking the Ashford tomb. A dark cloud forms around the broken stone, and then Marie Laveau appears in front of the cracked door. She's wearing an elaborate head wrap and a cocky smile, and her ankle bracelets clink in the air as she floats forward.

"You didn't really think you could do this ceremony, in my cemetery, without me, did you, Regina?" Madame Laveau doesn't look at her as she speaks, but at me. She winks, and my stomach sinks to my toes. Niki's arm falls away from my shoulders as both she and her brother turn to give me a questioning stare. Then her head snaps as she looks out into the crowd, the rain falling through her.

"What terrible weather for such a joyous event. Why does no one look happy? You're bringing new blood into this little coven of yours." She nearly spits the word, turning her glare on Regina. The witches standing closest to us all fidget, too confused to even speak to one another. The Deuxsang behind them have no idea what's happening, and they look even more uncomfortable than they did five minutes ago.

"Oh, I'm so sorry, I'm interrupting. I just wanted to give our new little priest a gift of blessing." She floats up to Eli, whose nostrils are flared to points. I can tell he's resisting looking back at me, and I keep silently urging him not to, barely moving my mouth. From the elaborate sleeves of her dress, she pulls out a flaming candle. It's no taller than my pinky finger, could easily fit into a pocket. I think its nothing, just a trinket, till the witches around us gasp. "I hear you're a talented projector, little priest. If you are ever in need of my assistance, light this candle and call my name. I pledge my allegiance to you."

Her glowing eyes cut to Regina, whose mouth has formed a line, though her eyes are twice their normal size. Eli turns to his mom, speechless, then back to me. I open my mouth to say something, but no words come to me. He turns back to Madame Laveau, and even though this sounds like a good thing, I feel like strings are definitely attached.

"Thank you, Madame Laveau. I accept your allegiance, and thank you for your gift." He doesn't sound like himself. His voice carries centuries in it as he bows his head in respect, and the Voodoo Queen does the same. Then she floats back to hover behind Regina.

"Let the ceremony proceed." I can see her bright smile from back here, especially when she turns it on me and winks again. I wish she'd stop doing that.

It takes Regina a minute to recover, and the storm is a nice distraction. Unnatural bolts of lightning illuminate the sky, followed by thunder crash after thunder crash. The sky is going berserk, but slowly the rain recedes until it's nothing more than an annoying drizzle. We're all soaked to the bone as Regina raises her flask and pours it out into her left hand. Instead of going everywhere, the water forms a magical sphere between Regina's fingers. Lucas pours the salt into his left hand and blows it across at Regina. The salt and water combine into a ball of shimmering power, waiting to be released. Meanwhile, Erik lights the candle with his right hand, and Mr. Ashford uses the flame to burn the sage. Then, he and Regina look to each other and start to move in time, tracing a circle around Eli once, twice, three times. When they return to their starting points, Regina raises her voice above the rain.

"Great Goddess, we present to you your son, Elijah Ashford, to become the newest High Priest in your order. We beseech you to bless him with your power, your wisdom, your purpose. Show him the way. Before our coven, Elijah offers his life to your service." At these words, Regina pauses, a tremble in her voice. "From this day, he accepts the responsibilities of the leader and the sacrifices his position will require. Mother Nature, he is yours, if you will have him."

The rain, before drizzling, starts pouring down around us. I can barely see through the fast and heavy drops, but I force my eyes to stay open. And I see it, the rain around Eli glows with light, golden and bright. His eyes are closed, and I wish so badly I knew what he was feeling. Does it hurt? Is he afraid?

He doesn't look at it. He looks like he was made for this moment, and I know that it wasn't a mistake after all. This is the way it's supposed to be. We are going to win.

Regina turns to face the coven, not leaving her place in the circle, and shouts out to the crowd. "The Goddess has anointed our new High Priest. Do you, too, accept him as your leader?"Cries of assent rise up from the crowd of witches. The wind stirs; fires pop up out of nowhere; the ground rumbles, and the rain dances. Regina wears a sad smile as she turns her back on them to return to her son.

It's odd, standing here now and feeling the magic of what I thought before was pure fiction. But now I know. Now I feel it all around me—the power—and it's intoxicating. I wish Ms. Rose were here to share in it. She and Eli had a private talk a few hours before we left, but Eli won't tell me what she said to him. All I know is that when he came out of her darkened room, he looked slightly more confident, but also more terrified.

When I zone back in, I recognize that the witches are chanting in an ancient language, almost swaying together in a type of trance. Niki and Dr. Cofi are on end, turning their heads every five seconds to make sure Lamia isn't about to crash in. Which she would do. I'm surprised she hasn't actually tried yet. I'm surprised some random walking by the cemetery hasn't tried to gate crash either. But it's like there's a shield around us, and for all I know, there is. The chanting grows louder and stronger, their voices more confident and powerful. I can't see Eli's expression, but Regina looks focused, staring intently at her son as she chants the same phrase over and over again.

That's when I feel the wind, gentle at first, as it always is, then surging, twisting around the cemetery, whipping through the tombs like a race. Eli's head leans back, and his eyes are closed, his hands curled into fists by his sides. The wind roars around us, breaking branches. The Deuxsang duck so as not to be smacked in the face—or impaled. Slowly the chanting comes to a stop as the witches observe their new leader in all his power.

But their masks of surprise match my own when Eli opens his eyes and turns back to me, stretching out his hand. I look to Dr. Cofi, then to Eli, then to the confused faces before steeling my jaw and taking his hand, stepping into the circle of Lucas's herbs beside him. I feel him pulling from me, but he's not taking any of my strength. In fact, I feel stronger than I've felt in weeks. As his wind continues, lifting up tombs as it passes, I paint an illusion of clear skies, of a peaceful New Orleans so that our entire audience can see the possibility of the future. If, and only if, we defeat the vampires. A future where we are safe. A place where both witches and Deuxsang know the truth, live in peace. Where there is happiness and no fear. The faces around us have gone moon-eyed, and Eli smiles.

Then I shift the illusion, to the present. I show them the truth about where the Deuxsang come from, the test tubes we're created in, the history of how we were actually massacred—not by the witches, but the vampires, our supposed protectors. Remembering all this, thinking about it so clearly, makes me sick to my stomach. Bloody bile rises in my throat as I shift again to an illusion of the opposite future where the vampires can all walk in the sun, can drink as much as they want, from anyone, at anytime—a future where humans are hiding in fear and the vampires have taken control of every aspect of society.

The last image I show, the one that's been haunting my nightmares for months now, is the Deuxsang, wiped out, bodies upon bodies. The witches go back into hiding, back underground. And though the world is saved and continues to survive, it is desolate and dark. I let that last image linger a while longer to let it sink in. Then it falls. I release my brain and let out a huge, unnecessary sigh. And everyone's left in a mixed state of horror, disbelief, and shock—mainly the Deuxsang.

There's more here than I initially realized. Or more have just collected while I was zoned out.

"We can offer you that first future," I manage to get out through a thick throat. "We can have peace and understanding and a world without control or fear. But we can't do that if we allow the vampires to continue with their plans of massacre and destruction and control."

"The future Cheyenne just showed you—that's the trajectory we are on right now," Eli's voice matches my own, still holding onto my hand. "We are headed to a society of fear and desolation, to a world where the Deuxsang no longer exist. And possibly the witches as well." I see mouths open to object, but Eli beats them to it. "I say now to the witches…" He looks back to my people, who are moving closer to the group. "Our forebears helped to create the Deuxsang. Our magic runs through their veins. But besides that, it is our duty to protect this earth and all those who wish to live peacefully on it. The Deuxsang wish to live just as we do."

"We want the same things," I say, keeping my gaze steady on both witches and Deuxsang. "Peace, the vampires gone, and to keep living. Your community has already done so much for my family and me. I would willingly die for the people standing up here with me, as they have risked their lives for me countless times. But that shouldn't be something that I'm thinking about, or any of us are thinking about. So please help us reach that first future. It'll only happen if we work together."

The silence stretches between them and us between our families, one behind us and the other in front. I can pick out my family's faces, staring at me like I'm a stranger. And I am to them now. They don't know me. If I'm honest, they never really knew me at all. But now we all realize, we don't even know ourselves. "We had this whole history concocted for us, and everything, everything has been a lie. That lie has put everything else into question. But it's time for us to make a future, a real future, not an illusion."

There are nods of agreement, people whispering to one another, and I could not be happier. Eli and I look at each other, and we can't help the smiles that stretch across our lips. We might've actually done it. And just like that the ceremony is over. Moments flash by as witches warp out in droves, and Deuxsang flit away. The only people left standing in the cemetery are our families. Now the trial actually begins.

***

They all encircle us, remaining silent, which makes me nervous. Then I see my dad step out of my family's circle, his chin raised high in contention, and I steel myself against what he's going to say. "How do you expect to defeat the most powerful creatures on earth? You're just kids."

Not even a moment to celebrate. Tears prickle behind my eyes. Mom grabs at his arm, but he shakes her off. Eli stiffens beside me, and I know he's thinking of all I've told him of my dad, things I probably should've kept to myself, but I was tired of doing that.

"We're going to do it together." I keep my face even, smiling at Eli.

"You're going to get us all killed." His words are biting, and I want to do nothing more than flit to him and smack him as hard as I can. But I can't, not with all these people watching.

"If we do nothing, then we are all going to die."

"All the vampires have is fear," Eli says. "We have strength and community. We have a cause to fight for, a future that we want more than anything."

"So do they—it's just not our future." I nearly hurl when Thomas steps up next to my dad, his arms crossed over his narrow chest. I was hoping I'd never have to hear him speak again. "The vampires are going to do anything to make their future happen. Lamia has been planning this exact moment for centuries. She's not going to fall just because you will it."

"We don't expect her to. But we have all of you. We have hundreds of minds ready to take them down. We believe she's planning an attack for Fat Tuesday when Mardi Gras is at it's most chaotic, the perfect cover."

"A second massacre." I feel faint as my mom speaks up. Everyone is silent as they turn to her. It's probably the first time a lot of them have heard her speak. I was honestly starting to forget what her voice sounded like. "Sometimes," her eyes flicker nervously, but she keeps going. "Sometimes late at night, the vampires would talk too close to where they kept us, thinking we were asleep and we couldn't hear them. They're planning to reveal themselves to humans. Show them who they are and what they can do—that they are in control now. At Mardi Gras, they'll get all the attention they need. The whole world will know within hours."

"Of course." Dr. Cofi speaks for the first time this entire evening. "Lamia probably has a whole host of vampires waiting in other countries for her signal to rise."

"It's not just here," Regina says, her eyes floating back and forth as the realization hits. "We're just one piece. She has a whole takeover planned." The idea that one woman can take over the entire world seems absolutely preposterous. Except I've met Lamia. And while it might be the most ridiculous thing I've ever heard, I know she wants it. And if we don't do anything, she's going to get it. That thought sends chills down my back and through my veins. Eli looks at me, and I look at him. This might be slightly bigger than we thought.

"So kiddos," Dad smirks. "What's your master plan?"

Twenty Two

Our master plan was getting everyone back to Grand Isle in one piece, which was mostly successful. Some of my family opt to leave, which I was kind of expecting. Eli looks a little disappointed when they say they won't stay and help us. But to my surprise, and pretty much everyone else's, Marilyn refuses to leave with her parents, who look torn down after Drake's death. I'm so glad they weren't there to see it happen.

But when Marilyn's family says they're leaving, she says, "No."

"Of course you are." My aunt looks like she'd just been slapped across the face.

"Of course I'm not. You didn't see what they did to Drake. I want them gone, and I'm going to help."

"Marilyn, I don't know if it's such a good idea to have Deuxsang who haven't been affirmed in their abilities fighting with us. I don't want you getting hurt," I say, the fear of losing more family lurking in my mind.

Her eyes shoot daggers at me, probably hoping I was going to be the one to support her. "What does affirmation matter now? After they're gone, there won't be anymore Ascensions or Affirmations. Right?"

I open my mouth to respond, but can't think of anything to say. I haven't thought about that...at all. Which is terrifying, because I most definitely did not think past getting rid of the vampires. I didn't think of the aftermath—how young Deuxsang are supposed to ascend and affirm, where we're going to get our blood supply from, how our population will survive... Eli sees me losing control, and that's when the witches warp all of us out of there, just as the storm is returning over New Orleans.

Now, my little group is sitting around a bonfire we built on the beach. Niki put up an illusion on the neighbors on either side of us so they wouldn't try to come up when they saw the roaring fire. Anne, Jason, and I sit with bottles of blood, but I'm too zoned out to drink mine. Eli's next to me, his fingers brushing through my windblown hair. No one's said anything in a long time. Everything tonight has been a blur. I'm so proud of Eli, and I know he's going to be an amazing High Priest. But just Marilyn's last words, they're haunting us all.

"Eli, dude, you were awesome up there, by the way." Of course Mason is the first to speak. It almost makes me smile. Almost.

Eli smiles for us both, though it's small and wry. "Thanks, man. It was mostly because of Cheyenne."

"Not true," I find myself able to say, though my voice feels foreign in my throat after so much silence. "You're powerful, Eli. You deserve this."

"I don't know about deserve, but we're doing this together." I curl in closer to him, holding my bottle of blood against my chest.

"Do y'all need a room?" Anne laughs. "Yes, you two are the all-powerful king and queen of the supernatural community of New Orleans. But we still have one big problem that your dad so kindly pointed out, Cheyenne—by the way, I really want to punch him in the face."

"Yeah, welcome to my life," I mutter, and Eli stiffens beside me for a moment. It took a lot of self-control for him not to take on my dad right there in that cemetery. I would've loved to see that, but at the same time, I very much want to be the one to prove my biggest anti-cheerleader wrong.

"Speaking of dads," Rove says, "your dad is a piece of work, Ashford."

Mr. Ashford and Erik opted to stay at the local motel on the other end of the island, thank goodness. But not before giving us another good berating for doing all of this without him. I understand why Regina left him now. Something about that man gives me the creeps.

"Yeah, you can say that again." Eli sighs, pressing his hands into his eyes.

The silence falls again as we think through the big question—how do we take down the vampires? We'll figure out the aftermath after we win. Rough waves crash on either side of our circle. It'd be possible for anyone to sneak up on us right now. I look over my shoulder at the sloping sandhill that leads to the main road. A thick wall of wild sunflowers lines the hill, almost serving as cover for lurkers in the night.

"What do we know?" Eli starts, sitting up slightly to focus better. "They're planning something for Fat Tuesday, one. They'll do anything to get Cheyenne, Jason, and Freddie back, two. They can walk in the daylight now. And, they're not just targeting Deuxsang or witches. Humans are part of this too."

"Maybe we should just spread the word that vampires are real, and everyone will start wearing turtle necks and scarves of steel." All I hear for a moment is the sound of the waves after Mason's ridiculous suggestion, and then I bust out laughing, picturing all of us running through the streets of New Orleans, yelling, "Vampires exist! Cover up your necks! Put garlic on your doors! Wear crosses!"

Then we're all laughing, even Jason, who I didn't believe knew how to laugh anymore. We collapse onto the sand in fits, holding our stomachs. I'd pay good money to see how people would react to that. Honestly, the people of New Orleans probably wouldn't even blink an eye at us—we'd just be another wacky part of someone's day. The tourists here for Mardi Gras would love us.

Our laughter dies off slowly, and then the heaviness of the question lays over us again. The fire is getting lower, and thunderclouds are forming over our heads. It's only a matter of minutes before the sky opens, and we're drenched again.

"What if a bigger army of us sneaks into the hotel?" Anne suggests. "Kill as many of them as possible, at least lessen their numbers." I cringe at the idea of killing, though I know it'll be necessary. There's just been enough death as it is.

"I think that's what they want," Eli says. "They're too confident right now. Lamia let us waltz into that basement and warp the Lanes out of there. Didn't call for back up, didn't try to stop us at all. And she knew locking the door would do nothing. No, we can't go barging in like we did last time. We have to be craftier than them."

"How do you propose we be craftier than a centuries-old vampire?" Rove speaks up for the first time all night. I was honestly expecting him to be one of my family members to leave. The fact that my parents are still here is nerve-wracking enough. I'd feel better if they were all gone, but I guess the more people we have, the better. But it's also more we have to lose. I don't want to lose any more.

Thunder rumbles over us, just a warning, not a real boom. Not yet. "To get Lamia, we have to think like her. She let us carry out our last plan. What if we take a page from her playbook?" Eli looks at me, then around the circle. He receives shrugs of half an agreement. "We send our people out into Mardi Gras acting senseless—"

"As one does at Mardi Gras," Mason chuckles, and the two friends nod, sharing a memory that none of the rest of us are in on.

"Right, but really we're all keeping an eye out for attacks. If we blend in with the crowd, they'll carry out their plan without question."

"You really think they don't know what we look like? They probably have a serial killer wall decorated with pictures of us." Rove shivers, scooting closer to the fire as the thunder strikes up again.

"It's Mardi Gras, Rove. We'll all be in masks," Mason half laughs. Every effort today is half-hearted, every smile and hug.

"We'll travel in pairs or groups—that's not conspicuous during Mardi Gras—and stop any attacks before they happen."

"And then what? We kill them all?" Jason asks.

"Yes," Eli says.

"No," I say.

We look at each other.

"What?" He looks at me like I've completely lost my marbles. Which maybe I have, but we can't kill all the vampires.

"First of all, we can't do to them what they're planning to do to us. We can give them the choice to be free and change sides. Second of all, there's always been too much bloodshed, and I'm getting sick of it..."

"We're at war, Cheyenne— " Rove rolls his eyes at me, and I'm not a fan of it.

"A war doesn't have to mean everyone involved dies just because that's how the history books tell us. Besides, if the Deuxsang have even a wish of living, we need some vampires."

Eli's anger and confusion halt at those words. "What do you mean?"

"We've been so focused on taking the vampires

down because, yes, they are monsters—but we didn't think about what would happen after they're all gone. For a moment, we'll celebrate. Then it'll hit. Where will the Deuxsang get blood? How will we Ascend and Affirm? How will we have more kids? Without the vampires' knowledge, there will be no more Deuxsang, ever."

Everyone stares down at their feet now, in shock.

"Well, maybe we can get the formula from Lamia before we..."

"I still can't live with killing all of them. Can you?" The group is silent as the two of us stare down, and I can see the fight in Eli's eyes. "There's no way that thousands of vampires agree completely with Lamia. They were humans once. Right?" I look around the circle, who all have their heads hung except Jason.

"You're right, Cheyenne." Jason's almost beaming. "Yes, Lamia does have some loyal followers, though one is now gone." He smiles to himself at the memory of Mirnov's death. "But there are others who follow because they don't know anything else. All the vampires I've ever known have been good to me."

"Jason!" Anne screams, and Mason jumps beside her, reaching for her hand. "They stole you from your family! How can you even say that?"

"I'm sorry, Anne." Jason stands from the circle, and we all follow suit, ready to take him down if he tries to flit. Rove inches closer to him, his arm stretched out to make for a grab. "But the vampires were the only family I ever knew. Lamia was my mother. She's all of our mother if you really think about it." He takes a moment looking at Rove, then me, and finally Anne. "I'm not going to run off to them, don't worry." Rove hesitates beside him, dropping his hand. "But I will not massacre the people who created me."

"And kidnapped you, and brainwashed you, and stole your blood, and created your baby without permission..." Anne goes on, but it's not doing any good.

"I'm going inside. It's been a long day." He breaks from the circle, and we all stare off after him as he slumps back to the house, where a group of adults stand watching us from the window, my dad the most disappointed of all.

"Well," Rove claps his hands together and falls back onto the sand, "that went well."

Twenty Three

The group disperses with Eli following Mason to Ms. Rose's room so that he can project to the ancestors—see if they have any advice on how to deal with the impending doom that we've created. Rove's gone to say goodbye to his parents since everyone that wants to leave will be fleeing in the morning. And there's just Anne and me sitting side by side, our arms linked as we lean closer to the fire, peering up at the sky as we wait for the rain to come. We haven't had a day without rain in a week.

"I remember," Anne breaks the silence suffocating us, "when the hardest thing I had to deal with was my mother being a helicopter." I snort, remembering the first time I ever met Mrs. Lacroix. That seems like a million years ago before we knew the truth of everything else.

"She put up such a fuss about your Affirmation party."

Anne's return smile is wry, but she laughs just a little bit. "Right. The dress had to be perfect. I had to be perfect so we could impress the vampires. The monsters who took my brother, who ruined all of our lives." The words rest between us. She's completely right. They did ruin our lives. But at the same time, we wouldn't have lives without them.

Our evil creators. "You sure we can't kill them all?" She swings her head to look at me, pressing her chin against her shoulder. Her wet eyes glitter, and I can feel her forcing away the tears.

"Not unless we all want to die too."

"Everyone's supposed to die at some point. It's natural."

"We're not natural, Anne." My words come out as a sigh. As much as I've wanted to be normal my entire life, to go to school, work, have a job doing...I don't know, being an artist maybe, I know none of that is really possible. Not right now. I keep trying to imagine what it would be like if the vampires get what they want—for the humans to know that they exist, the vampires to be in control. But we won't exist in that world, so maybe this all shouldn't matter to me. But it does—because Mason would exist, and Eli, and everyone else.

Anne rests her head on my shoulder, and I feel a teardrop onto my sweater. "Do you think Jason will turn on us?"

I open my mouth to answer but honestly can't. I don't know the answer to that.

We're both silent, staring at the dark waves.

"I don't know what would've happened to me if I'd been trapped with vampires for over a decade. Neither do you." I nudge her. "It's my nightmare to have them in my head." I shiver. "But just because I trust him doesn't mean we don't watch him carefully. Even if he doesn't want to fight for us, we can't let them have him. Or Freddie." She nods against my shoulder, both of us knowing how dangerous that would be if they got all three of us back.

Then we sit, letting the rush of the waves breaking on the shore crash over us. They seem to be getting bigger, stronger. I turn my head when I hear footsteps on the sand, and my heart sinks when my mom comes into view.

She smiles weakly as she sits down next to us, close but not too close. "What are you girls talking about?"

Anne can feel the tension settling in me and grows tense herself. "About how we could die soon, how my brother might be a turncoat, what it'd be like to be trapped by vampires for a decade. You know, normal girl stuff."

Mom's lips purse together, and she looks down at her bare feet. I don't think I've ever seen my mother without a pair of heels on, even when we were at home. They're small and pale, and I don't know why this matters. "I'm sorry you girls are having to go through this. No one should have to deal with what you're dealing with."

"Yeah, no—"

"Anne." I cut my eyes to her, and she shuts up, though it takes effort. My parents have certainly received the coldest of greetings of all my family members. I'm sure Eli and Anne have shared my history with the rest of the household. "Yeah, it's not been a great few months, Mom. Then again, what's new?"

"Cheyenne." Mom looks over to Anne. "Dear, would you mind giving us a few minutes alone, please?"

"Yes, I mind. I'm comfortable where I am. Besides, C will just come back and tell me what you said, so you might as well say it to both of us now."

I almost laugh, even though the situation isn't really funny. It's just small moments like these that make me very thankful for the friends I've made here.

"Okay then. Cheyenne, I know it's too late to apologize for everything..."

I knew this was coming, but I still don't expect it. I can't believe she has the audacity to say this to me. Now. Of all times. "Just a bit, yeah."

"Your father and I, we thought we were doing what was best for you. We thought Lilith knew what she was doing, trying to save you."

"You're talking about this semester? I didn't need saving this semester. I actually would thank Lilith for forcing the blood on me and the training. Without her, I wouldn't be who I am now. Do you want to know when I needed saving?" I detangle myself from Anne and spring to my feet, glaring down at my mom. "I needed saving the night of my Ascension when the vampires kept biting me over and over again. When I know for a fact that you all heard me screaming. I needed you and Dad to bust through those doors and save me then. But you didn't. You stood there, and then you never talked about it again. You treated me like a pariah after that."

I know my mom's crying now, but I can't stop. I've been waiting for this day for years, to have the courage to say this to her face instead of yelling it in my car over the blast of music.

"You failed me in every way; you continued to fail me once I got here, and there's really no way that you can apologize for all that. So I don't suggest trying."

Mom rises to her feet and reaches for me, but I deflect her hands. "Sweetie, tell me what I can do to fix this."

"Help us end all of this."

The moment I turn my back, I hear a whoosh of air and a strangled cry. Anne's eyes double in size, and she's on her feet in half a second, reaching for me. Thunder rumbles again as I turn around, and my heart sinks to my toes.

Lamia's long fingers wrap around my mother's neck, just barely lifting her off the beach. "Come, Cheyenne, your mother gave a moving speech. They were just doing what was best for you."

How did she know where to find us? I don't want to risk a glance back at the house, just in case she doesn't know exactly where we're staying.

Her long fingers squeeze tighter, and my mom gasps as a nail pierces into her delicate skin. "I see you've become quite the little revolutionary, my dear. Pairing up with your little priest, showing off your powers. It was quite a show, I must say." She smiles broadly, her eyes flashing in the light of the nearly full moon. "Yes, I was there, my dear." She drops my mom, who crumples against the sand, grasping at her throat.

"I'm not here for blood, Cheyenne. I'm here to

strike a deal with you since you've been ever so crafty and plotting with all these creatures in the most... charming of places." She glances over her shoulder at a fisherman sitting on the edge of the beach a half a mile down. I can smell him from here. "If you, Jason, and Frederick come to me before the start of Mardi Gras...." Her smile grows broader. "Your family and friends will go free and have nothing to fear from my family."

"That won't be happening."

She shakes her head and clucks her tongue in her mouth. "I'd think very carefully about this, my dear. There's more at stake than your little gang of rebels. You have a week. You know where to find me." I stand taller as she slithers up to me, her face beaming. She lifts my chin with two cold fingers, pinching the bones in my face. "What a masterpiece you are, my dear. I'm so proud of you. I know you'll make the right choice."

***

The moment Lamia goes, the three of us do a thorough search of the house to make sure there aren't any vampires lurking in the bushes, waiting on a surprise attack after our guard is down. I rip through the bare shrubbery and check the few palm trees that guard the house, but she's gone. Every nerve in my body is on end. My head's rushing, squeezing in on me, and I can feel my vision blurring. How did she know where we were? And why have they just let us sit here for this long?

Anne knows exactly what I'm thinking. She sees me from the other side of the house and flits over to take my hand as I start to sway on my feet. My mom joins my other side as they help me up the stairs and around to the back porch, which we know is open. I can't even speak when we walk into the sunroom where Dr. Cofi is reading, looking concerned, as always.

"Cheyenne, Anne, what's wrong?" he asks.

Mom and Anne set me down in one of the chairs as my vision gets worse. My head is pounding like there's a nail gun inside. Dr. Cofi kneels in front of me as Anne runs through the house, calling for everyone to meet in the sunroom. He checks my pupils and looks over me to make sure I have no visible injuries. My mom hasn't left my side, and I should check to see if she's okay too. But I can't move. I can't speak. I keep feeling Lamia's sharp fingers on my chin, and the way she looked at me.

Within moments, everyone is packed into the sunroom, looking confused, and all waiting on me to answer. My dad especially. I can't help but notice the glare he shoots at my mother.

"Cheyenne," Dr. Cofi is still in front of me. He shakes my shoulder in an attempt to knock me out of my trance. "What happened?" Everyone looks back at Anne, who's shaking worse than me now, leaning into Mason.

I squeeze my eyes closed hard until I see stars and take a deep unnecessary breath. "Lamia was just here."

The expected outrage of fear and worry rumbles through the house. Before I continue, all the doors are locked, windows are shut, and most of the lights are turned on. Not that any of that would prevent them from getting into this house.

My body starts to shake again, and my teeth chatter. I can't stop seeing her. Eli pushes through the crowd to sit on my other side, his arm sliding around my shoulders. I barely even feel him there.

"She was at the ceremony." I look up at him. "She's been watching us this entire time. She knows we're here, what we're planning to do. She knows everything." My voice breaks on the last words, and I lean into Eli, hiding my face in his side.

"That's it, we're getting out of here." My dad's rough voice sounds in the silence of our group. "Mary, let's go." He steps forward to pull my mom away from me, but she rips away from him and takes hold of my shoulder.

"I'm not going anywhere. I'm going to stay here and help my daughter. And so are you, Samuel."

I haven't seen Dad's eyes blaze at her like that. At me, all the time. But never at her. I've also never heard her speak out against him before now. He spins on his heel, searching out Kara and Thomas. Thomas won't meet anyone's eyes, and Kara looks like a puppy backed into a corner, holding onto Freddie for dear life, especially when Dad turns that glare on her. "Let's go," he growls and shoves his way into the hallway. Kara's lip quivers as her head bounces between mom and me and then to dad.

"I'm staying here, Dad. I can't leave Freddie." I'm almost as shocked as Dad when she finally answers.

"Fools." And then he's gone. But that part of me—the part of me that's been mourning my relationship with him for years—it's dead. This is just the final deciding blow. Silence creaks through the house minutes after he's gone, then slowly everyone turns back to Eli and me.

"Go on, Cheyenne. What else did she say?"

"Not much else. That I could either give myself, Jason, and Freddie up, and you all wouldn't be harmed, or we're all going to die." Again, silence. "I have a week to decide."

"Hold on." Eli's arm tightens around me. "This is not just a you decision. I'm not going to let you walk into their arms again and give them exactly what they want. That's just not going to happen. Don't even--"

"Eli, I didn't say I was going to." That shuts him down.

"Oh. Okay, good."

"Sorry, but I really don't want to sacrifice myself. Not that I don't care a lot about you all." I look back at all the faces staring at me, looking as scared as I feel and trying not to show it. "I think we need to play their game. If they're going to be this bold and open, then we need to do the same. Stop hiding. We need to go back into the city, show them that we're not afraid of them."

"I agree," Eli slowly nods, his eyes distant as he

tries to configure a plan. "Make our presence known that we're not backing down."

"Hold on a minute." I knew Regina would disagree with us. "You have to think about all the lives that you're putting at risk, Eli."

"No one is with us who doesn't want to be. They all know the risks. As you've all seen, you're welcome to leave."

Regina opens her mouth to argue with him again, but she has no comeback.

"I'm not going to cower in front of them. I say we go stay at Kara and Thomas's. We patrol the city as it gets closer to Mardi Gras." I hide my shaking hands in the long sleeve of my sweater. "Let's show these vampires who they're trying to destroy." Eli reaches down and takes my hand, but no one argues with us. Mom's hand rests on my shoulder, and for the first time, I think that we might actually be able to do this.

Twenty Four

The next two days are a blur of moving and sending out new information to all the Deuxsang and witches. We aren't trying to hide ourselves anymore or keep our location secret. Regina and Dr. Cofi rent three cars to get everyone from Grand Isle back to Kara and Thomas's house. They're arriving now. Eli throws our duffle bags over the landing of the stairs, even though they're quite light. I can't decide if that's a good or bad thing.

Dad's gone, and a few of my aunts and uncles are gone, along with all the young cousins. Marilyn is still here and has not left my or Rove's side for the past two days. It's only driving me slightly insane. She keeps asking me about having all four abilities, about drinking human blood, about all the things I really don't want to talk about. I have to focus, and her incessant talking is not helping me at all.

She's standing next to me now, talking about literally nothing. And that's not just because I'm not paying attention. When I zone back in, I still have no idea what she's saying. "Marilyn!" My voice is clipped, and I feel sorry about it...for a minute. "Please, for five minutes, please stop talking."

She looks at me like a wounded puppy, biting her lip, but I also can sense a bratty comment resting on her tongue. "I'm sorry, it's just really busy right now, okay?"

"Just cause you're special doesn't mean you can be a jerk." She crosses her arms over her chest then goes off to find Rove probably. Her words almost sting me, but I shake them off as Eli appears at the bottom of the stairs, planting a kiss on my cheek. I smile, letting some of the stress slide over me.

"Ready to do this?" He asks, pulling me against him.

"Of course not." Flashes of every way this could go wrong slide behind my vision, and I want to call it all off here and now. Tell everyone carrying bags to the cars to unpack. We're staying here. But I can't do that. It'll only be worse for us if we don't go on the offensive. "But we're going to do it anyway."

"And we're gonna win." He takes my hand and tries one of his bright smiles. They have been few and far between these past few months. But his confidence is infectious. Marilyn comes trailing back into the room after Rove.

"Alright weirdos, get a room." He scoffs, leaning against the wall to wait for everyone else.

"We're holding hands..." Eli laughs, though it seems a bit forced.

"Yeah, that's a little bit too gushy for me."

"Me too," Marilyn butts in, and I have to resist the urge to scream again. There's a reason I wasn't meant to have a little sister.

"Right, everyone shut up! I need a milkshake!" Everyone stops and stares at me and my outrageous outburst. I know milkshakes at a time like this is the most ridiculous thing in the world, but I can't help it. Milkshakes make everything better.

"Now we're talking, munchkin." Rove elbows Eli. "Cheyenne makes the best milkshakes."

"How come you've never made me one of your milkshakes?" Eli leans down next to my ear, and I shiver.

"I haven't exactly had the opportunity." I smile as I turn to him, just barely pressing my lips against his. "Now, we have the opportunity. Milkshakes for breakfast!" I yell, and I can hear Anne's shout of excitement from outside.

Everyone's waiting for us outside, most of them already loaded into the cars. Dr. Cofi drives one, Niki in the second, and Lucas in the last one. Jason's already been sat in the passenger seat of his car, and Mason and Anne are waiting for us in there with Rove and Marilyn. We climb into the last seats in the back, curled into each other, distinctly aware that Rove can't see us from where he's sitting and therefore not make fun of us. But something feels off in the air of this car. Like it's too stifling, and I don't even have to breathe. Eli feels it too.

Mr. Ashford and Erik watch all of us from the front lawn as we pull away. Eli meets their eyes out the window, and I give his hand a squeeze. "At least they're helping."

"Yeah, for now." His words are low, and there's a hint of concern behind them. But we can't worry about that right now. As long as they're helping instead of hindering, I'll take them.

Some of Monde Musique's songs play quietly in the background as they drive into the city. Lucas keeps glancing into his mirror at us, then to Mason. Rove and Marilyn have their earbuds in, and Jason seems oblivious. But Eli just seems on edge, his heart racing against my arm.

"You're gonna chew through your cheek," I whisper, watching the way the skin is sucked into his mouth. "What's going on?"

He releases his cheek but doesn't look away from the window. "My father isn't a good man, and it freaks me out that he's here. Now. Just out of the blue."

"So something we have in common then?" I try to smile, leaning into him, but he doesn't smile back.

"Very similar. But at least your dad isn't a horrible racist. At least your dad didn't give you a scar like Lucas's." The last words are barely words so that we're not overheard, but I know Rove and Anne are eavesdropping. They turn their heads just slightly for better sound.

"What happened?"

Eli shrugs, a short, jerky movement, as he adjusts himself slightly away from me. "Lucas was protecting our mom when she finally left him. They hadn't been okay for years. Then she met Andrew. When he found out, he just lost it. She was running out of the house with us. I was already waiting in the car, and Lucas was helping her carry the last of our bags. I should've been helping..." His voice breaks just slightly, and my heart hurts.

"He was coming at Mom with a knife when Lucas shoved her out of the way, and instead, Dad got a slice down Lucas's face. For a while, we thought he was gonna go blind, but the scar over his eye healed. Lucas hadn't seen him again before the other day. I've only seen him when I've gone to get Erik. That involves as little contact as possible."

I look back up at the driver's seat where Lucas is focused on the road now. We're in the city, and the place is a madhouse with people setting up for Mardi Gras, trucks all over the place putting up decorations on balconies. Lucas swerves to avoid falling signs and a few people running out into the road. We just need to get out of the Quarter, and it'll be better. But I can't believe he did that for his mom. And he's still here with her, hasn't left her side in all these years. What does he do for himself?

"Hey, Lucas, can we stop at the market before we get to the house? I need to get a couple things for milkshakes."

He snorts, shaking his head. "Is now really the time for milkshakes?"

Anne cuts me off before I can reprimand him. "It's always time for milkshakes. The vampires can take my freedom, but they are not going to take away my desserts."

The tension in the car lifts just a little bit as everyone laughs at Anne. I think I even see the corner of Jason's lips quirk up. "Fine. We're facing impending doom, but yes, we'll stop to get ice cream."

"Thank you." I laugh and say a silent thanks that Eli's relaxed, just barely. He rests his arm over my shoulder, and I lean into him. But I can still feel him grinding his teeth as we pull onto Magazine Street.

***

Mr. Ashford and Erik are waiting on Kara's front porch, and now that I've heard the truth, I want to be as far away from that man as possible. Hugo is helping Niki and Regina unload bags as Dr. Cofi carries Ms. Rose into the house. I offered to let her have my room, but they're keeping her in the lounge—easier escape route. We're all reluctant to get out of the car and face them. Jason is the first one out.

Mr. Ashford is looking down his nose at us as we approach. "Hello again," he says.

I don't say anything. I look to Erik, searching for some of the humanity I saw when he helped save me on Thanksgiving. But his face is blank like he's his father's puppet. He avoids my eyes at all costs.

"You don't look like much a queen, even of half-breeds."

I narrow my eyes. I wasn't going to say anything, but I can't not. "And you don't look like much of a man."

"Excuse me?" he growls.

"A man doesn't try to kill his wife and in the process nearly blind his son." Lucas stands behind me, and he sucks in a deep, sharp breath.

His face pales as he quickly glances up at Lucas, who looks just as embarrassed. "What do you know about it?" He takes a step forward at the same time

Eli and I do.

"She knows what I've told her about what kind of man my father is." Eli nearly spits.

Kara rushes forward at that moment. "Here, let me get some of those bags into the kitchen." I'm thankful for her compulsive hostess instincts, as she takes one of my bags, and we follow her silently into the house. Memories come rushing back. I look to the left, at the sitting room where I lost every ounce of trust for my family. I shake it off and continue to follow Kara into the kitchen. I definitely need a milkshake.

Eli's holding tightly to my hand as shouts break out from the porch. I can't make out exactly what they're saying, but Regina and Mr. Ashford seem to be yelling over each other, their voices rising louder and louder. We can hear them with the kitchen door closed. To block everything out, Anne cranks up music on her phone as Eli and Lucas exchange concerned glances. Rove "helps" me by dumping too much chocolate sauce into the blender. Add some vanilla and milk and a bunch of ice cubes, a dash of cinnamon, then my secret ingredient—a heck ton of chocolate chips. I hadn't realized how much I'd missed simple things like being in a kitchen. It makes me remember that I'm part human.

"I hope everyone likes chocolate." Rove helps me hand out full-to-the-brim glasses, and for the next five minutes, the only sounds in the entire house are our slurping. Eli settles next to me on the counter with a chocolate mustache.

"You've been holding out on me, Lane." He grins, and it's the first time all day he looks like he's not in pain. "This is the best milkshake I've ever had. No exaggeration."

I smile, wiping away the chocolate stache. "I know." But his lips still taste of chocolate when he leans in to kiss me.

"You two do realize that the world is coming to an end right now?" Rove butts in, grimacing at us. "This little show is not doing us any good."

"I disagree. I think it's important to find the light moments right now." Anne's head is resting on Mason's shoulder. "If we had nothing inspiring us, then we wouldn't be fighting."

"Fine, whatever, please continue to make out in front of your friends and family. It's totally fine and normal, but before you do that, can we please discuss what our plan is? And by that I mean, what the hell is happening here?"

As I have been my entire life, I'm extremely thankful for Rove and his comedic relief, even if he is being one hundred percent serious. It's just that, when he's concerned, he becomes even more ridiculous. He looks out of place right now, like he should never have a care in the world—just be a perpetual 18-year-old driving a convertible and serial dating. And yet he's here, and I love him for it.

Eli slurps up the rest of his milkshake, and I smirk at his look of disappointment at reaching the end. "So Mardi Gras is getting ready to hit full swing, meaning there will be thousands of people going crazy in the streets. They'll be lambs to the slaughter. We will be patrolling the streets and stopping the attacks."

"And then what, man? We can only stop people from being killed for so long. We're going to lose people in the process too." Mason surprises us all by speaking up. He hasn't played a huge part in the planning of all this, mainly because we aren't going to let him participate. He doesn't stand a chance against a vampire, even less of a chance than we have.

"Well..." Eli looks nervously at me, biting the inside of his cheek. "You're not going to be stopping any attacks."

"Excuse me?" Mason slams his glass on the counter. "I'm not just going to sit at home waiting for all of you. I'm not completely useless!" I don't think I've ever heard Mason raise his voice. He pretty much has two emotions—excited and then more excited, except when he's writing new music. Then he's just annoying and moody.

"I know you're not useless, Mason, but we're not talking about a fight in the school hallway..." Eli can't meet Mason's eyes.

"Don't patronize me, Eli. I know exactly what's going on, and I've been training with Dr. Cofi. Anne and I can fight together."

"We'll be fine." Anne takes Mason's hand as a sign of solidarity, but we've talked about this—I know she's not completely supportive. He beams at her, but Eli's not convinced.

"I'm not going to lose you, Mason. Your mom

can't lose you. Why can't you stay with her, protect her? That's definitely not being useless." That makes him pause. He looks back at Anne then at us. The rest of the room stays silent. "Your mom needs you too."

"Mom can...Mom will be fine on her own while we handle this. I'm protecting her by helping you."

"Mason..."

"Don't say my name like that, Eli. I'm tired of you looking down on me just 'cause I'm a human. In case you weren't aware, humans do make up the majority of the population. We're not as helpless as you think we are." Mason drops Anne's hand and takes a step forward. The rest of us take steps back, watching the two faceoff.

"I never said you were helpless. You're the one who keeps saying that!"

"Because that's how you're treating me!"

The door swings gently open, and Ms. Rose comes shuffling in. I haven't seen her up and out of bed in a while; she doesn't even come down to eat with us. Her face is blank as she looks between Eli and Mason, holding tightly to the doorframe to hold herself up before Anne and I rush to her side to help her stand.

"Now, what's all this yelling about?" Her voice is barely a whisper, rough with dehydration even though she's constantly drinking water.

Eli and Mason remain in their staredown, faces tight with tension. Ms. Rose sighs, letting out the weight of a lifetime. "Mason, honey, I know you want to fight, but you just don't understand what you're fighting."

"Yes, I do, Mom. I've been a part of this world as long as he has."

"I'm a year older than you." Eli smirks, and I swear under my breath. The world is coming to an end, and they're still this immature.

"Oh, my god!" Mason yells and raises his hands to shove Eli back, but Ms. Rose shouts as loudly as she can.

"Mason, you're not fighting against the vampires. They are centuries older than you, impossibly strong and fast. I'm sorry, but I forbid you from fighting them. I'm not supposed to lose you first." Her peaceful face contorts in pain and fear. She bites her cracked lips to keep herself from bursting into tears, and I want to squeeze her until all the sadness is gone.

"Mom—"

"That's the end of this discussion. You will help by staying here, protecting the house, keeping me occupied. But I will not have you out there. If it were up to me, I wouldn't have any of you out there." She looks around the room at all of us with bleary eyes. "But we've messed up. And now it's falling to the younger generation to clean up our mistakes. Now, you need to be searching for Lamia. You know how to end this right?" She looks at Eli and me with a pointed stare, and I know the answer. I just don't know how it's possible.

"Yeah, I know." We both nod, and I pinch my

eyes closed as a wave of fear rushes over me.

"That's the only way all this will go away. The rest of them are only following her. They are nothing without their leader. Without her, they'll be thrown into chaos, and we can all go on with our lives." She lets go of Anne's hand and reaches out for Eli, pulling us both so that we're standing in front of her. She has to tilt her head up to look at us. Her bony fingers press into our hands as she smiles, but it's a smile with a lot of sadness mixed in. "You two are meant to do this. You're the only ones who can, and I know you can. But please, oh please, be careful." She kisses each of our cheeks, then takes Mason's arm to lead him out of the room. I'm sure he's about to have a talking to. I wouldn't want to be part of that.

The kitchen is silent as they leave. Jason's eyes are to the ground, and Anne won't stop staring at him. Rove's eyes flicker around the room for a moment before he groans. "Damn." He bobs his head, sucking in his lips to erase his mouth. "I think I need another milkshake."

This disconcerting sense of being stuck in the past will not go away. Eli and I are out on my balcony, both of us in t-shirts because it's unseasonably warm for the end of January. It feels like a Virginia spring out here. I've drained two bottles of blood and one bottle of human that hadn't been discarded before the family was run out of the house. I haven't felt this strong in a long time—both the blood and having Eli beside me. Some of the witches and

Deuxsang have already been patrolling Mardi Gras and stopped several attacks, but they don't have numbers on how many vampires they've stopped. Or killed. I refuse to hear the accounts of how many vampires have been killed. If I had it my way, I'd just run them all out of town. But in the logical part of my mind, I know that's just a means to more destruction and death in a different city.

Eli and I are curled up on the floor of the balcony. His head's in my lap as he reads from some book that I've never heard of. It's the only way he can get his mind off of all this. Because tonight, we go into the streets ourselves for the first time. Tonight is the start of the peak of Mardi Gras when the largest flux of tourists hit the city for a weekend they may or may not forget. So all hands are on deck, except for Mason and Ms. Rose, who will be staying here with one guard that Mason does not and will not know about. Ever.

I run my hands through Eli's soft curls, twisting my fingers on individual ones, trying to think about nothing while simultaneously thinking about everything all at once. My head very well might explode in five minutes. Even though my door's closed, I hear footsteps creaking up the stairs and freeze as someone knocks on my door. Eli looks up at me, and I can feel everything that he wants to say without him saying—every dread, every fear, every...everything. I smile sadly down at him, pressing a kiss to his forehead, then he slowly rolls to his feet, dog-earing his page before leading me back into my room and throwing the book on my bed.

I'm waiting for Regina to be on the other side telling us it's time to go. But instead it's Lucas, looking as nervous as I've ever seen him. He's wringing his hands in front of him and not looking up when we open the door. "Hey, Lucas, what's up?" Eli asks, confused.

"Um, Dad wants to talk to you." His words are a mumble of nothing. I don't think he even opens his mouth.

"I don't want to talk to him." Eli says shortly, holding tightly to my hand and ready to slam the door closed when a large figure steps through the doorway, his hand poised in the air in case we tried to close him out.

"Stop being childish, son. It's time we had a talk."

Lucas turns on his heel and sprints down the stairs, unable to see Eli's glare against his back. Mr. Ashford lets himself into the empty room, looking at the blank walls that used to be my room. Now it's just haunted with memories.

He turns his beady stare on us, and it's hard to see how Eli came from him. I can feel his anger flowing at us like a wall. How can someone so dark create someone so full of light?

"What do you want to talk about Dad?"

"Your misguided ways, of course. So much like your mother."

"Wanting peace and security for all of us isn't misguided."

"All of us? She wasn't thinking about anyone but

herself and her own desires. Her desires to leave me and destroy our family, all for that half-breed downstairs."

The muscles in my face tense as I take a step forward in defense of Dr. Cofi. Mr. Ashford smirks, and I want to scream. "Seems you're following in her footsteps then."

"What do you want, Dad?"

"You've resented me all these years for wanting to keep my family together. And you chose your mother, even though she's the one who tore us apart."

"Mom did the right thing, leaving you. Lucas's scar is proof of that, of what kind of man you really are."

"That was an accident, and you know it, kid."

"If it wasn't him, it was going to be her!" Eli spits, and I've never heard him sound so completely hateful. It makes me hateful too, but worse, my heart hurts for all the pain he's been through.

Mr. Ashford is shaking slightly; his hands curled into white-knuckled fists. "Don't do this, Elijah. Don't be like her and think only of what you want. Don't destroy other people's lives to chase a fantasy."

"It's not a fantasy. The future we're fighting for may not be perfect, but it has to be better than this. You want our people to be cowards, just like you." Eli drops my hand and crosses his arms over his chest.

"I'm no coward, son." Again, Mr. Ashford takes

a step forward. But Eli doesn't move back.

Eli's nostrils are flared out, his jaw so tight it might nearly break. They're only a breath away from each other now. "Why...are you here?" For the first time, his dad pauses. He doesn't have an answer. "Did you just come to tell me what a screw up I am?"

"I'm here because no matter how much you hate me, you're my sons, you and Lucas. I don't want to see you get yourselves killed. You're fighting a lost cause. It's not right, but it's the way it is. Don't throw your life away for people who were never supposed to exist!" His boom of a voice shakes the thin, old walls, and the rest of the chatter downstairs stops.

Eli's face turns a purple-ish red color, but I put a hand to his chest to stop him from exploding. As calmly as I can manage, I say, "Mr. Ashford, whether I was supposed to exist or not, I'm here. Because of your ancestors. You are implicated in my existence, in my people's existence. And I, I am the answer to the vampires' centuries-long search. You can argue all you want that the easiest way to get out of this mess is to get rid of me, but, A—it's too late for that 'cause they already have what they need from me, and B—I'm a real person, naturally-created or not. I am just like you. Except, actually, I'm not just like you. If it were up to people like you, the world would be ending right now. The vampires would be running rampant while you hide. But thankfully, not everyone thinks like you. Thankfully, we have people like Eli, who know that people are people. And that is why we are going to overcome this."

And with that, I grab Eli's hand and pull him out of the room before I lose my calm and give Mr. Ashford a scar to match Lucas's. But before we can get down the stairs, Eli pushes me against the wall, and his lips are covering mine, hands holding my face against his. Too soon, he pulls away and smiles at me. "You're amazing, you know that?"

"No," I sigh, slightly dizzy from the kiss. "But I'm trying to be." He smiles again, snorting his understanding, then backs away so that we can go downstairs. And as I suspected, everyone is sitting in awkward silence, staring at the floor from overhearing our conversation upstairs. Lucas looks slightly ashamed. I know what having a father like Mr. Ashford is like. But I'm done hanging my head in front of men like him. And I'm done hiding from a woman like Lamia. I meant what I said upstairs. Because of the people fighting on this side, we might very well have a chance of setting the world right.

Twenty Five

Though my resolve slightly crumbles as the moments wear on, as Deuxsang pair off with witches and there are grumbles of dissatisfaction, looks of disapproval. My fingers tap against my leg as the minutes pass, minutes closer to being in the Quarter, closer to stopping Lamia. Closer to freedom.

I feel eyes on me, and when I look up to meet them, Kara is staring at me teary-eyed next to Niki, who looks like she wants to smack the tears right out of her eyes. She looks like she wants to take a step forward, but then stops herself, then starts again. She looks like she's talking herself up, and finally, she flits to my side. Eli flinches as she appears.

"Can I talk to you for just a second?" she asks quietly.

I look over my shoulder at Eli, then back at my sister, who looks completely pathetic and desperate. Who is this girl, and what has she done with my confident, perfect sister? "Yeah, sure." So I let her lead me into the study and shut the door, though I'd much rather it be open. "Let's be quick. I'd like to get going."

"I know, I'm sorry. I just...I never thanked you for saving us, which sounds cheesy, but I couldn't live with myself if I never said it. And for getting

Freddie back."

"You're welcome." My heart softens just a little bit because I know exactly what she is thinking, and I want her to stop. "Kara, I don't care how he was made. Freddie is your baby. He always has been, always will be."

She flinches and bursts into sobs. Definitely not what I was expecting. "I'm so so sorry, Sissy." She throws her arms around my neck before I can stop her and is sobbing into my black shirt. "I've been so terrible to you. We all have, not treating you right at all."

I'm stiff as she hugs me tighter and sobs harder. "You've only ever tried to be a good sister, and I've just been so terrible to you! Please forgive me, Cheyenne! Please." Slowly, I let my arms wrap around her, awkwardly patting her back.

"It's fine, Kara. Really. We need to go through." I try to push her away, but she clamps her hands down on my shoulders, her red, puffy eyes peering at me.

"Cheyenne, please. I just...I don't know what's going to happen tonight, and I need you to forgive me. Or else—" Her voice falters, and then she's just staring at me.

And part of me forgave her a while ago because that's what family does. Just as part of me has forgiven my dad for already walking out on me. But here, now, watching her break down like this, I can't keep holding on to this resentment. She did what she thought was right. It's not my fault; I don't see things the way she does. I can't fault her anymore.

"It's really okay, Kara. I swear." I take her hands from my shoulders and squeeze them in mine. "I know you were...trying to do what you thought was right. I can understand that. I promise that I forgive you. And I love you." She cuts me off with another tight, sobbing hug. "We're gonna get through tonight." That just makes her sob harder, and she doesn't let go of me until there's a knock on the door. "Come in!" I call over her cries. Please help me. Eli and Anne swing the door open, looking at me with raised and scrunched brows. Anne rolls her eyes dramatically, and I almost laugh. But then I'd feel too bad.

"We're, uh, handing out masks now," Eli says, looking extremely uncomfortable in front of my sobbing sister. She nods, wiping her running nose on her sweater sleeve; I don't think I've ever seen her look more un-Kara-like than she does at this moment. She attempts a smile, but her face is all ruddy and swollen.

"Why don't you take a minute?" I suggest and hug her one last time before leaving her to collect herself. She walks over to Freddie in his crib. She'll be staying here tonight with him, out of the fight.

It was Mason's idea for us to wear masks whenever we're out on the streets. That way, we'll at least blend in a little bit more. I highly doubt that the vampires are going around wearing masks. Either way, Deuxsang have always been able to tell when vampires are near. It's like our version of spidey-sense. Eli's already chosen my mask for me, no surprise there. I trust his taste much more than my own. I don't even get a look at it before he swoops it over my eyes to rest on my nose and ties the silky ribbon behind my head. His smile as I turn to face him is a mixture of sad and smugly pleased. I walk into the entryway to get a look at myself in the mirror and gasp.

He's picked out a beautifully simple light purple mask with hints of gray in the sparkle. The eyes come to sharp points, and only one side is decorated with a silvery feather reaching past my head. I can't stop looking at it, comparing it to the other extensively more elaborate masks than my own and just thinking how perfect it is. And then I think how much more I'd rather be wearing this to go enjoy the night, instead of using it as an actual disguise.

I feel him behind me, waiting for my opinion. "It's perfect, E. Thank you." I kiss him gently. It's kind of hard to kiss with these masks on—they might need to work on the design a little bit. But he beams with pride.

Suddenly, Mason is beside us, clearing his throat. "So when you all make your victory speech tonight over the vampires, I'd like you to mention the brilliant efforts of your extremely useless normal human friend whose brilliant idea it was to make you all wear masks. If you don't add this to your speech, I swear that I will destroy my guitar and never play music again. That is now on your conscious." His gaze bounces from Eli to me back to Eli.

"Perfect," I say shortly. "I didn't have enough on my conscious already." I force a smirk and roll my eyes, wondering how visible that is through the mask.

"It's a great idea, Mason." Eli pushes him away, laughing. "You'll definitely get an addendum in the victory speech."

"Freaking fantastic," he mutters as we walk back over to the rest of our group—a mixture of mine, Eli's, and Anne's families, all here, all working together—looking to us.

"Alright, everyone. I know this is the night that we all have been dreading, and wishing would never come. But it's here, and we are ready to do this. Tonight, we take our freedom, we atone for the sins of the past, and we show the vampires who they're underestimating." I don't know where all these words come from. I've been struggling with what to say to people for several days now. But this comes naturally. The words feel right. "Tonight, we ascend, and we affirm our place in this world as free beings!" I don't expect the roar of support that follows, even from Regina and Dr. Cofi. I spot Mr. Ashford and Erik, silent in the back of the room, watching all of us. I want to flit back there and invite them not so kindly to leave. But at this point, I don't want to lose the numbers. Not when we're this close.

Eli scans the room, meeting each and every gaze. "Let's show them what we're made of."

Twenty Six

Never in all my life have I seen anything like a New Orleans Mardi Gras celebration. There are people covering nearly every square inch of the French Quarter, but not as many as I expected wearing masks. Girls' necks are weighed down with beads, and not one person walks by without a drink in their hand. I have never felt this city more alive. Even more bands and performers are out on the sidewalks and in Jackson Square. We walk by a magician who's managed to captivate a dumbfounded crowd of fifty with a cheap trick. I can hear the music from the clubs on Bourbon Street all the way from the square, and the sun hasn't even set yet.

Eli won't let go of my hand as we weave our way through the mass of people, and the more I look, the more relieved I am to see people wearing masks. So this wasn't a total waste and hindrance. But Eli and I are on high alert. Every unusual sound that hits my ears makes me swivel and search it out. But most people are just cackling drunk or falling over their own feet. Eli's tension rams into my own, and I feel like my neck is about to snap in anticipation.

The tiny cobblestone streets are packed to capacity, and even the alleys are full of people. Well, most of the alleys. And the ones that aren't—those are the ones we decide to turn down. And that's where we hear it—nearly silent cries for help, and at the end of the lane, I see a guy pressed up against the wall by his throat, and one of the vampires relishing the sunlight that's just barely touching the tip of his hand. And he's not burning. I still can't get used to that sight.

All of a sudden, Eli disappears beside me, finally releasing my hand. I creep up behind the vampire so that the guy can see me, holding a finger up to my lips. But he's too terrified to do anything but try to scream. Then I flit between the vampire and the wall, keeping my eyes wide open as the vampire looks down at me—just what I wanted. In a matter of seconds, he's trapped in my compulsion.

"Put the man down," I say slowly, articulating each word, and regretfully realize that I'll need to be more specific. The vampire quickly releases his hold on the man, though I can feel him fighting against my compulsion now, aware that he's under it. The man screams as he starts to fall, but Eli's waiting under him and catches him before he smashes into the cobblestones.

Eli reappears as he sets the man down and turns to me, "Do you want to make him forget?"

That's something I hadn't thought about—should we be compelling them to forget their run-ins with vampires? But I think no. I think they should remember something like this. It's unfair to take their memories away, even if it's a haunting one. So I shake my head no.

He nods his approval and says, "Run, go find your friends." The man hesitates, looking between the three of us like he has a question but then really doesn't. And then he bolts, tripping over himself to get as far away from this group of freaks as he can. I'm still holding the vampire in my compulsion, keeping him from attacking us, though my hold is waning.

"Eli," I say through gritted teeth. It was easy to think through half of our plan. Stop the attack. Boom. Then what? I don't want to kill anyone. I don't want Eli to kill anyone.

"We'll let you go free if you swear to abandon Lamia's plan. No more attacks. Leave the city. No one will chase after you."

For a minute, the vampire is silent, and I think he's actually considering our offer. But then his face contorts into a creepy smile, and a cackle erupts from his mouth. "You thought that would actually work?" His voice raises two pitches as his cackle continues. And then it stops, and he glowers down at me, taking a step forward, and I feel like I'm pinned against the ground. "You're gonna die, little princess. All your friends are gonna die. Your family. Everyone you love. Should've just turned..." And then his head snaps to the side at an unnatural angle, and he falls to the ground.

Eli reappears, standing behind where the vampire stood a second ago. He pulls his stake out of his back pocket and stabs it into the vampire's still chest. In moments, he disappears into dust

"He wasn't one to save, Cheyenne. He wasn't going to see reason."

"Yeah, I know." I stare down at where the vampire fell, wishing this was easier.

***

We try to blend into the crowd, stumbling through the hordes of people with Eli's arm wrapped around my waist. Everyone else couldn't be less aware of their surroundings, but Eli and I have never been so on edge. I look at every face that passes by me to see if it's one of the vampires I can recognize. Eli keeps his eyes on the alleys and balconies.

But even with us constantly on alert, I don't hear anyone come up behind us. I don't know anything's happening until the small delicate hand grabs me by the scruff of my neck and pulls me out of the crowd, Eli following after me. We're thrown into one of the dirtiest alleyways, the road covered in muck and alcohol and trash splashing against my face and clothes. I spit the trash away and look up at a group of the vampire kids. It's weird seeing them now, knowing what I know. Madame Laveau's children, stolen from their mother, all because she was a threat.

"Where's Jason?" The one girl asks as we stand up.

"How am I supposed to know?" I brush myself off, but Eli looks like he's about ready to attack. I hold up my hand to stop him. "They're fine, Eli."

"What do you mean? They're vampires."

"Yes, but… They're also Marie Laveau's kids." He looks at me like I'm nuts, but there's not really time to explain right now.

"We need Jason."

"Well, you're gonna have to go find him yourself."

"Why do you need him so badly?"

Then Arlo is there, rolling his eyes, while the others look nervous, checking over their shoulders. "We're not taking anyone back to Lamia. We need Jason so we can kill her."

"What are you talking about?" I say to him, who just looks bored with the conversation.

"If we drink from both of you, then we'll be able to walk in the day, and we'll have your strength and all the abilities. We might just be able to take her down."

I look back at Eli, contemplating. "Look, Arlo… I know you're Madame Laveau's kids, but…"

"Cheyenne," he steps in front of his brothers and sisters, looking more human than I've ever seen him. "Lamia killed us. She took everything from us. We want nothing more—nothing—than to see her dead."

"Please, believe us." One of the younger girls actually looks genuine, and it makes me stop. "I swear, we'll go to our mother, and you'll never have to see us again. I've forgotten what the sun feels like." I don't want to break it to her that she probably won't even feel the heat once she can walk out in it. And that's when I realize that I'm going to do it. I'll give them what they want, and if they turn on us, then... we'll do what's necessary. And if they don't, that's five fewer in Lamia's army. Maybe five more on ours.

"Okay, let me find him."

"Cheyenne!" Eli yells, turning after me as I pull out my phone to call Anne. "You're not actually serious."

"Yes, I am. They're kids, Eli! Kids who've gone through hell and back, who were taken from their mother. And they want to help us. I'm not going to say no." He looks back at them, fighting the sympathy that I know he has to be feeling. He wouldn't be my Eli if he didn't feel something for them.

"I don't like this," he says simply.

"I know. But my gut's telling me that I'm right. I need you to trust me." I meet his eyes as I bring the phone to my ear, ridiculously compelling Anne to pick up the phone from blocks away.

She picks up on the second to last ring. "We're a little occupied right now, C." I can hear grunting and punching in the background.

"Where's Jason?"

"With Regina. Why?"

"Stay safe!" I slide the phone back into my pocket and turn to Eli. "Call your mom."

"What? Why?"

"Because she's with Jason."

As Regina answers the phone, I watch Eli's face change dramatically, losing all of its color. "We have to go. Now."

"Why? What's happening?"

He looks back at the group of kids, who've dropped their gazes to the murky ground. "Did you know about this?" Eli's in Arlo's face, pushing him back against his shoulders. "Was this just a distraction?" Eli shoves him again, and the kid just lets him. Why isn't he fighting back?

"No! But yes, we knew she was going to do this," one of the other kids says, one who hasn't spoken up yet. "We just didn't know when."

"What's going on?" I yell, just to be heard over the roaring crowd. And then I realize that everyone around us is running in one direction.

"Lamia took over the Endymion parade. We have to get to Canal Street now. Text Anne and Rove. Tell them to meet us there." We start to take off, but the youngest girl stops me.

"Please, just a taste. I want my momma." I don't know if it's possible for vampires to cry, but this girl looks like she's about to break down. I look away from her to the other four kids, who are all trying to hide their own disappointments.

"I'll tell you what—if you help us end this, I'll let you have the cure. Do we have a deal?" I turn to Arlo. They'll go along with whatever he says. And for a moment, I think he might laugh in my face, prove my gut instinct wrong. But he stares, stone-faced, biting the inside of his cheeks.

"You have to swear that you'll help us. Swear on the high priest's life." His red eyes flash to Eli, but I don't even hesitate.

"I won't go back on my word."

"Alright," he sighs. His siblings nod their acceptance, "Let's go take down Mommy Dearest."

Twenty Seven

It's like Lamia cast out a giant compulsion to bring everyone to Canal Street. Eli has a tight grip on my hand, and I keep checking over my shoulder to make sure the kids are following us. It surprises me every time when they're still on my heels, running easily beside people who are panting but can't seem to stop.

The moment the crowd empties onto Canal Street, I comb faces and backs of heads for anyone familiar, anyone fighting for us. I vaguely recognize a few of the witches that I've seen over the past couple of months, who were definitely at the ceremony. Then there are some of the Deuxsang families, looking battered, but alive. Way down the street, I can see the amazon Regina holding onto Jason's arm, looking around wild-eyed for one of us. I swear I can hear her cry when she finally lands on Eli. Across the road, there's Lucas and Anne, and farther down, I see Rove's curly head. We need to stay spread out because whatever this is, it's going to be brutal. I wave to Anne, and she looks relieved when she sees me and elbows Lucas so he can see us too.

Eli spins on his heel, yelling over the music. "What is she planning?" The kids look nearly sick to their stomachs as they stare down the road, the peak of the parade starting to come into view.

"She told us it was just an illusion. But I'm not so sure. You need to break the compulsion and get these people out of here." Arlo says, looking grim.

"How are we supposed to break her compulsion? She's the most powerful vampire in the world."

"I don't know, but you better do it, or this road's going to become a bloodbath," he growls.

"Eli, stay here, with them."

"No, we're not splitting up." He tightens his grip on my hand.

"I'm just going to flit over to Anne and your mom, tell them that we have to get these people out of here."

He's shaking his head the whole time I'm talking. "Cheyenne, no, these people aren't going to leave the Endymion right before it starts. This is what everyone's been waiting for."

"Yeah, including Lamia."

I can hear the music getting louder; lights are flashing, and there's screaming. Please don't be death screams.

"I'm going with you."

"No, stay here and make sure they're with us. I'll be right back." He barely loosens his grip, enough for me to pull away and flit across the streetcar tracks to Anne. "We have to get these people out of here. They're under a compulsion. Tell everyone." She doesn't have time to react before I flit to Rove and then to Regina.

"Where's Eli?" She asks desperately, reaching for

my arm. "And Lucas?"

"They're fine, and they're safe." I'm yelling at the top of my lungs now, and I can see the front of the parade, moving slowly toward us. Maybe about a block down. "Those vampires kids—they're with us."

"No, they're not. You can't trust them!" She still has a tight grip on Jason, who's wincing away from her, begging me with a look to take him away. But I can't handle watching him and the vampires.

"They're Laveau's kids. They want Lamia dead. I promise they're not going to cross us." And that's when I notice the figures patrolling along the side of the streetcar line. The vampires keep their heads down, but their eyes are roaming the crowd, searching for someone in particular...me? I grab Regina's shoulder, horrified, unable to move.

"Go! Get to Eli now!" She shoves me into a flit, and I brace myself weaving through all the people that are smashed together, bouncing around, sloshing their drinks. I keep my eyes open, searching for where Eli was standing in the crowd with the kids, but I left them on Royal Street. The kids are there, but Eli's not. I skid to a stop just as rain starts pouring down. The kids are looking around, their heads throwing from side to side, searching for him too.

"What happened?" I yell over the rain and the music. "Where'd he go?"

"I didn't even see it!" Arlo yells. "They just flitted in and out, and then he was gone." The youngest one is crying, holding onto her brother.

I look back up at the parade, at the first float, and everything in me goes woozy. Lamia is at the front of the float…with Eli. She waves her queenly wave, smiling down at the people she's planning to eat. She looks right down at me, her smile even bolder than before. Her arm is linked through Eli's as he stands stock-still, not looking left or right or down. I try screaming his name, but it's pointless over the rain and the music. I'm drenched from head to toe and don't bother fixing the mask that's fallen around my neck.

The wind starts to whip around the crowd, and I don't know if that's from the storm or the witches stirring something up. Then lightning strikes bold in the sky, and some of the people break out of the compulsion with echoing screams. Several small groups break into a run, back toward the Quarter, toward cover. But the majority stand stock-still. The float continues, and then I notice it. The vampires are filching people from the crowd one by one. The float is getting fuller, stuffed with people who are still in a daze.

Then there's the screaming, and I'm sure the vampires have started their attack. Except they haven't. There's a bright red blaze coming up Royal Street. Flames stretching taller than some of the buildings race each other, but don't touch the bricks and aren't put out by the rain in the least bit. A crowd of people finally notices the fire and scream, pushing over one another to get out of its way. The flames slow as it approaches the people, guiding them away from the vampires and whipping out at any monster that tries to grab someone running away. Then I feel the heat on my side, and two more fire witches are coming up this side, ushering people away from the parade and back into cover. The compulsion's broken. Everyone's screaming, scrambling over one another, doing anything to get away from the fire. In the distance, I hear sirens whooping and whirring, but once the whole crowd has filed out of Canal Street, the fires dampen, and they're just witches, panting, bending over their knees to catch their breaths and cool down.

Lamia has stopped the parade with a hand held calmly in the air. She approaches the edge of the float, pulling Eli after her. "You disappoint me, my dear." She shakes her head clucking her tongue in shame. The music is gone, but the storm still roars around us. "I truly wish you had made the right decision." The vampires on the float are holding tight to their humans, who wouldn't be moving anyway because they're still under the compulsion. And then I look down at the floats following her and realize that this isn't the only float with hostages. They're all filled, farther back than I can see.

Eli's jaw is square as he looks down at me without moving his head.

"Every choice we make has a consequence, my dear." She smiles as if she's offering me the greatest salvation. "If you want your little priest…" She turns to Eli then, taking his face in her hands, and he squirms under her gaze, trying to pull out of her grasp. "Meet us back on Grand Isle, at the dock." And then in a flash, timed perfectly with the biggest bolt of lightning yet, the entire float is gone. An illusion. It was all an illusion. And then the only people left standing there are witches and Deuxsang, awestruck and dumbfounded.

***

Canal Street is now empty, the road covered with debris, piles of dirty beads, and who knows what else. Hundreds of Deuxsang and witches close in together. The vampire kids are glued to my side, wary of all the dark looks they're getting from everybody else. I want to blame them for letting her get Eli, but I can't. They're part of this team now.

Regina storms up to me, absolutely livid, her hand raised as if she's about to smack the life out of me. I stand, waiting for it to happen because I deserve it. It's my fault. I shouldn't have left his side. Mr. Ashford is right behind her, steam rising off of his body with a murderous look in his eye. But just before Regina reaches me, someone pulls me back, and Dr. Cofi leaps in front of his wife.

"Regina, what are you doing?" he yells as I turn to look at my mom. She's got cuts and bruises all over her face, and I can't help but hug her. I never thought I'd feel so happy to see my mom alive.

"Lamia has my son! Because of you!" She roars, lunging at me over Dr. Cofi's shoulder. Mr. Ashford is right behind her, ready to kill me when she gives the go-ahead.

"Regina, stop. This isn't Cheyenne's fault, and

you know it." Dr. Cofi is calm, despite the hundreds of confused stares. This is just what the vampires wanted—for us to fall apart. This alliance was so fragile to begin with that they knew it would be easy to break us.

"But he's...he's my baby." She collapses into Dr. Cofi in tears, and there's an uncomfortable shuffle of murmurs from our army.

"Regina, I'm not going to let her have him." I say, stepping out of my mom's arms.

"It's a little late for that!" She screams through her tears, and I feel the weight of blame on my shoulders. I don't care what Dr. Cofi says. This is my fault, and it would be better if Eli and I were together. Everything just goes terribly wrong when we're apart. And I think Lamia knows that, and that's why she took him.

I step closer to them and step up onto a bench so that everyone can see me. The rain has let up, but just barely, just enough that people can hear me now. "I know that this is my fault, and I'm going to fix it. We're going to Grand Isle to get our High Priest back, to save all those innocent people, and to end this for good. I am sick of their games! I am sick of their control, and there's no way that I'm going to let Lamia get what she wants. Now, you don't have to come with me. You've done your part. But I'm going to Grand Isle. I'm going to get our High Priest back, and I'm going to set us free." I step down from the bench, expecting the majority of them to leave without even looking back. But everyone's still standing, watching me, watching Regina and Dr. Cofi, waiting for me to go.

Twenty Eight

The weather is even worse when we land on Grand Isle. The motel behind the dock is firmly rooted in place, but I can hear the stilted houses groaning against the pressure of the wind. The boats are crashing against the side of the docks from the force of the waves beneath them. But Lamia is there, with all her vampires and their human hostages, lining the dock to the edge, where she's standing with Eli, protected from the vicious rain with a gigantic white umbrella covering all of them.

"Oh, good, you chose to listen this time around." The lightning dancing behind her illuminates her wide smile. "Of course, I knew you wouldn't abandon your little priest."

"I'm here, Lamia. We're here." I look over my shoulder for Jason, who joins my side. "Now let them all go. That was the deal."

She laughs quietly, but the wind carries the chilling sound to my ears. "No, I believe the deal was, if you didn't come, I would most certainly kill them all. I never said I wouldn't kill them if you did come." Eli tries to wrestle out of her grip pointlessly.

"Why are you doing all this, Mother?" Jason says.

"I'm doing what I have to do, darling—for our

future." Her eyes are glowing red, and I know she's feeling all the power right now. She has hundreds of humans trapped; she has us right where she wants us. In her eyes, she's already won.

But I won't let her. I'm about to flit up the dock, grab my boyfriend, and dive off the dock when a chill runs down my spine, and a familiar ghost floats up to my side. "Cut the shit, Lamia. Everyone here knows your true raison d'etre."

Lamia's head cocks to the side, trying to hold back her anger with pursed lips. "And what might that be, Marie?"

"Power. Pure, blind, purposeless power. And this little girl right here—" Madame Laveau's ethereal hand passes over the back of my head, "is going to stop you. With help, of course. She's only one girl, after all. A powerful one, I'll give you that. You sure did put some extra bit of something in her." They're both looking at me like I'm the prize-winning science experiment. Hundreds of witches and Deux-sang behind me are restless, wanting something to happen.

And I do feel something happening. I scan the dock for movement and catch sight of the vampire kids creeping up the other dock that no one's paying attention to. Mr. Ashford and Erik are behind them, and I have a terrible sense that I know what they're about to do. I know we didn't have a plan when we came here, but this shouldn't be a plan at all. I tense myself, ready to flit after Eli and prevent whatever aftermath is about to happen. I just have to keep them talking.

"I don't know about all that, but I am going to stop you. All this cruelty ends today. I'm sorry not sorry to say that you will not be taking over the world." Each of the kids has settled behind a vampire, the same with Erik and Mr. Ashford. Arlo is right behind Lamia. He nods once, but it seems that tiny gust of movement alerted Lamia. She whips around and snaps Arlo's head off before I can even scream.

Then Madame Laveau is next to me, wailing in the most awful way that I feel down to my core. "My baby!" All the other kids scramble before the vampires can get their hands on them and hover behind us.

Marie turns to me, her ghostly face covered in anguish. "Take her down now."

"How?" I look at Eli for help, but he's as confused as I am.

"You have to destroy her from the inside out."

When Lamia spots us, she knocks Niki to the side as if she's an old rag. She turns to us, and the lightning seems to crackle around her as she moves forward. I can do this. We can do this. Eli and I interlock hands, holding tight to one another until our hands are forever imprinted with the other's fingerprints.

Lamia laughs as she gets closer, throwing her head back, her whole upper body shaking. "I would look closely before you two lovebirds do anything rash." She turns her head to the right, and we follow her gaze. Off to the side of the dock, three vampires are guarding, Kara, Mason, and Ms. Rose, who's definitely unconscious.

One of the vampires leaves the group and strolls over to Lamia, carrying Freddie. I look on in horror as Kara rails against the vampire holding her, screaming Freddie's name. "You wouldn't want anything to happen to this precious child, would you?"

I have no words.

"You really think you can stop me? I made you. And I can end you just as easily."

I look to Eli, petrified. "We can't do it while she's holding him," I whisper. "He'll get hurt."

"No, no, we can do this. You just do what you have to do and trust me."

I stare at him, look at the scene around us, our side, and their side rearing for a fight, my sister being held back from her child. It's not that I don't trust him. I have to trust us.

"Do you trust me, Cheyenne?"

"Of course." I don't have any other choice. So I take his hand and turn back to Lamia, blocking out her taunts.

The surge of magic tingles at the bottoms of my feet as I reach for my power, shooting up through me, but when I send out the infliction, searching for her mind, she brushes off my attempt to breach her walls like I'm a feather. Eli feels the deflection and reaches out to his ancestors, asking to channel their power, praying for their help to get us through these next moments. And I can feel the change. Their ancient magic surges through me, the magic that's angry from being tricked by this monster, the vengeful magic ready to make amends for their mistakes. That power settles inside Eli and me. He forms a wall of wind between Lamia and us and blows away anyone who tries to get in our way.

When she tries to step through the wall of wind, it just blows her back. I try again, even though the urge to grab Freddie is almost overwhelming. I breathe, squeezing Eli's hand tight in mine, and reach for the power that starts at my base and works its way up and up, roaring through me. It almost knocks me off of my feet as it rushes out, headed straight for Lamia. Then I hear the screams. "You can't be doing this!" She curses, pulling Freddie tight against her while her other hand grabs for her head. "This is impossible!"

I hold tighter to Eli, trying not to focus on Lamia's arm around Freddie, pulling more ancient power from Eli and combining it with my own. Slowly, her defenses are down, and her mind is open.

I start with her ability to inflict, drawing that out of her internal system, the neurons that run through her muscle. And as it's pulled from her, it passes through me, and I force it out, into the storm. And then, I find compulsion and begin to work it out of the framework of her brain. It tumbles out and dissipates in the rain.

I'm surprised by how strong her dreamwalking ability is, featured at the back of her mind, the most peaceful, untouched part of her brain, holding dreams of the woman she was before all this, before centuries of endless life passed. She holds onto that part the hardest, fighting me every centimeter of the way as the dreamwalking slides out her mind and through me.

Then there's just the illusion, sitting at the back left cortex of her brain. I open my eyes long enough to see her on her knees, pounding her head against the dock. I desperately search for Freddie and follow Eli's gaze. And there's my little nephew, floating in the air in front of everyone. I give Eli's hand one last squeeze, a silent thank you, and turn back to the dark queen who nearly ruined everything.

"You can't do it," she mutters. "You don't know what you're ruining. Everyone will die without me. I'm the reason you're all still alive."

"No, we're alive in spite of you. And we intend to live much longer without you ever crossing our minds again." I don't even have to say it loudly. I know she hears me. And in one final surge of power, I rip illusion from her, and there's a chorus of screams as the last of her dies, rips through me, and disappears forever.

Thunder shakes the beach, and lightning crackles in a circle around us, illuminating Lamia's limp body. And slowly, everyone stops their fighting. They turn, vampires, witches, Deuxsang, and they look to me. Marie Laveau is floating a distance away, surrounded by her kids who are all crying into her ghostly form.

Eli and I look around us, accounting for everyone

that we love, and from what I can tell, everyone is still standing. I stand, waiting for everyone to break into fighting, but off to my right, the vampire holding Kara has released her, and she flits to Freddie's floating form, hugging him tight to her chest, and I want to cry. But hundreds of faces are staring at me. I turn back to look at Lamia's lifeless form one more time, assuring myself that she's really gone.

All this time, I've been trying to think of something to say that's clever or commanding or absolutely brilliant that will go down in the Deuxsang history books. But my mind is fuzzy, and I'm barely able to keep myself on my feet. The only reason I'm standing is Eli's arm around my shoulder. So I say the only thing I can think to say.

"It's over. Lamia is gone." I never thought I'd be able to say those words. "The vampire reign is over. The Deuxsang are free to live our lives. The vampires can either join us, or be part of our community, or you can leave and never show your faces to any Deuxsang or witch ever again."

Eli hears my voice wavering with exhaustion and steps in. "If you swear an oath of loyalty to both the Deuxsang and witches, swear never to harm our kind, and swear to the keep the peace in the world, Cheyenne and Jason have offered their blood. That way, you will truly be part of our communities. The choice is yours."

Hundreds of vampires now realize that they're surrounded. Our words have given the witches and Deuxsang enough time to move silently around them. Fire witches are positioned strategically around the circle, their hands ablaze and pointed directly at the vampires.

They all stand around, snarling, some mooneyed and lost without their leader. Eli's holding his breath, and my back tenses like a rod, waiting for someone, anyone to step forward.

And then one does, and I slowly unravel, until he starts speaking. "This isn't what Lamia wanted!" His thin line of a mouth growls. "She might be gone, but the cause isn't. I'm going to finish what she started." His eyes pin directly on me, then he's snarling and rushing forward, about to break into a flit. But then there's a rush of wind and a blaze of fire. Erik's standing in front of me, panting, and the vampire that was is now just a pile of ash.

"Anyone else want to carry out the evil queen's plan?" Erik growls, a flame springing up from his palm.

Murmurs rush through the vampires, and again we're waiting. Erik stands in front of me, and then Mr. Ashford is in front of Eli, blocking us from the vampires. Then my mom is standing next to me, and Regina is next to Eli, Dr. Cofi, Niki, and Hugo behind us.

Slowly, like a miracle, vampires begin to kneel, dropping like a giant wave. The hundred or so left standing look around them, confused, and look to us, fighting off visible anger. I see the decision in their eyes, and before I can say anything to change their minds, they break into flits, leaving bursts of empty peace in their wake.

Around two hundred vampires are left, just about the amount that we were hoping for, though we prepared for much more. “Please stand,” I say, summoning all my strength just to utter those two words. They all look around at each other from their bowed heads, then they all stand as one, looking to Eli and me and our little posse of protectors. “Are you all willing to swear an oath of loyalty to the Deuxsang and witches?”

A moment of hesitation, and then, “Yes.”

“Do you swear to never harm a Deuxsang or witch?”

“Yes,” hundreds of voices echo.

“And do you swear,” it takes all my strength to project my voice, “to keep the peace in the world, the peace that the witches have worked so hard for, that the Deuxsang now believe in, and that we are going to achieve?”

We’re all tense and exhausted and near tears when two hundred vampire voices echo, “Yes, we swear.” And I fall into Eli with relief.

He’s smiling and holding me tight as he says, “Then come forward to collect your dose of sun.”

Mason comes forward carrying a box that holds small vials of a mixture of mine and Jason’s blood, just enough to give them the ability to walk in the sun but not make them so strong that we couldn’t take them down if necessary.

And one by one, I watch our victory as the vampires line up to accept their vials. It feels like a miracle. It is a miracle. That I'm alive, that Freddie's alive—that all of us have made it out of this horror story with our lives. The vampires drink their dose in front of us with a small thanks and then flit away, except for those that choose to stay with us, milling awkwardly about the weird conglomeration of vampires and witches. And for once, in months, I feel the peace. But that only lasts for a moment.

"NO!" I twitch, turning toward the end of the dock where Anne was waiting with Ms. Rose. Now, neither of them are standing. I break into a flit, pulling Mason and Eli with me.

"Anne, what's wrong?" I kneel next to her, where Ms. Rose is lying on the wood, unnaturally still, fighting to keep her eyes open.

Mason falls to his knees beside his mom, taking her hand in his. "Mom, what's wrong? Talk to me." He brushes her graying hair away from her face, but she just smiles back at him.

"It's my time to go, baby boy."

Tears gush down his face. "No, it's not. We've won. Cheyenne and Eli won! So you have to stay because now everything will be better."

She slowly turns her frail neck to Eli and me. I take her hand in mine, trying to see her through my tears. "You both did so well. I knew you would do it. You've saved us all."

"No we haven't!" I cry, barely squeezing her hand. "You can't leave us now. I still need you."

Slowly, she looks around at all of us, memorizing each of our faces. "You all are amazing, the most beautiful children in the world. And I'm so honored…" she takes a deep, labored breath, closing her eyes for almost a moment too long, "to know and love all of you. But my time on this earth is over, and I leave it with the lightest, fullest heart."

Anne's holding Mason as he shakes, leaning over to kiss his mother's forehead. When I look back, a group has formed around us—Regina, Niki, Dr. Cofi, Erik, Rove, Mom, Jason, even Kara, holding Freddie close. Then Madame Laveau floats around all of them and hovers over Ms. Rose as her breaths become shallower.

"Are you ready to leave, beautiful lady?" Marie asks quietly. And slowly, Ms. Rose nods, just barely, and a new round of sobs escape all of us. I lean into Eli, crying into his shirt as I still clasp her cold, bony hand.

"No!" Mason roars. "She can't leave me!"

"Child," Madame Laveau floats in front of Mason, "your mother has fought this fight for a long time. Her body is tired, her soul is ready to go. But you know that she will always be with you, and you can visit her, with the help of the little priest. But for now, her human self is ready to go. So let her." She backs away, to give us all a moment, and the four of us lean over her, hugging each other, our tears mixing.

"I love you all." Ms. Rose whispers, smiling her small, gentle smile. "Thank you for saving us. I'll talk to you on the other side." And then Madame Laveau floats through us to face Ms. Rose, placing her ghostly hands over the lovely woman's heart. Slowly, almost as if I'm dreaming it, her eyes close, her breath no longer puffs, and her chest stills. And then the world disappears.

Twenty Nine

Then there's a soft knock on the door, and my group is standing in the doorway—Eli, Anne, Rove, Mason, and Jason. I bury my face in a pillow, trying to hide my tears. Even though we won, we defeated the big bad evil, it all feels pointless. Our rock is gone. They all climb onto the bed with me, Eli curled up against me, pulling me into his chest.

"It's over, Cheyenne. We did it," he whispers into my hair, rubbing circles into my back. I know he has to be hurting worse than I am. Mason has barely said five words since last night.

"But Ms. Rose..." I manage through a gasp.

"I know," he holds me tighter, and Anne squeezes my hand. "I know, but like she said, she was ready to go. She got to see a miracle. And besides, thanks to me, we can talk to her whenever we want." I feel his smile against my back.

I'm finally able to stop the tears, drying my face on the old blanket, and look everyone in the eye. "Thank you all...so much for all you did and all you've done for me. I don't deserve this, but— "

"Stop saying that, Cheyenne." Anne cuts me off, pulling on my hand. "You're amazing. You did this. You beat Lamia, and now, because of you, we're all free."

I shake my head, looking down at my pillow before I meet Eli's gaze. "No, it's us. We all did this. Neither of us could've done anything without you all." I look at Mason directly. "All of you." He blushes a little bit, but nods in acceptance, wiping at his red eyes.

"Well," Eli sighs. "Everyone is waiting on the beach. Madame Laveau wants to talk to us."

We all stand, and I allow a giant group hug, even though it's cheesy and ridiculous. But right now, I need that. And then I pull Jason aside as everyone else files out of the room.

I look down at my shoes. "How are you doing with all this?"

"I'm fine, Cheyenne. You're amazing, and I owe…everything to you. You gave me my life back." He squeezes my shoulder, and we follow the group outside to the beach. Marie Laveau is surrounded by her children, all looking nervously as the sun starts to rise.

The youngest girl flits to me with a small smile and throws her little arms around my waist. "Do you think it worked?"

"Only one way to tell." I hold out my hand for hers and lead her over to the group as a little peak of sun starts to rise behind them. I look back at the little vampire girl who smiles as a ray of sunlight hits her skin, and she keeps smiling when she doesn't burst into flames.

I turn to Madame Laveau then, who's beaming down at her daughter. "I don't know how to thank you for everything. You saved us."

"No, dearie. I'm just a ghost. You saved them. You and the little priest. Rose was right to believe in you." She smiles back at Eli, who's talking quietly with Erik. "I wanted to thank you for trusting me and listening to me. I know it wasn't easy to do what I asked, knocking Regina out of her position, but I was just doing it for you all."

"I know that now. Thank you for making me do it."

She bows her head at that unnatural angle, but I smile regardless. "It was my pleasure, dearie. If you need anything else, you know where to find me." I smile, nodding, wanting to say more but not wanting to keep a ghost around much longer. "But... try not to need anything else." And with a tinkling laugh, she turns into mist and floats away with the early morning breeze.

I start to turn back to the group, but Eli cuts me off, pulling me farther down the beach, away from the craziness of the group. Our hands fall into their natural interlocked position, swinging gently between us. I'm not really sure what to say, and I don't think he is either. So we keep walking.

"How's it feel to be a High Priest at the young age of 19?" I finally ask, unable to handle the silence.

"How's it feel to be the savior of her people at the age of 17?" He retorts with a smile.

"Well, aren't we astounding specimen. I think we should try not to let it get to our heads, yeah?" I smile too, squeezing his hand in mine.

He stops us, pulling me tightly against him.

"You're right. You are astounding. Because of you, we did it." And then he's kissing me, and I've never felt so accepted or loved. I throw my arms around his neck until we could not possibly be any closer and will the whole world away. "I love you," he whispers against my lips.

Never in a million years did I think I'd be here, completely in love with a witch who helped me defeat the most powerful vampire known to history. But here I am, saying, "I love you," right back. He lets out the most carefree laugh, dragging me to the soft sand. We're both laughing nonstop as I brace myself over him to look down at this face that has never once given up on me, who's fought for me, and loved me, and I don't know how I got this lucky.

And then, of course…

"Hey, the house is about three miles back that way," Mason calls with a chuckle. I roll my eyes, and we both sit up, smiling at our group of friends.

"Why do you always seem to pop up at the most inconvenient of times, man?" Eli jokes, shoving him away as Mason sits down next to him. Anne plops down next to me, with Rove and Jason on the other side of her. We all look up as a shadow approaches, and Erik is standing in front of us.

"Mind if I join you?" We're all silent, everyone looking to Eli and me. We look at each other.

"Yeah, man, come on." I give him a small smile as he sits next to Mason.

On one side, Eli's hand holds tight to mine. On the other, Anne's arm linked through mine and her head rests on my shoulder. And in this moment, I can think of nothing more that I want. In this moment, we are carefree. In this moment, life is perfect. In this moment, we are forever.

The End

The Author

As the recent recipient of a Master's degree in Writing for Young People from Bath Spa University, author Hannah Rials has dreamed of being an author since childhood. A native of Maryville, TN, Rials began writing her first YA novel at age twelve. That same novel, Ascension (Book One in a three-book trilogy) ultimately became her first published book at age 19. Published by Aletha Press in 2017, the Ascension series is a saga of modern-day teenage romance filled with "double-blooded" vampires and revenge-seeking witches. Her second YA thriller in the Ascension series, Clandestine, was written and edited while she was a full-time college student at the University of Tennessee at Chattanooga. When not writing YA novels or selling books at Mr B's Emporium, Hannah can be found roaming around England in search of unique bookstores and coffeehouses to experience.

Connect with her on Facebook, Twitter and via her website. www.hannaherials.com

HANNAH RIALS

CPSIA information can be obtained
at www.ICGtesting.com
Printed in the USA
FSHW021316090220
66878FS